RAVENCREST ACADEMY

MAGIC BOUND

THERESA KAY

Cover design by Christian Bentulan of Covers By Christian
Book design by Inkstain Design Studio

RAVENCREST ACADEMY

MAGIC BOUND

ALSO BY THERESA KAY

Broken Skies
Fractured Suns
Shattered Stars

TO REGAN,

who never stopped believing in this story

(or talking me into writing when I just didn't wanna :)

CHAPTER 1

The thing about shifter parties is they're really only fun for shifters... and maybe swingers. There's no booze, everyone's super touchy-feely, and couples or groups often disappear only to return slightly rumpled and smiling. Unfortunately for me, I'm neither a shifter nor a swinger, and it's getting harder to remember why in the hell I let my cousin, Reid Donovan, convince me to come here. The party's not a bad scene, a roaring bonfire, fresh air, good music, but it's Sunday night and I have to work tomorrow. Plus, the jerk ditched me the second we got here so he could go be one of those disappearing couples with his girlfriend, Lana.

Last party of the summer or not, I would much rather be in bed right now than standing here alone watching shifters—most of whom I don't even know—having fun around me. I'd leave, but Reid drove, and 'random field somewhere off 151' isn't exactly an Uber pickup location.

When I find him, I'm going to wring his neck.

From the edge of the trees, I scan the shifters gathered around the bonfire, hoping to catch a glimpse of my auburn-haired cousin. No luck. There are no familiar faces of any kind, and I'm not interested in starting up a conversation with a complete stranger. Explaining my presence here and my relationship to the Blue Ridge regional alpha, my adoptive uncle Connor Donovan, is not something I feel like doing tonight. Being adopted into the pack does not a pack member make, and being a Blank—a person with two witch parents but no actual magic—adds an extra level of complication.

Don't get me wrong, being taken in by Aileen and George, Connor's sister and her husband, was the best thing to ever happen to me. Witches are supposed to raise their powerless children, but more often than not they foist them on unsuspecting humans. If I hadn't been taken in by the shifters, I would have been stuck in the human world, and the minuscule bit of power I do have—a heightened sense of supernaturals—would have been more than a little confusing. But at the end of the day, I'm not a shifter. And, magic or not, if anyone here besides Reid knew my birth parents were witches, things might get a bit sticky.

I sigh and take a sip of my bottled water then cast another glance at the large group of shifters closest to me. They're dancing, chatting, and generally having a blast. I can't hear much of what they're saying, but the bits of conversation I manage to catch are all about the upcoming school year. Most of them are off to the local high school, a few are headed to college, but one of them is headed to an OSA (aka the Order of Supernatural Affairs) training academy, quite a feat since very few OSA academies allow shifters.

I'm nearly eighteen, and if I were a witch, I'd probably be headed to one of the OSA academies as well, but instead I have my senior year of high school ahead of me. Technically, the academies are only for those supernaturals who want to join OSA or use their abilities as part of their future careers, but nearly *all* witch children end up attending. However, the Order of Supernatural Affairs doesn't give a crap about me. I have nothing to offer them without magic. Though, I'm sure they'd be quite interested to know which one of the 'upstanding' covens abandoned a Blank infant on a shifter's doorstep.

The wind changes direction, sending a cloud of smoke from the bonfire my way. *Awesome.* I'm going to smell like a campfire for the next three days. I cough and squint against the burning in my eyes. Time for me to find a new location to be bored out of my mind in. I drain the rest of the water, then toss the empty bottle in a nearby bin, and walk around the edge of the party until the haze of smoke no longer threatens to choke me.

It's another ten minutes of not-so-subtle people watching before I catch sight of Reid and Lana returning from the woods on the opposite side of the fire. *Finally.* They're red-faced, breathless, and wrapped in each other's arms, both of them wearing wide grins. It's sickeningly adorable.

I don't begrudge my cousin his happiness. He's also my best—and damn near only—friend, but I'd be lying if I said I'm not more than a little jealous he has a connection, a type of belonging, that I'll likely never have with another person. I've had a couple human boyfriends, but nothing serious. Connor so far has been steadfast in his refusal to allow me to take the Bite, the only way for someone who isn't born a shifter to become one, so I can't be with a shifter. Witches pick only from among their own, something I never will and never want to be, not after my cowardly birth parents deserted me because they were ashamed of the fact I have no magic.

And vamps? No. Just no.

Lana catches my eye and waves before poking Reid with her elbow. He gives me a mock salute and tugs Lana in my direction, but the two of them are pulled into a conversation, their forward progress slowing before stopping completely. *Wonderful.* I'll never get out of here if I don't go over there and hurry him along.

I make my way in their direction, but when I'm halfway through the crowd, someone steps in front of me and forces me to stop. The unfamiliar shifter in my path shoots me a rakish grin, his dark eyes glinting with interest. His hair is a deep shade of black, only a few shades darker than mine, and he's definitely attractive in that rugged, broad-shouldered way most shifters are. He's also damn near powerful enough to become an alpha if he isn't one already. In other words, not someone I should simply brush off. Insults between packs or pack members aren't taken lightly.

And this is just the kind of social dance I spent the last two hours trying to avoid . . .

"Hi there," he says, holding out a hand. "I'm Zeke."

"Selene." I take the offered hand, and the essence of his power prickles against my senses.

"You looked a little lonely standing by yourself over there." He tilts his head toward the trees. "Fancy a run?"

Great. Now I need to come up with a polite way to clue this guy in on the fact that, despite my presence here, I'm not actually a shifter. I'm opening my mouth, most likely in preparation for putting my foot in it, when a heavy arm lands across my shoulders.

"Beat it, Zeke," says Reid. "This one's ours."

Zeke narrows his eyes, and for a split second I think he might try to argue—two alphas almost always butt heads—but instead he simply shrugs and shakes his head. "No worries. I was just talking to her." He rakes his gaze over me. "She's that charity case the regional beta took on, right?"

My cheeks heat, and Reid stiffens.

Whether Zeke knew all along and was messing with me or he just now figured it out, I have no clue. Either way, what he said is not only an insult to me but an insult to the entire pack, including the boy standing next to me.

And because I'm *technically* the regional beta's daughter and Reid is the future regional alpha, we can't let this go. *Oh the joys of shifter power plays . . .*

Reid tilts his head toward me and speaks in a low voice, "You wanna handle this, or should I?"

My only answer is to slide out from under his arm and take three steps forward until I'm directly in front of Zeke. I'm a good six inches shorter than him, and the guy probably outweighs me by almost a hundred pounds. I wouldn't be able to take him in an actual challenge even if he didn't shift, but training with Reid and my parents has made me strong enough to handle what's required for the petty slight Zeke threw my way.

"You've insulted me and my pack. I claim the right of first blood." My voice is steady, but inside I'm some weird combination of pissed and scared out of my mind.

He laughs. He frickin' *laughs.* "You...you...want to . . ." His words trail off in another fit of laughter. Finally, his shoulders still shaking with mirth, he straightens and holds his hands out at his sides. "Take your best shot then."

I give him a predatory smile and slam the heel of my left boot onto the instep of his right foot. A sharp cross to his diaphragm has him huffing out more in surprise than in pain, but it also has him instinctively curling inward and leaning forward. I link my hands together behind his neck and hold his head down so I can slam my right knee into his nose with a solid crunching noise.

I relax my stance and take a step backward as he straightens with one hand over his nose, blood dripping down his chin. The broken nose will heal in the next two minutes or so, but it'll probably hurt like a bitch until then.

Zeke grins. "Aren't you full of surprises, little one?"

Reid clears his throat.

"Yes, yes, yes," says Zeke, waving one hand through the air in a dismissive gesture. "I apologize for the slight and all that."

I accept the apology with a dip of my chin, and a wave of relief washes over me. That wasn't too bad.

Reid moves up behind me, placing his hands on my shoulders. "Run along now. Go find someone else to sniff after."

Zeke's gaze hasn't left me, and where there was a kind of bland attentiveness in his eyes before, now there's a flare of true interest. Shifters aren't violent by nature, but power, physical or otherwise, turns them on, and that little challenge was practically foreplay. He grabs my hand and rubs the back of it down his cheek then flips my hand over and presses his nose to my wrist, his gaze never leaving mine. "If you ever decide to accept the Bite, please find me."

A low rumble starts in Reid's chest, but Zeke ignores the sound. He simply lets go of my hand and disappears into the crowd without another word.

Reid releases my shoulders. "Your right elbow came a little too far up, but otherwise that was perfect."

"Really?" I poke him in the stomach with the offending elbow. "I pull off my first minor challenge—quite epically I might add—and you're going to complain because my *elbow* wasn't absolutely perfect?"

"It left your side open and took power away from the hit, so, yes, I'm going to complain. This was a minor challenge, and the guy wasn't actually going to try to fight you. In a real fight, this wayward elbow"—he squeezes it—"could be the difference between winning and losing."

"But I'm never going to be in a real fight, now am I?" I yank out of his hold and spin to face him, my words growing sharper as my prior irritation with him resurfaces. "Your dad won't allow me the Bite, and no shifter will seriously challenge a *human*. Hell, if I hadn't shown up here with you, reeking of alpha wolf, I wouldn't have had to worry about insulting Zeke. I could have just told him to get lost. But no. I had to worry about how that might reflect on my pack, the pack that got stuck with me because their beta and her husband couldn't bear to part with the infant abandoned on their doorstep."

His brown eyes soften, and he pulls me into a hug. "We aren't 'stuck' with you. Aunt Aileen and Uncle George love you like their own. My dad has done everything possible to treat you like one of the pack, and I know he thinks of you that way, as well as thinking of you as his blood niece. I don't know why he won't let you take the Bite. You're old enough now to make the decision, and even though you're not a Born wolf, you're family. The only reason I can think of is that there are still risks, and if Aileen were to lose you . . ."

"Yeah. I know," I say, my voice soft as I nod against his chest. Before they adopted me, Aileen and George lost a son and were never able to have any more children of their own.

A moment passes in silence, and then Reid releases me and leans back, the corner of his mouth curling upward. "So 'reeking'? Isn't there a better word you could have used?"

I shove him in the shoulder, a smile tipping up the corners of my mouth, then glance around at the various groups of people by the bonfire. "Where's Lana? I thought you two planned to be attached at the hip for the remainder of the evening."

"I saw you with Zeke and figured you might be in a bit of trouble. How did you end up on his radar?"

I shrug. "I didn't search him out. He must have been watching me for at least a little while when I was standing by myself and then used my heading in his direction as an opportunity to talk to me. Who is he anyway? I've never seen him before."

"I don't know a lot about him, but I met him at a pack gathering last year. He's from one of the higher packs in the Southwestern Virginia region. I forget which one."

Not surprising. I definitely felt the near alpha level power coming off him. As much as I hate to admit it, I probably wouldn't have confronted him without Reid at my back. Just because it's illegal for shifters to attack humans doesn't mean there isn't the occasional hiker that goes missing or fight that gets out of hand. Much like in human society, not every shifter chooses to follow the laws. Attacking a witch is the worst crime of all, an automatic death sentence if caught, and lately that's been happening way more than normal.

I shove Reid's shoulder again. "Go get your girl."

He wiggles his eyebrows. "Well, I'm supposed to meet her out behind the barn to—"

I wave frantically. "Okay. I got it. No need to explain further. I don't need the mental image to go along with that. Can I have your keys so I can wait in the truck?"

"Sure," he says as he pulls the keys from his pocket and tosses them to me. "You know how to get back to where we parked, right?"

"Yeah. Definitely." I gesture vaguely in the direction we came from when we arrived. "It's just through those trees over there."

"Try not to get into any more altercations with shifters on the way, yeah?"

I roll my eyes. "I will give any shifters I run into a wide berth." I poke him in the shoulder. "I'm giving you one hour. If you aren't back to your truck by then, I'm driving it home. I can't guarantee your clutch will make it through my attempt at driving stick, so you might want to be on time."

"I've seen you try to drive my truck. You wouldn't make it out of the parking lot." He lets out a laugh. "I'll see you in an hour. Thanks for coming out here with me."

"Yeah, sure, whatever. Get moving. I'd like to see my bed before the sun comes up."

He kisses the top of my head and then wades into the crowd closer to the fire. After sneaking up behind Lana, he grabs her by the waist, lifts her into the air, then runs off toward the forest with her as she giggles. I smile as they disappear then make my way toward the narrow trail between the trees that leads to the gravel lot.

As I reach the end of the trail and the first line of cars, the sound of voices hits my ears. I glance up to see four shadowy forms ahead of me. By the looks of it, three of them are ganging up on the fourth—one shifter standing against three witches who have absolutely no business being here.

Reid told me not to get into any altercations with shifters, but how would he feel about me getting into an altercation with *witches?*

CHAPTER 2

To say shifters and witches don't get along would be a bit of an understatement. Especially in the past twenty years or so since the Coven Council has been pushing OSA, which governs all three supernatural races and deals with any conflicts between them, for more oversight of the shifters, something shifters are adamantly against. Some of them so much so that there are rumors about a group of renegade shifters who've been attacking witches. It's a stupid thing to do, and it doesn't help their cause, but no one's been able to root out what pack or packs might be doing it. All I know is it's not anyone from the Blue Ridge pack because Connor would never allow something like that to happen in his region.

But even though we're currently on Blue Ridge pack lands, the already tense relationship between shifters and witches makes the little spat going on in the parking lot a bad idea on *both* sides: the three witches for being here at all and the shifter for not simply walking away.

Getting involved is probably a bad idea on my part too, but I recognize Bridget, a slender, preppy looking witch in the group, and I might be able to defuse the situation.

Bridget, who's taking the lead in the argument, is from a midlevel witch family who owns a nearby horse farm. I have the misfortune of seeing her quite often at the coffee shop where I work during the summer months, but what she's doing here is a complete and utter mystery.

All four of them fall silent as I approach. Bridget and her two lackeys send me death glares, and the shifter girl crosses her arms over her chest.

"Hi, Bridget." I walk up to the group, stopping beside the shifter girl and glancing at her from the corner of my eye. Brown eyes. Light-brown hair. Like Zeke, she's unfamiliar. What's with all the new shifters in the area tonight? "What are you and your witch friends doing on pack lands?"

Bridget gives me a saccharine sweet smile, her nose wrinkling. "Move along. This is none of your business."

"I think it *is* my business, especially when you're—"

"I don't need your help," bites out the shifter girl. She tilts her chin up, her dark eyes flashing with anger. "I can handle these weaklings on my own."

Before I can open my mouth to point out that, regardless of strength, this fight is three against one, Bridget speaks up. "Oh, yes, you're the Donovan pack's pet human. Selene, right?"

The insult stings, but this isn't like earlier with Zeke. There's no formal type of response for outsiders. But her catty words also give me my one and only card to play.

"Yup, that's me." I step slightly in front of the shifter girl. "A human... Who you're forbidden from using magic on, so why don't we break this up and all go our separate ways? You know you're not allowed on pack lands without a formal invitation."

Bridget laughs, and the two other witches join in. "Aren't you cute." She looks from side to side with an exaggerated motion. "But who's around to report me? Better yet . . ." Her voice drops low, and she adds a bit of a simper to it. "I was just trying to defend myself. The human came after *me*. She was raised by shifters, so who knows what kind of violent tendencies those animals might have instilled in her."

Rage brews in my stomach. How dare she call my family animals. She's nothing but a—

The shifter girl wraps her hand around my upper arm. "Get out of here. It's okay."

"You should listen to her. This is witch business," says Bridget. "If you leave now, there's no hard feelings. K?"

"Go." The shifter girl widens her eyes and pushes me to the side.

Bridget huffs. "You'll get out of my way one way or another." She pinches two fingers together as if pulling something from the air—*magic*—and flicks her index finger my direction.

The small ball of concentrated magical energy hits me in the abdomen and pushes me to the side. The skin where the magic hit tingles, a feeling that walks the edge of pain, and I suck in a breath as I wait for the feeling to pass. But the feeling doesn't pass. Instead, heat and electricity surge through my limbs and I fall to the ground with my arms wrapped around my middle. The pain is like nothing I've ever felt, a raging inferno flooding my veins, a building pressure that makes my skin feel too tight, and a wrenching pain like something's breaking inside me.

"What'd you do?" yells the shifter girl. "What kind of spell did you throw?"

"It wasn't a spell. I just...I just . . ." stammers Bridget. "It was a tiny zap, just enough to get her out of the way. I didn't . . ."

"You dumb bitch." The shifter drops to her knees beside me, muttering under her breath things I can't quite hear as she grabs hold of my face and tries to get me to look at her.

The pressure in my chest is getting worse, so bad that it feels like I might explode. There's another cracking sensation deep inside, and I whimper as another wave of pain washes over me. Tears run down my face, and my muscles have gone rigid.

The shifter girl runs her hands over my arms, down my legs. Looking for what? Her words come in and out. "A necklace? A bracelet? Something!"

I try to shake my head. I don't understand what she's asking.

Her hands go to my face again, forcing me to meet her eyes. "You have to let it go," she says. "You can't hold it, and you don't have a talisman."

The words themselves make sense, but I have no idea what she's talking about. Let go of *what*? A talisman? Isn't that some kind of magical item? Another wave of agony shoots through my body, and this time a cry of pain rips out of me.

From the corner of my eye, I see Bridget and her two friends slowly backing away, eyes wide, confusion and maybe a tiny bit of fear written on their faces. The initial blast of magic Bridget threw is barely a blip on my radar compared to the fiery power locked in my core.

Wait a second...power? In *me*?

My head spins at the idea, but I focus on the heat in the center of my chest, finally recognizing the feeling for what it is: magic. But that's *impossible*. I'm a Blank.

Another blast rages against the confines of my body, and my chest feels like it's going to crack open. I can't breathe. I scratch frantically at my throat, willing air into my lungs, but the only thing filling me is more and more pressure. More and more *magic*.

"Let it go!" yells the shifter girl. "You have to *let it go*."

There's no air for me to form words, so I can't tell her I don't know how. The realization that whatever's happening to me right now is going to kill me if I don't do *something* is enough to clear my head and let me think. Some instinct tells me not letting go isn't really the problem. It's...it's opening a valve, releasing the pressure. *Directing it.*

I raise one arm to the side, my palm facing—I hope—toward the trees. As the next back-arching surge of pain crests, I will the force of it into my arm, as if throwing a punch and the magic is the follow through. A burst of power explodes from my hand and finally drains the pressure from my chest so I can pull in a full, gasping breath.

A good thirty seconds pass before I can push myself to my hands and knees, coughing, sputtering, and completely exhausted. Shifter girl yanks me to my feet as soon as I catch my breath.

"You need to get out of here," she says. "Get in your car and leave before someone comes."

"What?" I sputter. "I...What the actual hell was that? How?" Nothing makes any sense. My head is full of fog, my limbs are numb, and my chest feels like it's on fire.

She shakes my shoulders. "You don't have time for this. If they catch you here ..."

"Catch me? Who?"

"I don't know...OSA? The Coven Council? *Anyone?*" She gives me another shake. "Pull it together!"

My gaze travels over her shoulder to the three witches lying on the ground near the edge of the gravel lot. "Did I...?"

"*Yes*, you idiot. Do you know what the penalty is for using that caliber of offensive magic against a fledging witch, *in public* no less?"

We're technically on pack land, not in public, but I'm not sure if that's better or worse for me. I know enough to know it's bad, so I nod and blink my eyes.

"Then go!" She gives me a somewhat gentle shove then shifts into a large, gray wolf before disappearing into the woods.

Well *shit*.

My legs are begging me to sit down, and my head is pounding like there's a woodpecker inside trying to find its way out, but I'm not a complete idiot. I can't stand around. It won't matter to OSA that I had no idea what I was doing, no idea I even *had* the ability to use magic. All that will matter was that I used it on someone, and I'm sure Bridget will tell the story in a way that paints me in the worst light possible.

And even if I'm able to avoid any consequences, if the Coven Council finds out that shifters raised a *witch* child, no matter how the situation may have come about, it will be my parents who suffer. Witches, particularly those old money families who run the Coven Council, aren't known for being understanding. They'd no doubt find a way to spin my adoption as something criminal.

I need to find Reid and get out of here before Bridget and her friends wake up. I need to get home. Now.

I locate the trail leading back to the party and run toward the noise and the lights. Everyone's still huddled around the bonfire, dancing and chatting like nothing at all happened. And nothing did happen to them. My life has completely changed, and they still get to be normal. The thought makes my stomach churn with nausea.

I scan over the partygoers. Reid is nowhere to be seen, but neither is Lana, so they're probably still out behind the barn.

He's going to kill me for interrupting. I might be better off attempting to drive myself home, the stupid clutch be damned. A half-hysterical giggle breaks past my lips as my feet carry me in a mostly straight line toward the barn at the top of the hill on the other side of the bonfire.

I find Reid and Lana wrapped together, attached at the lips but, thankfully, fully clothed.

"Reid," I croak out.

They spring apart. Reid sends a glare in my direction, but the expression quickly turns into a look of concern and then, after a twitch of his nose, a look of pure confusion.

Lana, a little mussed, offers me a small smile. "Is everything all right?" she asks. Her nose twitches too, a shifter taking in an unexpected scent. She glances back and forth between Reid and me. "A witch? I thought she was human."

"So did I," I say. I sway on my feet but catch myself with one hand on the side of the barn.

Both of them rush forward. Reid places a steadying hand on my shoulder, and Lana grabs my arm to keep me from falling over.

"I need to go home. There's another shifter. A girl. And witches. I . . ."

The two of them share a look, and Lana nods. "Get her home. I'll talk to you later."

The tension and terror that has kept me going drains away now that I'm not alone and something is getting done. Both a good thing and a bad thing because I feel much better emotionally, but physically there's nothing holding me up anymore. My legs give out, so Reid sweeps me up into his arms and cradles me against his chest.

Lana kisses him on the cheek and runs a hand over my head. "Take care of yourself, girl. I'll be looking forward to hearing all about this tomorrow."

Reid glances down at me with a wry smile. "You have so much explaining to do."

I shrug. I'm not the only one with explaining to do. As much as I hate to admit it, there's no way my parents, no way *Connor*, didn't know anything about this.

CHAPTER 3

It's a thirty-minute drive to get home. The first ten minutes Reid spends cursing at his phone for not having service. The next ten minutes, after he manages to get a very brief call through to his dad, he spends cursing at his truck for not going fast enough. The last ten are spent in near silence as he vacillates between looking like he's terrified for me and looking like he's terrified *of* me.

Hell, I'm kind of terrified too. Of what this means for me, for my family, for everything . . .

The second Reid pulls into my driveway, three people rush out of the moderately sized two-story house and over to his truck.

Mom reaches the vehicle first. She yanks the passenger side door open, her blue eyes scanning over me frantically, only relaxing when she's sees I'm in one piece. She runs her hands over my hair and down my arms then takes a step back, wringing her hands. "I'm so sorry. It wasn't supposed to happen like this. You must have been so scared."

Dad walks up behind her and wraps an arm around her shoulders as I slowly climb out of the truck.

"There's—we—I—" He sighs and stares down at his feet.

It isn't until Reid's dad, Connor Donovan, a large, red-haired man, steps around them and looks down at me with a worried expression that I realize none of them are surprised. None of them are sniffing the air, trying to figure out where the magic smell is coming from.

And none of them will meet my eyes.

They already know. They've *known*. For exactly how long I have no idea, but they knew I'm not a Blank, that I'm an actual witch, and they kept it from me. But *why?*

Closing my eyes, I take a deep breath. The entire way here I hoped I was wrong, that they didn't know any more about this than I did. I wasn't sure how it would be possible for them not to know, but...I had hope. That hope is dead now, and the confirmation of their betrayal is like a block of cement in my stomach. I'm not sure how to react. I'm angry, of course. Downright pissed. But, most of all, I'm absolutely gutted.

Why would they keep a secret like this? Why would they lie to me my entire life? There has to be some explanation, right?

I open my eyes and study the three adult shifters in front of me. Mom and Dad look more sad and scared than anything else, but Connor looks almost resigned, as if he knew this day was coming.

Well, of course he did. The Blue Ridge regional alpha is nothing if not pragmatic. He knew I was a witch and allowed me to be taken in anyway. But *why?*

Reid runs around the back of the truck and then stops beside me. He sends a look of frantic desperation at his father. "So, what do we do? How do we fix this? Selene can't possibly be a witch, right? There's no way those assholes would let . . ." His voice trails off as he takes in the faces around us. "You're kidding me."

A strained laugh breaks past my lips. *At least I wasn't betrayed by my best friend too. That's a bright spot in this awful evening.*

Connor shakes his head and gives his son a stony stare.

"Have you always known?" Reid's voice is low with an edge to it that borders on a growl.

"Yes," says Connor, short and succinct, as he rubs at his forehead.

Reid takes a step backward. "I can't believe you." His gaze moves to my parents. "Any of you. Someone could have gotten hurt! Selene could have died! And if the witches find out about this . . ."

"More like *when* the witches find out," I say in a flat voice. "Since I laid three of them out this evening and one of them knows exactly who I am."

Dad's eyes widen. "You did what?"

"They were going after a shifter girl. I stepped in. It got ugly, and one of them blasted me. That's when . . ." I throw my hands up and let the words trail off as my eyes burn with tears. "I just don't understand why you never told me."

"We were planning to tell you. It wasn't meant—" Mom starts.

"No," yells Reid. "You don't get to explain this away. What gives any of you the right to keep this kind of secret?"

The lump in my throat prevents me from saying anything else, and I'm immensely grateful Reid is here asking all the questions I can't find words for.

Connor places a hand on his son's shoulder. "I think you should head on home, Reid. There are things we need to discuss with Selene."

Reid's eyes narrow, and his jaw tightens. "You're not leaving me out of this. Clearly, none of you thought this through. The last thing she needs is for you three to gang up on her."

"The 'last thing she needs' is to be taken to a shifter party after I specifically forbade you from doing so," says Connor in a low voice. "If she hadn't been there, none of this would have happened. How did you get around my command?"

Reid tilts his chin up, defiant, and shrugs.

"Tell me *now*," Connor says, throwing the power of an alpha command behind the words.

Speaking through his teeth with a snarl, Reid says, "Your command was to say no if she asked to go to one. She didn't ask. I did."

Leave it to my crafty cousin to find a loophole...

Connor's eyes narrow, and his nose twitches. "Go home, Reid," he says in a soft but dangerous voice. "We'll discuss your disobedience later."

Reid ignores him and holds his gaze, the ghost of a snarl still lingering on Reid's lips.

"It's okay," I say, one hand on Reid's arm. I don't want him to go, not really, but I also don't want him to fight with his father. There's been enough turmoil this evening. But Reid's gaze doesn't leave his father, and a low growl rumbles in my cousin's chest. I shake his arm. "Really. It's fine. I'll call you later and fill you in, okay?"

Connor bristles, his chest puffing out. "Go home, Reid," he repeats, this time in a voice that demands obedience.

Reid scowls, clearly unhappy about the order, but not even he can disobey a direct command. He walks around the front of the truck, still glaring at his father, and hops into the driver's seat. Reid's attention moves back to me, worry creasing his brow. "Everything will be okay. We'll figure this out. Call me if you need me."

"I will," I say in a soft voice.

I wait until his truck disappears over the next hill before I turn to face the three people who have been lying to me for pretty much my entire life. My initial anger has faded and been replaced by utter exhaustion. Now, like Connor, I'm resigned. I'm not going to like what they have to say, but there's no doubt I need to hear it.

There are too many questions clamoring for attention in my mind for me to pick just one, so I cross my arms and simply say, "I'm ready for an explanation any time now."

"Let's get you inside. You should probably sit down." Mom shuffles forward and reaches for my arm.

I pull away, and she flinches.

"Please," she says, and I allow her to lead me through the front door and into the living room while Dad and Connor file in behind us.

I take my normal seat on the couch and curl my legs underneath me. Mom sits next to me, and Dad and Connor take the easy chairs on either corner across from the couch. This whole thing feels like some weird-ass intervention or something.

Everyone's looking down at their hands, but my eyes are drawn to the coffee table where a pendant necklace sits. It's a simple thing, a thin gold chain and a fingernail-sized shiny stone that looks something like an opal.

"I want to know why tonight is the first time I've felt even an inkling of power, why you've told me I'm a Blank my entire life, why you've all lied to me." My voice is laced with a cold detachment even I don't recognize. I glance at the necklace on the table, and after a moment of strained silence, I add, "Or I guess you could start with the talisman."

Connor raises an eyebrow. "Where did you hear about talismans?"

Because that's the important question here. I scoff. "The shifter girl at the party. When whatever happened started happening, she asked me about a talisman. I figure that's what the necklace there is."

"It is," says Connor. "It was given to us in the event something like this were to happen."

"In the event…So this was always a possibility? And none of you thought to warn me?"

Mom swipes a finger under her eyes. "We didn't mean for it to happen this way. We were supposed to have more *time*." She sighs and glances at Dad. "When she came to us with you, this helpless little child, I couldn't say no, not after all she'd done for us. Helen—"

And rage rears its head again. "Wait a second. Do you mean my birth mother? You know who she is?"

"Who she *was*," says Connor softly. "Her name was Helen. She was a friend of the pack."

Friend of the pack…a special designation for an outsider who's been granted protection by an alpha. In this case, it must've been Connor.

"What? How?" I rub a hand over my forehead and blink back tears. My throat tightens, and I rise to my feet to pace to the opposite side of the room, the sense of betrayal digging deeper into my stomach. They always told me I was abandoned on the doorstep, that they had no idea who my family might be. "And my birth father? Have you been keeping his identity from me too?"

Connor slowly shakes his head. "We don't know who he is. Helen never told us."

Can I even trust that's the truth? Probably. Since it seems everything else is coming out tonight, why would they bother keeping that information from me now? I lean against the wall as far from the three of them as I can get and choke out one more word. "Why?"

"It was for your protection," Mom whispers. "I hated lying to you, hated that I could never tell you…She wanted you far, far away from the witch world, even if it meant you had to hate *her* in order to stay away from *them*."

The lump in my throat is practically choking me, and I'm drowning in questions I don't know how to ask because to voice them feels like a betrayal to the people who raised me. What was she like? Did she love me? Why did she leave me? I fight back tears—and curiosity—and try to focus on what's going on right now. There will be time for those kinds of questions later, but there are other things I need to ask right now. "How?" I ask. "If I'm a witch, how is it that I'm only accessing my powers now? I mean, I know witches don't *fully* manifest until at least seventeen, but there's always...something."

"Your powers were bound when you were an infant. They were never supposed to manifest at all," says Connor. "Helen didn't fully explain the circumstances, but she said your magic was different, that it was powerful... and dangerous." He looks away. "And that it would be better for everyone if you lived your life as a Blank." His tone is so matter of fact, so bland, that I simply don't know what to do with this information.

Better for everyone? What the hell is *that* supposed to mean? And what gave my birth mother the right to make that decision? She left me. She... she...I give my head a hard shake and walk back to the couch, sit down, think for a second, then stand up and pace to the other side of the room. Back to the couch again, my temper ramping up and coiling in a knot in my chest. No. Not nerves. *Magic.*

It's happening again. Heat flares in my chest, and the pressure builds. Not quite as bad as last time, but still...

Dad slips the pendant over my head, and the feeling vanishes. He places a hand on my cheek. "The talisman will help for now. It has some sort of containment spell on it so you won't lose control." He pauses and waits for me to meet his dark eyes. "I'm sorry we kept this from you. I'm sorry we didn't prepare you. We failed you, but we'll get through this. No matter who gave birth to you, you're still our daughter, and you always will be."

I nod woodenly, my mind still spinning with all the new revelations. I'm not a Blank. I'm an actual a witch. The other shifters will never understand. I was already an outsider. Now, I'll be an *outcast*. My stomach twists, and I sit back down on the couch.

"What happens to me now?" I ask in a small voice, the force of my anger deflating to make room for the scared teenager I am.

Connor glances at my parents. "There's a contingency plan, one I've already put into motion."

"What are you talking about, Connor?" asks Dad, leaning forward and grabbing Mom's hand.

"I couldn't risk the safety of the entire pack on a single binding spell, no matter how strong it was," Conner replies. He holds my dad's gaze for a moment before glancing away. "And I couldn't risk Aileen's safety on one talisman and the slim chance that tonight's events would stay secret." He reaches across the space between us and wraps one of his big, scarred hands around mine. "You'll be going to an OSA training academy. There are people there Helen trusted. One of them is on his way to pick you up. You'll be safe there, and you can learn to use your magic."

"You mean I have to *leave*?" Of all the things I expected to come of this craziness, that's one outcome I hadn't anticipated.

"I'm sorry, but now that your powers have manifested, now that you're a fully-fledged witch, you can't stay on pack lands." Connor pins me with his gaze. "Even if I were to issue a formal invitation for you to stay, our laws can't protect you anymore. *I* can't protect you, but the school can."

"I can go with Reid to New York. We—"

"No," says Connor. "The Coven Council is going to hear of all this very soon. They'll be breathing down our necks, and they'll also get OSA involved, so we need to be proactive. We hid you for as long as we could, but that's over now. Shifter laws and protections don't apply; the sanctuary of pack lands doesn't apply. The only place you'll be safe is the school."

I sputter, trying to think up another option, an excuse, *something*. "But I don't know anything about how to be a witch!"

"You'll learn," says Connor in his alpha voice. "You don't have a choice here, Selene. You're not the only one who might suffer consequences."

My entire body goes cold, and my gaze moves from Mom to Dad and then back to Connor. "The witches...They'll come after you, won't they?"

They nod in unison.

Connor speaks first. "The Coven Council will call it kidnapping. At best. They'll go after your mom and dad first. Probably won't take a shot at me for a while. They will have a hard time getting through the protections of shifter laws even with the pending legislation." He rubs a hand over his head. "But if you're still here, the Coven Council has every right to come on to my pack lands and take you. Now that you're a witch, you're considered under their authority. Not mine. If they get their hands on you, I don't know what they might do. They can go against me, against pack laws, but they can't go against OSA."

"But I don't want *any* of this." My hands curl into fists, and my cheeks heat. "Let me take the Bite. None if this will matter then because I won't be able to use magic anymore."

Mom's eyes are wracked with pain. "He can't," she says. "The punishment for biting a witch and stripping them of their magic—"

"I'm *asking* him to."

"It doesn't matter," says Connor, shaking his head. "The pack's actions in regard to you are already going to be viewed as interference in witch business."

There's a knock at the door. Connor walks over to open it before returning with an elderly man whose presence tingles against my senses. A witch.

"This is Basil Kostis," says Connor. "He's with the OSA academy."

The man has on wrinkled pants and scuffed shoes, and his white hair floats around his head like a cloud. He looks more like someone's eccentric grandpa than what I'd expect in an OSA employee.

"Nice to meet you?" I say, hesitantly.

Basil's mouth spreads into a warm smile, and he rushes over with his hand out. "Hello, hello," he says, shaking my hand rather vigorously as he continues to beam at me. "I'm so pleased to meet you. I'm the Head of Admissions at your new school, Ravencrest."

My eyes widen. *Ravencrest?* It's nice to know I'm not being forced across the country. Ravencrest is in the Shenandoah Valley, only an hour or so away, but it's the most elite of all the OSA training academies. Only the best, the brightest, and the *richest* end up there. It's where all the old money and high-society type witches end up. Who was my birth mother that she was able to arrange my admittance to Ravencrest as a *contingency* plan?

"Ah, I see you've heard of it," says Basil with another too-perky grin. He moves toward me, studying the pendant hanging around my neck. "May I?"

The niceness he exudes on top of everything else is unnerving to the point of stupefying me, and all I can do is nod.

He lifts the pendant away from my chest, brushes a finger over the stone, and whispers something I can't hear. "There now. The talisman will hold until we get you to school."

"What exactly *is* a talisman?" I blurt out. It's probably a dumb question, one with a stupidly obvious answer, but if Basil is put off by my ignorance, he doesn't show it. In fact, he actually smiles.

"A talisman is a spelled object, generally something that can be worn." His eyes twinkle as he examines the pendant again. "This one helps the wearer contain or hide their magic, and it was some of my best work. I'm surprised the spell didn't hold up better. Oh well, nothing to be done for it now."

My head spins with all the new information clamoring for attention in my brain, but the first words to make it out of my mouth are, "*Your* best work?"

"Oh, yes," says Basil. "I prepared that talisman for Helen when she decided to leave OSA, though I was under the impression she was the one who was going to use it."

"You knew my birth mother too?" The question is barely a whisper.

He nods, and a hint of sadness creeps into his words. "I knew her quite well. She was one of my best students when I was still teaching at Ravencrest."

He claps, back to the jolly old man again. "But all that is a story for a later date. We must be going. There's so much to do, paperwork to fill out, books to gather, a schedule to be arranged . . ." His brows lift when I don't move. "Well, go get your stuff together. We need to get within the boundaries of the school wards before the refreshed spell on the talisman wears off, lest your magic draw any unwanted attention."

CHAPTER 4

My head is a mess of confusion, anger, and hurt, so packing is more like shoving the first few pieces of clothing I lay hands on, my running shoes, and a pair of flip-flops into a bag. I don't have the brain power to think too hard about what I need or what I should bring. Nor do I really care. Once I manage to wrestle the zipper closed, I sit on my bed and stare down at my shaking hands.

When I woke up this morning, I had no idea my entire life was going to change. And right now, I'd give almost anything to get back that blissful ignorance. I wish I'd never found out about my powers and lived the rest of my life as a Blank. My life wasn't overly exciting, but it was happy and it was *mine*. Now...I don't even know who I am anymore.

My mind is an endless string of what if questions. What if I hadn't gone to that party? What if I'd just stayed with Reid? What if I hadn't stepped into that fight? What if...

The door to my room opens, and Mom comes in. She sits down beside me on the bed and grabs my hand.

"I know this isn't what you wanted. It's not what I wanted for you either, but you can do this." She places a hand on my cheek. "You're my strong, smart, beautiful girl."

I crack a weak smile.

"It won't be easy, but I know you'll find your place. You might even enjoy it," she says. Her voice grows softer. "All of this was a shock to you and you're angry, but I hope you know your dad and I love you and that everything we did, every secret we kept, was to protect you."

Tears flow freely down my face, Mom's too. She pulls me into a tight hug and holds me there as my shoulders shake and my tears dampen her shirt.

Dad appears in the doorway and knocks his knuckles against the frame. "Can I come in?"

"Of course." I sniffle and wipe at my eyes.

He sits on my other side, drops an arm over my shoulder, then presses a kiss to the top of my head. "We'll miss you, sweetheart. Every moment of every day."

I nod. "But we can still talk, right?" When neither of them respond, I lean back and glance from one to the other. "I can call you, right? This isn't . . ."

Dad shakes his head. "Ravencrest doesn't allow students to have cell phones on campus, and Connor...He thinks it's best if we cut all communication for now. At least until you get settled and some of this blows over."

"No." I jump to my feet. "That isn't fair. You can't just upend my entire life and then expect me to be okay with that. I'll be all alone. I'll have no one. I can't...I can't . . ."

Dad gets up and places his hands on my shoulders. "You *can*. It won't be forever."

"You don't know that. What if . . ." I can't even finish the question, and I don't want to start crying again, so I focus on my anger instead. I pull away from Dad and grab my bag. "I'm going to take this outside."

The two of them follow behind me but wait just inside the front door as I walk to Basil's car to shove my bag in the trunk. The old man is sitting in the driver's seat, giving me a sympathetic look—no, a *pitying* look. And I hate it. I walk back into the house to finish my goodbyes. Mom hugs me tightly, and Dad wraps both of us in his arms as he presses a kiss to my hair. I stand there stiff and awkward, willing my arms to move, my mouth to say goodbye and tell them I love them, but I'm frozen in place. There's so much I want to say, so many questions I still have, but Connor tells me it's time to go and steers me out the door.

In the driveway, he places his hands on my shoulders and waits for me to look at him. "Don't blame your parents for this. It's—"

"They're not really my parents anyway," I snap, glad to finally have someone I can yell at. "I'm just some stupid charity case you all took on."

He waits, his head tilted to the side, as I process my own words. Connor Donovan is good at that, the silent look that tells someone to think things through.

I wipe at my eyes with the heel of my palm and look away.

"You know that's not true," says Connor in a low voice. "Your mom and dad love you."

"I know," I say quietly. "But all this . . ."

"Sucks, I know." He waits until I meet his eyes again. "I'm sorry it all had to turn out like this, but...things will be okay. You know, I love you too, kiddo." He wraps his big arms around me. "Take care of yourself. You can do this. I believe in you."

"Okay." The desire to fight, to argue, drains away, and I get into the passenger seat without another word. I don't know quite what to think about any of this. I'm equally angry, terrified, and devastated. Going to an OSA academy and probably being forced to *join* OSA was never part of my life plan. And doing it like this, because there's no other option? I feel like an animal caught in a trap, like my life and my choices aren't my own anymore.

I stare out the window at the passing trees as I travel farther and farther away from the only home I've ever known and the only people who've ever loved me. I'm about to be alone in a school filled with a bunch of uptight witches who probably won't look too kindly on my upbringing. The thought makes my stomach roil.

The late hour and everything else is starting to catch up to me and weigh my eyelids down, but every time I close my eyes, I feel like the air is closing in around me and squeezing the breath from my lungs. I want to scream. I want to cry. I want to do anything at all besides be in this car. But I can't.

Basil chatters on about something, but I'm too spent to really listen. From the overly upbeat sound of his voice, whatever he's discussing probably isn't horribly important anyway. I'd love it if he'd just shut up so I can take some of this downtime to be alone with my thoughts. But he barely stops for breath, and I'm not going to be rude, not after he's been so insufferably nice.

The next thing I know, the car is parked in a small lot next to a stone wall and a large iron gate. I must've managed to drift off at some point.

"End of the line, I'm afraid," says Basil. "We have to go the rest of the way on foot because of the wards."

"Wards?" I've heard the word before, but I don't actually know what they are except they have something to do with magic.

"They're woven into the gates and the walls to protect the school, keep out intruders, and to ensure the no cell phone rule is followed. All staff vehicles are kept here outside the main gate. There's a garage for student vehicles near the back gate." He gestures for me to get out of the car and then strolls around to the trunk to grab my bag.

I stand slowly, my muscles sore and overexerted. From the magic maybe? Can using magic do that?

Basil pushes my bag at me and urges me forward with a hand on my lower back. "Now, just remember what I told you, and you'll be fine."

What he told me? In the car? I'm opening my mouth to ask him what it was when the gate swings open and he gives me a little push. As I pass through the gate, there's a sharp jab, uncomfortable but not quite painful, at the place deep in my chest where my magic exploded from.

The air shimmers to reveal a long, meandering drive lined with recessed lights and bordered by perfectly manicured grass that leads up to a group of buildings at the top of the hill. Walking up the entire drive takes ages, and the buildings that looked normal-sized from the gate keep growing larger and larger until the full scope of them becomes clear. There are three buildings, at least ten stories each, making the shape of a 'u' with a sizeable, grassy square in the middle and a few smaller buildings scattered around behind them. The bigger buildings are all gray stone with ivy curling up the sides, and the windows are all dark—probably because it's at least 3:00 a.m. if not later.

It's all rather pretty. And ridiculously fancy looking in that old money estate type way. I don't know if I've ever felt more out of place in my entire life.

My parents aren't poor. Everyone in the Blue Ridge region does pretty well for themselves thanks to the various businesses Connor has set up to support the packs.

But the way I grew up was nothing like this. This is...rich. *Freakishly* rich.

I glance down at my jeans and try to recall what outfits I might have thrown in my bag, suddenly wishing I'd taken a bit more care with packing. The black boots I have on are decent enough, but I don't think running shoes are going to cut it. And flip-flops? I cringe.

Basil points at the building on the left. "The boys' dormitory." To the building on the right. "The girls' dormitory. The first floor of each is made up of various common rooms: theaters, study rooms, game rooms and the like. Anyone can use those. The athletic fields are behind the main building there in the center, and starting by the corner of the boys' dorm there's a trail that goes around the lake. All classes will be in the main building, and that's where staff offices are as well, but the top floor is faculty housing and off limits to students."

This is all so overwhelming...What the hell am I doing here?

"Why Ravencrest?" I finally ask.

"Because it's where Helen went? Because it's the best? I can't tell you anything for sure except that Ravencrest is apparently what Helen wanted for you. Otherwise she wouldn't have included me as part of her contingency plan. She left the Order only a couple months after she graduated and didn't confide in me regarding her plans—or regarding you. I was just as surprised as anyone when your uncle called me this evening," says Basil, his voice going quiet for a moment before he puts his cheery smile back on and pats me on the shoulder. "Don't worry. I'm sure you'll fit in just fine."

Yeah. Right. I want to ask more questions, find out more about my birth mother, but I don't have the energy to process any of that right now. I'm sure I'll have plenty of opportunities to get more information later. Like after I've had a good night's rest and my head has stopped spinning.

The tour continues, but I only listen to half of it, managing to catch where the dining hall and the library are located before he starts blabbering on about the history of some stairwell. Trying to remember all the room numbers and information he's throwing is just making me dizzy again, so I tune out his voice and focus on figuring out how I'm supposed to deal with all this.

I want to go home. I want this night to have never happened. I want to be in my own bed so I can wake up to Mom cooking pancakes and Dad ruffling my hair.

But instead I'm here. *And I was too angry and too selfish to give them a real hug goodbye.*

"There, there. It won't be as hard as you think. You'll have a map and a student guide," says Basil brightly as he hands me a piece of cloth. A handkerchief.

The burning in my eyes and the dampness on my cheeks finally registers. How embarrassing. I must be more exhausted than I realized.

I offer up a tight smile and wave away the offered cloth before swiping my hand over my cheeks. "I'm fine. Just a little overtired."

He nods. "Very well then. We have a little paperwork to take care of, and then you can get settled."

"Okay. Sure." Nothing is really 'okay', but there's no point in arguing about it now.

He leads me into the middle building and up a narrow corner staircase. Six flights of stairs later, we exit into a darkened hallway. The air is a little musty in that old building kind of way, but the carpet is plush, and art pieces line the walls. At the other end of the hallway, Basil stops in front of a door and runs two fingers over the wood as he mutters something under his breath. There's a click before he pushes the door open and gestures for me to follow him inside.

"Most doors at the school are simply warded, but as an extra security measure my door is spelled as well," he explains.

I smile and nod as if that makes sense.

The office is quite large with overflowing bookshelves lining every wall. Lopsided piles of paper cover the desk located in the far corner, and yet more books are scattered throughout the room in tall piles that appear as if they might tip over at any moment.

My brows rise as I take everything in.

"Now where did I put it?" Basil totters around the room, running his fingers over the bookshelves, flipping open a few covers of unshelved books, and rifling through a few pieces of paper. He scratches at his temple and looks around the room again. Distractedly, he motions at a chair. "Please have a seat, dear."

I lift a stack of spiral-bound notebooks from the chair and glance around. There's not really anyplace to put them, so I set them on the ground next to the chair and take a seat, letting my bag rest on the floor.

"How long is this going to take?" I drag a hand over my face. "I'm exhausted."

Basil's gaze moves over me, and he raises a finger. "I know just what you need. I'll be right back."

He hustles out of the room before I can say anything. A few minutes later, he returns and shoves a mug into my hands. "Here, drink this."

I tilt the mug up and take a large sip then immediately start coughing as liquid fire burns its way down my throat. "What the hell?"

"You should probably slow down. That's my best brandy. More of a sipping drink really," says Basil.

Another cough works its way from my chest. "No kidding. A warning would have been nice. I thought it was coffee."

His brow furrows. "No. I don't drink caffeine. It's awful for you."

My mouth opens, but I swallow the words at the last moment. There's no use in trying to argue with him. I don't know much about Basil, but I've come to realize he doesn't quite follow things the way other people do. I take another sip, a *small* sip, and this time the liquid goes down much better, the warmth of it curling in my stomach and sending out a pleasant feeling to the rest of me. Brandy definitely isn't something I'd pick for myself, but I guess it will do.

"So . . ." I say as Basil flips through a stack of papers on his desk and then sifts through his drawers. "What's next?"

No response. He pushes his glasses up his nose and continues fiddling with the papers.

"Do I get a room or something? I'm really tired."

"No, no, no," he says, shaking his head. "You haven't been admitted yet. There's some paperwork here somewhere . . ."

Admission paperwork? You'd think with the late night cloak-and-dagger antics, filling out paperwork would be unnecessary. I snort under my breath. This situation keeps getting more and more ridiculous. Next he'll be telling me there's a placement test. Wait...*Is* there a placement test? Well, if there is, I probably won't have to deal with it until tomorrow—or next week at this rate—so there's no use worrying about it now.

I stand and walk over to the desk. Sitting just on the edge is a thin sheaf of papers stapled together, clearly marked as admission forms. It even has my name across the top in shaky capital letters.

"Is this what you're looking for?" I ask, holding the forms up pinched between two fingers.

His face brightens with a grin. "Yes!" He grabs the papers out of my hand before setting them on the desk. "A pen...a pen...Where did I put that pen?"

I gently tug the forms out from under his hand and grab one of the pens in the narrow holder hidden behind a pile of notebooks. "I've got it."

"Wonderful." He directs me around the desk and gestures for me to take the chair. "You can use my desk. I'm sorely lacking in any other space in here."

No kidding. I eye the haphazard piles of books and the desktop nearly covered in stacks of paper. Him missing the form is understandable. I glance at my name written across the top. *Almost* understandable.

The first page is simple enough, asking for basic details like birth date, address, parents' names—I put down George and Aileen—and things like that. It isn't until I get to the second page that I have to pause. Power affiliation? Concentration area? Manipulation scores? Clearly, there's a lot more to being a witch than I know.

"I'm not sure how to fill the rest of this out," I say, handing the papers back to Basil. "I don't know any of that stuff on the second page. I don't know much about being a witch in general."

He takes the papers and pats my arm. "No worries, dear. I've already notified Director Burke. He'll arrange for any necessary testing to get the rest of this filled out. It should be fairly routine."

Fairly routine. *Right.* Like anything about any of this has been routine.

"Let's get you to your room. You should probably try to get a little sleep before you meet with the director in the morning." He pauses. "Oh yes, let me take that talisman off your hands for now. It won't do much within the boundaries of the school wards."

A sudden sense of loss coils in my chest as I slowly remove the pendant before handing it to him. "Will I...get it back?"

"Of course, of course," he says. "It does belong to you after all."

Huh. I guess it does since it was my birth mother's.

Basil places the pendant inside a small box on his desk and then makes a shooing motion with his hands as he ushers me out of his office before I have time to say anything else. We go down the stairs and across the quad to the building he previously identified as the girls' dorm. I follow him up five more flights of stairs and down another long hallway to a door at the end marked 513.

"This will be your room for the duration of your stay here. You have a roommate, Isobel Cardosa, but she'll probably be sleeping at this time of night." He presses his fingers against the doorknob and motions for me to go in as the door swings open. "It'll be keyed to you once you're fully registered. Get some sleep, dear. Director Burke will be expecting you at his office, room 419 in the main building, at 8:00 a.m. *sharp*. He'll key the wards to your magical energy, set you up with some uniforms and books, and tell you about your classes and school procedure and all that."

He pats me on the head and gives me a gentle push into the room. He's gone again before I can find enough words to form any of the million questions flying through my mind. I suppose I'll have to wait until the morning for more answers.

I take in my surroundings. The room is simple but cozy. Two beds, two desks, two dressers, and two narrow doors to what I assume are closets. The side of the room farthest from the door is decorated with simple solid colors, mostly teal and yellow, and there's a person-shaped lump underneath the geometric design on the comforter, most likely my roommate. The fact that she's asleep already is almost a relief. I don't know if I have it in me to deal with anyone else tonight.

I flop down on the empty bed, tossing my bag on the floor, then eye my roommate's cluttered desk. There's a precarious-looking stack of books on the desk and one fairly thick book left open in the center. That's quite a lot of reading for this early in the school year. Is the course load going to be that heavy?

The lingering anger that's held me together is fading into a deep hopelessness. One of the tears I've managed to hold back escapes and tracks its way down my cheek. I sniffle and eye my sleeping roommate. Will it wake her up if I completely lose it right now? Does it really matter?

Another sniffle. Another tear.

By habit, I reach for my phone to text Reid. But my phone is gone. Next week, Reid will be in New York, and who knows what's going to happen with my parents.

Connor said they'd be in touch as soon as they could.

And I have no idea when that might be.

The fragile hold I have on my emotions shatters, and the tears come down full force, followed by a hiccupping sob.

I can't do this. I don't want to be here. I want to go home.

CHAPTER 5

When I wake up, the person-shaped lump in the other bed is gone. I'm not normally one for sleeping in, but after everything that happened last night, I must've been more tired than I realized, because I could sleep for another twelve hours. But the brightness of what has to be at least mid-morning shines through the window.

Which means I'm late. Very late.

Crap.

I really could use my cell phone right about now, if only for its alarm clock feature.

My eyes are gritty and my head is pounding from not getting enough sleep, but staying in bed isn't an option. There's too much at stake for me to mess this up. I need to put on a happy face and just do it. Push through adversity. Don't let the witches get me down and all that...*Ugh, I sound like a motivational poster.* If nothing else, today I need to figure out what the deal is here so I can try to make it work. Emphasis on *try*.

I jump out of bed and search frantically through my bag for an outfit that isn't wrinkled beyond recognition. No luck, and even if I had time, there's no iron in sight. Once again, I'm hit with a large dose of regret for not taking the time to pack properly. I pull on yesterday's jeans, shove my arms into the dressiest-looking shirt I brought, a pale-yellow, short-sleeved blouse, and pull on the first pair of shoes I can find: my flip-flops. This is certainly not the most fashionable outfit, but who do I need to impress? Basil mentioned uniforms, so I'll only be wearing this until someone issues them to me. I can deal with it until then. Right?

There's a paper cup sitting on my desk with a short note.

Tried to wake you, but you weren't budging.
Hope you like vanilla lattes.
-Isobel

I don't know much about my new roomie, but even though she's a witch, she's my favorite person in the world right now, no contest. The latte is cold, but I down it anyway, willing the caffeine into my system as quickly as possible.

Feeling a little better even if it is only psychosomatic, I pull my unruly mass of dark hair into a messy bun and put on enough makeup to look somewhat presentable: eyeliner, mascara, and a touch of lip gloss.

I grab the admission forms Basil gave me and rush out the door, realizing only as the door shuts behind me that I don't know how to open the thing. I grimace. Basil mentioned something about getting the wards keyed to me, so hopefully I don't need anything else from the room until either that happens or I meet up with my roommate for an actual conversation.

I dash through the hallways—the *empty* hallways—and run down the stairs to the ground floor.

Administrative offices are in the middle building, but what room did Basil say I was supposed to go to? I have no freaking idea. Glancing down at the admission forms, I flip through them. Maybe Basil wrote the room number on here. *Please, please, please.* No luck. I guess I'll—

I slam into someone. Everything in my hands goes flying, and I land on my butt on the ground. Dammit. I should have been paying more attention.

The guy standing over me, clearly another student as he's wearing what must be the school uniform, stares down at me. As in, literally looks down his perfect, lightly freckled nose at me. His hair is barely on the blond side of dirty blond, neatly combed, and trimmed close to his head at the sides and a little longer on top. Golden-brown eyes the color of dark honey go from the top of my head to my flip-flopped feet and my purple toenails. I'd say he's the hottest guy I've ever seen if his lip wasn't curling in distaste. The expression makes the high cheekbones and sharp lines of his pretty face turn into something cold and hard.

"Sorry," I say, offering a weak smile and a shrug. "I'm late, and I wasn't looking where I was going."

His gaze makes another pass over me, and then he huffs and steps around me without a word, leaving me to gather the scattered papers alone. Wow. What an ass. But pretty much what I expected from Ravencrest and witches in general. I hope he's not in any of my classes.

Admission forms reassembled, I brush off my jeans and make my way to the main building. The door is locked. Crap. Basil did warn me to be on time...

There's a pad by the side where students are supposed to scan IDs or something like that, but I clearly don't have one. I glance frantically around, but the quad is deserted. I give the door another shake, and it rattles in the frame. I resist the urge to kick it. More because I'm wearing open-toed shoes than from any sense of decorum.

Behind me, someone clears their throat. I spin around to face a guy with an amused look on his face. He has tan skin and dark, glossy curls that tumble over his forehead, the kind of hairstyle that looks effortless but really isn't. A fancy watch graces his wrist, and his clothes, a perfectly fitted pair of navy-blue trousers and a white button-down shirt with a blazer bearing the school crest on it, look like they were made for him. Another student then. Here's hoping this one isn't an asshole too.

His gaze flicks down to my flip-flops. "Are you lost?"

"Um, yes? Well, sort of. I'm new and I'm supposed to meet with the director, but I'm late and don't have a student ID yet." I shuffle from foot to foot and give him a nervous smile.

"A student ID?" His brows pull together, and a hint of mirth flashes in his dark-brown eyes.

I gesture at the pad beside the door. "To get in."

"You don't need an ID. It's a ward." He places two fingers against the pad, much like Basil did with the doorknob at my dorm room, and there's a soft click. "Your magical energy will be keyed to it, and any other doors you're permitted access to, once you're fully registered."

So that's what Basil was talking about. My cheeks heat, and I shrug. "Yeah well...this is all a little new to me."

He tilts his head to the side and rubs his chin. "New to wards? How is that possible? All witches learn the basics as children. What, were you raised by wolves or something?"

He means the words as a joke, but I can't help a flare of anger. "Actually, yes," I say. "I was supposed to be a Blank, so my witch parents deserted me, and I was raised by shifters."

He blinks and gives me a curious stare then chuckles as his face breaks into a warm smile. "Well, that's certainly going to shake some things up. I can't wait to see the looks on everyone's faces." His expression shifts to intrigued as he crosses his arms over his chest and leans against the door. "And what is your name, Ms. Raised by Shifters?"

"Selene," I say, holding out a hand as relief washes over me. Maybe not everyone here will be a complete jerk.

"Adrian Dumont." He straightens and takes my hand in his then presses a light kiss to my knuckles. "It's been a pleasure to meet you, Selene, but it appears we're now *both* late." He places his fingers on the pad again and then holds the door open for me, gesturing for me to step in ahead of him. Once inside, he starts off down a hallway.

"Excuse me...?" I call out.

He turns, amusement sparking in his eyes. "Yes?"

"Where's the director's office?"

"Fourth floor, Room 419," he says with a wave. "Good luck."

Good luck? What do I need luck for? I shrug off the worry and start toward the stairs.

Four floors later, I tick off each room number as I go past until I reach the end of the hallway where I find 419. I knock softly.

"Come in," a chirpy voice says from inside.

I enter a small office with a man sitting behind a desk. He grins at me, and a wave of relief washes over me. He looks nice enough with that open expression and friendly smile. Being late might not be quite the disaster I thought it was if he's not glaring or yelling.

"Director Burke? I'm Selene. I'm so sorry I'm late. I must've—"

The intercom on the desk clicks on. "Is that her?" asks a voice in a clipped British accent.

"Yes, sir," replies the man at the desk who I'm now realizing must be a secretary or assistant or something.

"Send her back." The director does not sound happy.

The guy at the desk shoots me a sympathetic look before tilting his head in the direction of the door to his right. "Go right in. He's expecting you."

No kidding. I pull my shoulders back, plaster a smile on my face, and walk through the door into the director's actual office.

The man behind this desk is somewhere in his fifties, with gray sprinkled throughout his dark hair. He has on a pair of thin-framed glasses that he peers over as I enter. His mouth pulls into a tight smile, and he rises to his feet. "Director Desmond Burke. I'm pleased you could make it this morning." He holds out a slim-fingered hand, and I shake it hesitantly. He gestures to the chair in front of the desk. "Have a seat."

I do, offering up the best smile I can muster. "I apologize for being late."

He sits back down and waves away my apology. "You have the admission forms?"

"Yes." I hand him the somewhat messy stack of papers over the desk. "I wasn't sure if—"

He holds up a hand, and I clamp my mouth shut. His gray eyes skim across the paper as he flips through the admission forms with no expression. He reaches the end, places the stack on his desk, and leans back in his chair. "Basil tells me you're an Andras witch. Is that correct?"

"Um...If that was my birth mother's last name, then yes?"

He sighs. "Is that a question or a statement? Because if you're planning to stay at my school, you must own your identity as a witch of the Andras line or you have no chance of success."

My brows pull together in confusion. "Why? What's so special—"

"Your presence here, starting late, all of it"—he gestures to my somewhat disheveled appearance—"you will have enough problems without having a high-powered name to protect you. The admission criteria is very strict. With your lack of knowledge, I can't pass you off as a scholarship student, therefore you need to be presented as a member of an elite family. The Andras line is well thought of, and we can spin you as a long-lost distant cousin or something."

Lost? *Spin?* What the hell is going on here?

"But I wasn't lost. I was *left.*" The last word is sharp, and I narrow my eyes.

He gives me a hard look, one eyebrow rising. "Semantics," he says. "What you don't seem to understand, Miss *Andras*, is that you're in a very precarious position here. As am I. As are your adoptive parents, the Blue Ridge alpha, and perhaps the entire pack. The only reason the Coven Council hasn't already carted you away for 'questioning' is because I pulled the strings that got you enrolled at Ravencrest. As a student here, you're under the jurisdiction of OSA, and that offers you some protections. As an Andras, you have even more protections. But if you continue acting like you don't belong here, eventually someone will decide that you're correct. You do not want that."

It's on the tip of my tongue to say that I *don't* belong here and I *do* want that, but not at the expense of something bad happening to my family. I'm here to stay—whether I like it or not. And I better make the best of it.

I hold his gaze for a beat before looking away. "Fine. We'll do it your way. Tell me what I'm supposed to be doing."

"Besides showing up to appointments on time and going to class?" He raises a brow. "You need to fit in, find a place you can belong, because even if it's not said outright, I'm sure the Coven Council will be less inclined to press charges if you're able to become a productive member of society despite your less than ideal upbringing."

"Who do you think—"

He holds up a hand. "Save your vitriol for someone else. I have nothing against shifters, and I am not your enemy. I'm sure you're quite capable of finding some of those on your own. What I *am* is responsible for this academy and its students. Disrespect and disobedience will not be tolerated, not by me and not by your instructors."

I glare at him but hold my tongue.

"Your class schedule," he says as he slides a piece of paper across the desk. As I'm skimming over the list, he continues. "Now that you're considered fully registered, the school wards will be keyed to you, allowing you access to your dorm, your classrooms, and any other areas you are permitted to be in. You'll be issued five sets of uniforms, but due to the lateness of the day and the fact that classes have already started, your current outfit will have to do for today. After today, though, we expect you to present yourself in a more... proper manner." A pause. "I'm going to be frank with you here: You're behind, and it will be a struggle for you to catch up. And I'm not only talking about the fact that classes started last week. I'm sure the shifters do things very differently, and you know very little about witch culture or society."

"I know enough," I bite out even though he's technically correct.

He doesn't look convinced. "Be that as it may, I can only do so much. I placed you in the basic classes and scheduled you tutoring sessions with Basil every morning as he can hopefully get you up to speed. Most of it will be up to you, however. The competition for grades and class ranking is stiff, and you'll be battling it out with witches who have been involved in this world their entire lives. At *least* their first three years of high school were spent preparing to attend this academy. Granted, much of their prior studies have been on only the theory of magic, but you don't even know that much."

"I'm a fast learner." I jut my chin out.

"And you'll need to be." He leans back in his chair. "As you know, this is a two-year program meant to prepare you to use your powers for the benefit of the Order. The classes are semester based, and you will have, at minimum, a Wards and Sigils class, a Potions class, and a Physical Education class every semester. For the moment, your morning tutoring session with Basil will take the place of two other required classes, Government and Spells. The dining hall is the large building behind this one. Breakfast hours are from eight to nine, lunch from twelve to one, and dinner from six to seven. If you miss a meal, you're on your own. Off campus privileges are granted on a per student basis, and for the time being, you don't have any. Work hard, Ms. Andras, and you have no reason to worry for yourself or your adoptive family."

Before I have a chance to ask any questions—and boy do I have *a lot* of them—the office door swings open and the blond boy I ran into earlier comes striding in, his face set in an irritated expression. I don't see much more of him beyond a set of broad shoulders, a trim waist, and a very nice ass in those fitted uniform slacks, because he pays me absolutely no attention as he saunters into the office like he owns the place and throws a piece of paper down on the desk.

"Desmond, what is the meaning of this?" he asks with the barest hint of a British accent.

Director Burke sets his jaw and raises an eyebrow. "Contrary to what you might think, Mr. St. James, my friendship with your family does not entitle you to storm into my office and make demands of me as if I am your servant."

"Des—" The guys huffs. "*Director Burke*, I am not in a position to act as a student guide. I have too much on my plate already with—"

"Too bad," says the director, shaking his head.

The guy slams a hand onto the sheet of paper. "It's unacceptable. My parents would never—"

Director Burke rises to his feet. "You will not speak to me as if you are above me. This is my school, and I set the rules. If you aren't happy with it, go somewhere else." He leans over his desk. "Now, since you have barged into my office and interrupted my meeting with the very student whom you are going to be guiding, I believe some introductions are in order."

Shocked golden-brown eyes finally turn on me, noticing me for the first time. Those same eyes travel from the tips of my purple toenails to the messy bun on top my head. *Again.* The look he gives me this time isn't quite as harsh as the one earlier, but it's not much better. It's slightly hidden disdain instead of open disdain.

"What is a new student doing here after the term has already started anyway? And who is she? Certainly no witch I've ever met."

The level of arrogance dripping off this guy is ridiculous. And I've dealt with moody alpha level shifters. It makes me want to punch him. Hard.

I wiggle my fingers in his direction. "Selene"—a glance at the director— "Andras."

Now Mr. St. James looks at me like I'm dirt under his shoe and lets out a huff. "Descended from some by blow a couple generations back then? The Andras line has no academy-aged heirs and hasn't for at least two decades."

"I'm thinking it's more around eighteen years to be exact," I say, gesturing at myself. "I'm a direct descendant of Helen—"

"You have got to be kidding me." He turns back to Director Burke.

Director Burke sighs and stares as the ceiling. "This is not up for debate." His gaze moves back down, going from my face to the boy's, and the director's lips ghost into a smile so small I almost miss it. "Selene, meet your student guide, Tristan St. James."

The final repetition of his last name makes something finally click together in my mind. *St. James.* The super-rich, old money witch family who heads the Coven Council and is leading the charge on the proposed anti-shifter legislation that would strip the protections of the shifters' pack lands and require reginal alphas to subordinate themselves to the laws of OSA.

In other words, this guy is probably the absolute last person in the world I'd want to associate with, and now I'm stuck with him. *Wonderful. Just wonderful.*

CHAPTER 6

Tristan no longer bothers to hide his disdain. It's written on his face for anyone to see, and I'm sure my expression isn't much different. I'm all for having a guide—there's no way I'll find my way around on my own—but pairing me up with Mr. Uppity Asshole is not what I had in mind. I open my mouth, prepared to argue against this insane idea, but Director Burke holds up a hand.

"It's not optional." He directs his next words more toward Tristan than me. "It will do you both some good to broaden your horizons a little."

Broaden my horizons? I'm not so sure pairing me with a witch who more likely than not hates shifters is going to improve my opinion of the Order or witches in general. But saying so at this point won't do me any good.

"Fine," I say.

Tristan narrows his eyes, and his lips press into a thin line. "Fine," he repeats without looking at me.

I rise to my feet and shoot him the best smile I can manage before gesturing to the doorway. "Lead the way."

He glances in my direction, sends another scathing look at Burke, and then spins around and quickly exits into the outer office and then the hallway, not so much as looking back to see if I'm keeping up. I grit my teeth and speed up. The last thing I'm going to do is ask him to wait for me.

I follow Tristan through the maze of hallways. He still hasn't so much as looked at me since leaving the director's office, but I can hear him muttering something that doesn't sound complimentary. I'm pretty sure the mumbled curses are directed toward Burke and not me, but I wouldn't be surprised to hear my name in there somewhere *if* the jerk even remembers what it is.

We go down to the second floor, and he stops in front of a closed door and shoves my schedule into my hands.

"You have lunch hour after this, and then your next class will be on the bottom floor in room 142. I assume you can find it?"

My answer should be no because I'm *not* entirely sure I can navigate on my own, but getting him out of my hair now is worth maybe having to beg someone else to help me later. "Sure. I've got it from here."

"Great." He shuffles his feet a little. "Have a nice day or whatever." With a dismissive wave, he heads off in the opposite direction. He certainly won't be getting any awards for congeniality or hospitality. Not that I'd expect either of those things from a St. James.

I wait for him to disappear around the corner before turning to the door in front of me. It is, I assume, locked, so I need to use the ward thingy to open it. Director Burke did say they were all keyed to my magical energy now, so that shouldn't be an issue, but he didn't exactly explain *how* to use it, and I damn sure wasn't going to ask Tristan. Could opening a door really be that hard?

I place my fingers against the pad in a similar position as that guy Adrian did when he let me in the building earlier. Nothing happens. I press down and whisper, "open sesame," under my breath. Still nothing. I sense the ward beneath my touch, kind of like a little spark of magic. A switch maybe? Hmm...I close my eyes and concentrate on that feeling of a switch.

It's definitely there.

I poke at that place in my chest where my magic resides, willing it to do something. Again, nothing. I lean my forehead against the door. This is so, so stupid. I don't belong here. I can't even open the stupid door.

But I don't have a choice now, do I? I *have* to figure out how to do this. If I don't, my family might suffer the consequences. I straighten and study the pad again. Maybe the ward isn't so much a switch as a reaction and magic is the catalyst? What if I just...

I pull up some magic, dragging it from my center and down my arm to send at the ward. The door still refuses to open. Am I unconsciously holding on too tightly? I take a deep breath and try to relax. Nothing.

Anger surges through me. *Dammit to hell!* I slam my palm down on the pad, and a burst of magic flows into the ward. The door clicks open— *finally*—but there's also a sizzling sound, and a thin stream of smoke rises from the pad. Oops. I guess I used a little too much. I bite at my lower lip and look into the classroom. Every single eye of the maybe thirty students is on me, a few openly hostile and the rest completely disinterested.

I wiggle my fingers in an awkward wave. "Hi, um, I'm Selene. I'm new."

A ripple of quiet laughter passes over the room, and they all look to the front. I follow their gazes to find a slim, dark-skinned woman with glasses giving me a disapproving stare.

"I'm Ms. Anderson. If you're quite done being a disruption, class has already started. Please find yourself a seat," she says.

Forcing my lips into a smile, I nod and walk inside to find the room is set up like a lecture hall, with five rows of seats rising toward the back. I scan over the seated students, hoping to find one friendly face. No luck.

Well, I'm definitely not sitting in the first or second rows which are filled with what I assume to be the preppy elite. Perfect hair. Tailored uniforms. A general aura of money. There are some empty seats near the back, though, so I head in that direction. The sound of my flip-flops is like mini explosions in the silence, and another wave of laughter passes over the room.

I take a seat in the second to the last row near the middle of the room. As soon as my butt hits the chair, the teacher starts speaking again.

There are a few diagrams on the board, and she seems to be explaining one of them, but half of what she says makes no sense. I pull my schedule out. The class is called Geometry of Wards and Sigils, so some of it makes sense now. This is a math class. But one that apparently talks not just about angles and degrees but ley lines and power levels. Math isn't my best subject, but it's not my worst either.

I focus on what the teacher is saying. I have no way to take notes, and I don't have any books yet, so I'm not sure how much of this lesson I'll actually retain, but paying attention is better than doing nothing.

"Last week, we went over the basics of wards and what they are; I'll spare the rest of you the refresher and suggest our new student get up to speed on this information as soon as possible." She draws another diagram on the board, a circle with three intersecting lines inside. "This is a locking ward. Easy to draw, easy to implement, and easy to use." She gives me a hard stare. "A ward like this and like the one on the doorway to our classroom requires only a slight touch of magic. As they grow more complicated, a stronger touch is needed and sometimes a specific touch or a specific sequence. There are blood wards that can only be opened by witches with a certain blood type or of a certain bloodline, but they're much more difficult to create and not often used."

She faces the class. "For the remainder of the period, I want you to find a partner and work on drawing the simple locking wards from page ninety-three in your textbooks. We're not actually infusing them with magic yet. That won't be covered until later in the quarter. Right now, I want you to just practice drawing the correct lines and angles."

There's a flurry of activity in the room as the other students pair up. No one offers to partner with me. Fine. I'll do it by myself. How hard can it be? But there's one problem...

"Ms. Anderson," I say as I raise a hesitant hand. "I don't have a textbook yet."

She shrugs. "Next time, come to my class prepared and on time or not at all."

I take a deep breath through my nose and clench my teeth to hold back the argument I want to make. Antagonizing her any further won't do me any good. Maybe when I can prove I'm not a complete spaz, she'll go easier on me. For today, I'll sit here and bite my tongue until the end of class.

And I do. I spend thirty minutes staring down at my desk as the other students work around me. As soon as a soft tone signaling the end of the period sounds, I'm on my feet and heading toward the door. I have a while until my next class starts, but I want to grab some lunch, and I'm hoping I'll also have time to grab a pen and some paper and maybe a uniform and a textbook. I'm dashing past the second row when a purse slides into my path, the strap tangling around one of my feet. I go stumbling down to my hands and knees.

A jolt of pain travels up from my knees, feeding into my already on-edge temper. I leap back to my feet and spin around in a much more graceful move than I should be able to achieve in flip-flops—thank God for all that time training with Reid—and find the girl sitting at the desk next to the purse, smirking at me.

"Clumsy much?" says the vaguely familiar-looking brunette, and two girls to her right giggle.

The thin-lipped smile on her face finally clicks in my memory. For the life of me, I can't remember her name, but she's Bridget's older sister, which means she knows damn well who I am and where I came from. I already told Adrian that I was raised by shifters, but he seemed nice enough since he helped me with the door and all. If I asked him to keep quiet, he probably would. This girl, however…Burke might be able to "spin" my identity as a distant relative of the Andras line but he's out of luck if he's hoping to keep my upbringing a secret.

I scowl and try to ignore the heat gathering in my chest, but everything in me wants to smack the smile off her face. Someone wraps a hand around my arm, squeezing gently, and I turn to the new arrival in surprise.

"It's not worth it," says the girl next to me. She's a short, curvy Hispanic girl who I don't recognize and I'm pretty sure isn't in this class. When I don't say anything more, she continues, "Basil sent me. I have some time before my next class. Why don't I show you where to pick up your books?" Her brows rise expectantly.

She has a point. Bridget's sister isn't worth getting into trouble over, and something tells me I'd be the one blamed no matter who started it.

"Yeah. Sure." I take a deep breath and follow the new arrival from the room without another word to the still-smirking brunette.

"I'm Isobel by the way, your roommate," the girl says as she leads me around to the stairs. "Sorry I wasn't awake last night to greet you. I was trying to knock out all my reading for class and practically passed out on my desk. It was all I could do to crawl into bed."

I return her smile, grateful. She seems friendly enough. I certainly could've ended up with a worse roommate. *Thank you, Basil.* "Thanks for rescuing me from making an even bigger idiot out of myself back there. I'm not used to people being mean for the hell of it, or at least not without consequences. And the coffee this morning...You're a life saver."

"No problem," she replies. "Let me see your schedule. I can help you figure out where to go after lunch."

"My lackluster guide told me my next class was down on the bottom floor somewhere. I'm pretty sure he was telling the truth, though we didn't quite hit it off, so I wouldn't put it past him to lie either. He wasn't happy about showing me around."

"Guide?"

"He wasn't much of one. He was way too busy scowling at me for existing. Plus, he's a St. James, so I think I'm supposed to dislike him solely on principle."

"Ah, the illustrious Tristan St. James, huh? It's a shame he's so vile when he's so pretty." She laughs and pushes open the door at the bottom of the stairs.

"You can say that again."

"I think we're going to get along just fine." She links her arm through mine.

"I think you're right." I grin. "I'm so glad not everyone at this school is a jerk. This is not how I planned to spend the next year, navigating a bunch of stupid social niceties while trying to fit in and deal with all these new classes. I can't even open a door correctly."

She pats my arm. "No worries. I can help you out with that. You're here, so you must have plenty of power. You simply need to learn a little finesse. How long has it been since you manifested?"

I mime looking at a non-existent watch. "Oh about sixteen hours."

"Are you serious?" She stops dead in her tracks. "How in the world did you get through all the admissions testing already?"

"Uh...I didn't?"

She starts walking again. "Explain."

Knowing the way rumors spread, my not-so-secret is going to be common knowledge before long, so I have nothing to lose by telling Isobel the truth. "I was raised as a Blank. By shifters. My powers were bound or something, and they only showed up last night. The next thing I knew, I found out my parents had been lying to me, Basil showed up at my house, and I was whisked off here. I don't know all the details, but my birth mother was from a fairly important witch line. She was an Andras witch."

"An Andras? That must've been one hell of a binding spell to keep that kind of power under wraps." She casts a glance at me from the corner of her eye, assessing. "How is it you got stuck with a roommate like a peon? Not that I'm complaining—I'm here on scholarship, and this place is sorely lacking in down-to-earth people—but I'd expect you to have one of the private rooms since the Andras family has more money than...well, pretty much anyone but the St. James family."

"Director Burke suggested I use the name since it means there's less of a chance of me having to explain exactly how I got here, but they aren't really my family, at least not in the way I think of family. I'd much rather room with you than be stuck with a bunch of rich, uh, witches."

She laughs. "I take it growing up with shifters was not of the 'more money than God' variety like most of the students here."

"Definitely not. My uncle is the regional alpha, but we still lived pretty simply." I sigh. "And we were never lacking love."

There's a lump in my throat now, and I have to pause to take a deep breath.

"It's hard being away from family." Isobel places a gentle hand on my arm and offers up a small smile. "My little brother and I were raised by our grandmother. When I was given a scholarship to attend Ravencrest, I almost turned it down because I didn't want to leave them behind. I'm sorry you had to leave yours so suddenly."

I return her smile. "Thanks."

Steering the conversation toward less depressing things, she tells me a funny story about her little brother and a pair of hair clippers. She goes on to tell me more about Ravencrest and how the student body is fifty percent the 'richer than God' variety, about forty percent 'as rich as God,' and the last ten percent is made up of either moderately rich students sponsored by richer family members or scholarship students. Her stream of friendly chatter continues as she leads me back to our room. The distraction is exactly what I need. I don't know what made Basil choose Isobel as my roommate, but I'm beyond grateful that he did.

When we reach our room, Isobel winks. "And now to teach you the amazing feat of opening a door."

CHAPTER 7

After my door opening lesson and scarfing down some snacks my roomie had in a box under her bed, I try to get in a quick nap before my next class while Isobel heads to the library. Everything is still catching up to me, and I'm starting to drag again, no matter that I had another two cups of coffee. I rummage through my bag, throw on a pair of leggings and a loose tank top, then curl up on my bed and promptly fall asleep.

Sometime later, Isobel's frantic voice rips me away from sleep. "Selene!"

"Huh? What?" I sit up quickly, rubbing at my eyes. *Dammit.* I really should have asked Isobel about setting an alarm...

"Have you been asleep this whole time? You missed your potions class."

"Crap. What time is it?" I drag a hand over my face. This isn't good. I fumble at my desk for my schedule and squint at it. "I've got phys ed next."

"You have time to make it if you leave like *right now*," says Isobel.

"I'm going. I'm going." I give my head a shake and go over to my bag.

The leggings and tank top will be fine for PE, but I grab a sports bra and wiggle it on underneath my top. I redo my hair, pulling it into a high ponytail, and search out my running shoes. Thank goodness I shoved those in my bag. PE in flip-flops wouldn't have been fun. Once I'm ready, I shoot Isobel a quick wave and run out the door.

At least this is a class I can probably do okay in. I'm used to training with Reid most days, so how different can magic PE class really be? A part of me is looking forward to it.

That is, until I actually arrive at the athletic field behind the main building.

The entire class is decked out in navy-blue shorts or leggings and white tops with the school crest on them. Gym uniforms? Really? Is this *middle* school?

My steps slow as I draw closer and take in the various groups. There's a flash of familiar dirty-blond hair in one of the groups—Tristan. The group he's with is made up of seven or eight others, all of them with that certain kind of shine that comes with being rich and popular. Perfect hair. Perfect skin. Perfect teeth. And Tristan with his arrogant attitude and pretty face should fit right in with them.

Except...he somehow *doesn't*. His expression is bland, his arms crossed over his chest, and he's just silently standing there in the middle of the group as the others talk around him. Even though he's surrounded by others, he's alone, as if he's playing the part of the popular guy but doesn't actually want to be there. It's weird.

There are a couple smaller groups around the edges, and on the far side, Adrian is standing with another guy. Interesting. With Adrian's dark good looks and friendly personality, I'd expect him to be one of the popular kids. If the flashy watch he was wearing earlier is anything to go by, he's certainly one of the rich ones.

I shuffle my feet. What now? I know all of two people in this class, and

I'm damned sure not going to try to hang out with Tristan whether he's my supposed student guide or not. There's only one option then...

I plaster a smile on my face and wander over to where Adrian stands. "Hey, um, we met earlier. Selene."

He gives me a wry grin. "Oh, I remember. Did you get your 'student ID' situation straightened out?"

"Yeah, pretty much. I'm still one step behind everyone else though," I say, gesturing down at my clothes.

"No worries. Sometimes standing out can be a good thing," he says with an amused glint in his eyes.

I scoff. "Yeah, sure. Whatever you say."

Adrian's friend grins at me and holds out a hand. "Devin Ames. I'm Adrian's roommate. You're the girl raised by shifters, right?" He shares a look with Adrian. "We've heard quite a bit about you."

I cringe. "The rumor mill's that bad, huh? I can"—I wave a hand at an empty patch of grass near one of the other groups of students—"go over there or something."

"Please, stay." Adrian winks. "I imagine you'll be the most entertaining part of this class." He pushes a hand through his hair, and the sun glints off the fancy watch on his wrist, further solidifying my opinion that he belongs with the group of rich, popular kids.

"Why aren't you two with the others?"

"Haven't you heard? I'm the stereotypical black sheep." Adrian holds his arms out to the side. "My family name got me in, but I'm not much of a 'joiner,' and I certainly don't care to cater to the expectations of others. And Devin here is, gasp, a scholarship student. The lemmings over there don't know what to do with us."

Devin nudges his friend with a shoulder. "And there's the fact you tend to hit on anything that walks on two legs."

Adrian shrugs. "What can I say? I have a healthy appreciation for the physical form no matter the gender."

All three of us laugh, and I don't feel quite as awkward anymore. These two are outsiders kind of like me.

The teacher, Mr. Davis, a broad-shouldered man with close-cropped black hair, starts us off with a few laps. I keep pace with Adrian and Devin for the first one, but I pull out ahead by the second one, and by the third, I've almost lapped them. I'm not trying to leave them behind, but I'm used to running with Reid or my mom, and they don't know the meaning of a slow pace.

"Too bad we don't have a track team," says Adrian as I pass him. His breaths come easily, so he could go faster if he wanted to.

I wrinkle my nose. "Not much of a joiner."

Unlike Adrian, my breaths, though regulated, come fast and hard, and talking isn't easy. I slow my pace just a bit and turn around to face him, moving backward at a slow jog.

"Show off," says Devin, smirking.

"What's the matter? Can't you two—"

My back crashes into someone, and we go down in a tangle of feet. The air is knocked from my chest as I hit the ground. I fumble around until I can flip over onto hands and knees, my legs still half-tangled with the other runner's.

"Get the hell off me," says a voice I'm coming to know better than I'd like to. *Tristan.*

Adrian clicks his tongue against the roof of his mouth as he draws up beside us. "St. James, it's always nice to see you on your knees, but that's no way to talk to a lady."

"Piss off, Dumont," says Tristan. He shoves to his feet and goes back to running without another word.

"Jackass." I brush dirt off my leggings.

"So true," says Adrian. "But can you imagine how hot the hate sex would be?"

Devin shoves him. "Hot or not, don't mess around with St. James. His parents would have your head on a platter, and I rather enjoy having a roommate who doesn't have a stick up his ass about money." His gaze moves to me. "The St. James family has certain 'expectations' of their son, and they tend to...clear the field of obstacles."

I arch an eyebrow. "So what you're saying is he's a spoiled brat who will go running to Mommy and Daddy?"

"Pretty much," says Devin. "And Mommy and Daddy have enough influence—and money—that they have practically the entire OSA at their beck and call."

Some pieces of the exchange in the director's office earlier suddenly make more sense. As does my earlier observation about Tristan being alone in a crowd and the fact that he's currently running entirely by himself. Is it because he has no real friends because of who his parents are or because he doesn't want any friends?

Mr. Davis claps his hands. "All right. Let's see what you've got." He has us arrange ourselves into two parallel lines, and I end up between Adrian and Devin.

Relief seeps into me, and I find an actual smile on my face. As horrible as my other class went, at least I have friends in this one.

"Now, turn toward the center of the field and face the other line."

I do as directed and find myself staring at Tristan. A sense of foreboding oozes into my stomach.

"The person directly across from you is your partner for this exercise."

Wonderful. Having friends in this class does me no good at all if I have to partner up with this asshole. What did I do to deserve this punishment?

"We're going to take things a little easy today," says the teacher. "A few practice shots, nothing major. And we're concentrating on defense right now. Offensive skills won't come into play until later. Everyone on this side"—he gestures toward Tristan's side—"will pull a little magic and send energy balls at the other side as they defend themselves accordingly. Energy balls *only*. No spells."

I suppose it's a good thing I'm not the one expected to use any magic since I'm still not exactly sure how to do it, but I also have no clue how to defend myself from magic either. Apprehension must show on my face because Tristan smirks.

Devin leans to the side so he can speak into my ear. "It's nothing to worry about. All you have to do is defend yourself."

"All I have to do is defend myself?" I repeat.

"Yes," confirms Adrian from my other side.

Defending myself sounds easy enough, but there's gotta be a catch. I don't have time to figure out what it is though. The teacher sweeps his arm down through the air in a motion that I guess means begin. Everyone in the other line goes into action, each of them moving their hands in different ways.

Tristan only uses one hand in a motion that looks as if he's scooping something from the air, and then he tosses whatever that something is in my direction. I don't see what he threw, but damned if I don't feel it when it lands on my arm.

I wince and hiss out a breath. What the hell? How am I supposed to defend myself from something I can't see?

His hands are moving again. This time, I step out of the way when he tosses another burst of magic at me. I'm not letting him land another one of those things.

"You're supposed to be defending, not avoiding," he says, his upper lip

65

curling.

"Well, excuse me for not knowing the rules," I mutter under my breath. To Adrian, I say, "Defend myself, that's the only rule, right?"

"Yup," says Adrian as he flicks his hand out like he's batting something away. Which he probably is. Duh.

I focus my attention back on Tristan and give him a sugary-sweet smile. "Let's do this then."

He makes that scooping motion again, this time balling something up with two hands before lobbing it at my face. I dodge to the side and move forward. The magic brushes by my head, and the smell of burned hair hits my nose. He threw magic at my *head* and *singed* my *hair*. What the hell kind of game is he trying to play?

As Tristan gathers up more magic, I stalk the fifteen feet or so across the field and shove him in the shoulder. "You could have really hurt me with that!"

He shrugs. "You're supposed to be defending yourself from my very, *very* basic attacks. If you can't cut it, why don't you leave?"

He doesn't need to know how much I'd absolutely *love* to leave this place, but I'll certainly show him how I 'defend myself.' I set my feet, raise my hands, and send my fist at that stupid, smug face of his. He makes no effort to dodge or block or do *anything* but stand there as my punch lands and sends him backward onto his ass. He doesn't even look like he knows *how* to do anything to defend himself without magic. Are all witches this dependent on magic to protect them? If so, that's ridiculous.

Tristan scowls up at me from his position on the ground as he wipes a trickle of blood away from his mouth with his fingers. I tentatively reach out to help him up, but he smacks my hand away and stands on his own.

"I'm quite capable of getting up without your help."

"I know that, asshole. I was just trying to be sportsmanlike."

He snorts. "The mongrels taught you manners then? Or what passes for them among animals I suppose."

My skin goes cold, and anger curls into my stomach. "My parents are not mongrels. They're good people."

"People." He scoffs and pushes his hair away from his face. "I think that's giving the canines a bit too much credit." His fingers are moving again as if he's plucking delicate strings from the air and weaving them together. He flips his hand palm side up and flicks his wrist toward me. Another ball of energy comes racing my way, but I step to the side.

He makes a slashing motion with his other hand, and a wave of energy flies up from the ground under my feet. I stumble backward. He tosses another energy ball in my direction. I avoid it again, but only barely. His movements get sharper and more precise, and his eyes narrow in concentration as he observes my movements for a second.

The corner of his lip twitches, and he jerks one hand toward my feet and the other off to the side...Of course, it's the side I step to in order to avoid what he threw at my feet.

An electric current rips through me, and my teeth slam together, just missing my tongue. Muscles seizing, my legs give out and I go down, the ground jarring against my kneecaps. I catch myself before I faceplant on the grass and push back up immediately. Now I'm pissed.

Without even thinking, I dart forward on light feet, plant my left leg and send my right leg in a side kick directly into his abdomen. The air leaves his mouth in a whoosh, and he falls on his ass. I move closer and press my foot against his throat. "Why don't you stay down there this time?"

He bares his teeth and grabs my ankle, trying to fling me off. I press my foot harder into his throat.

Someone grabs my shoulder and pulls me back. "Let him up, Ms. Andras.

THERESA KAY

Physical violence is not tolerated here."

"What?" I sputter as I turn to face the teacher. Everyone else has stopped practicing to stare. "What do you call what he was doing to me? A gentle massage?"

"Magic," says Mr. Davis.

"You're the teacher. You know I'm new here. Aren't you supposed to *teach* me how to use magic instead of just throwing me into this situation? What did you expect me to do?"

"Magic," he says again. "This was a very basic exercise using a skill you should have already mastered. It's also the only acceptable method of defense and offense in this class. That is, if you want to have a place at this school."

And that's it, the thing that finally pushes me past the line. I didn't ask to come here, and I sure as hell don't want to be here. Everything, every goddamn thing at this place, is awful. I've met only three—four if I count Basil—decent people here, and the rest are complete and utter assholes.

Just as I expected.

"Well, maybe I don't want a place at this school," I snap before stomping off the field.

The entire way back to my room, my mind races. What do I do now? How am I going to cut it here? *Can* I cut it here?

And what happens if I can't?

68

CHAPTER 8

B arely thirty minutes after I arrive back at my room—and open the door on my own, go me!—someone comes knocking. The sound makes me wince. What the hell was I thinking? *Of course* I'm going to get in trouble, hopefully not enough that I get kicked out, but there are damn sure going to be consequences. My actions were pretty stupid, especially after what Devin said about the St. James family, but I couldn't help myself. From the very first moment I met Tristan, he irritated me. The fact that he's a St. James just makes it all the worse.

I rest my forehead on my palms and shake my head. How am I possibly going to make it here all year? I haven't even been here a day and have managed to piss off probably the worst person possible. I push to my feet to answer the door and find the smiling secretary from the director's office posed to knock again.

He gives me a sympathetic smile. "Director Burke would like to see you in his office."

I nod and gesture for him to precede me down the hall. Clean clothes might be nice, but what would it matter? There's a chance I might not be here much longer, and I've already made all the first impressions I'm going to. I let the door shut behind me and follow the secretary in silence all the way to Director Burke's office.

Unsurprisingly, Tristan is already sitting in the office, wearing a sour expression. *He* had time to shower and change somewhere in the last thirty minutes, and I could kick myself for not doing the same. I feel extra gross compared to him as I sit down in my damp and dirty gym clothes, but the sight of his fat lip makes the situation not entirely awful.

I give Tristan my best sugary-sweet smile. "How's the mouth?"

His honey-colored eyes narrow, but he doesn't answer. He simply sits there and scowls at me. Who knew such a pretty face could twist into something so ugly?

Burke clears his throat. "I assume you know why you're here?"

I meet his gaze, conjuring up confidence I don't actually feel before speaking. "I'm not going to apologize. I did as I was instructed and defended myself. He's the one who took it too far."

"*I'm* the one who took it too far?" Tristan exclaims, his voice rising and his face twisting with anger. It's the most genuine, naked emotion I've seen out of him all day. He curls his hands around the arms of the chair. "You punched me in the face, you mangy—"

The director slams his hand down on his desk. "That is *enough.*" He glares across at me. "From both of you." He sighs and rubs at his temples. "This is not what I needed this afternoon. Or this school year, really."

We sit in silence for a minute as Tristan and I exchange glares, and then Basil comes bumbling through the door. He beams at me. He beams at

Tristan. Does the man know how to do anything but beam at people?

Tristan raises his eyebrows, and for once, I think we might have at least one thing in common: Basil's cheeriness in the face of, well, everything baffles both of us.

"Have you made the preparations?" asks Burke in a monotone voice.

Basil claps his hands, a delighted smile resting on his lips. "I have. It'll be perfect. Two birds with one stone and all that."

Burke looks skeptical, and I glance back and forth between them in confusion. What's going on here? What am I missing?

Basil pulls out a small bag and then lines things up on the desk: a piece of chalk, a white candle, a few odds and ends I don't recognize. Tristan must recognize them though because his eyes go wide.

"No," he says. "Not happening. You will not—"

"Be quiet, St. James," thunders Burke. "I already warned you this morning about showing proper respect. I'm not in the mood to go over that conversation again. This is not up for discussion. I assigned you as her student guide for a reason. The fact that you managed to weasel out of your responsibilities and get into a fist fight . . ." He trails off, shaking his head.

"I showed her where her class was," says Tristan, the words clipped and bordering on petulant.

I snort. "And that's about it."

"You shouldn't be so flippant about this." Tristan turns his irritation on me. "Do you know what they're planning?" He sniffs, and his upper lip curls. "No, you probably don't. I'm certain your upbringing didn't teach you much about witches. They're going to do a binding spell."

"And that's so awful because...? Isn't that like what I had on me before?"

Tristan huffs in irritation. "Binding you and me. Together. Like squabbling siblings."

"As in we'll be handcuffed to each other like in some stupid rom-com? For how long?" This is not what I signed up for. The guy and I can't be in the same room without arguing, and they want to *force* us together?

"Until you learn to get along," says Burke.

"But...How will I get dressed? How will I shower? How—"

"It's not literal," says Tristan, implying the word *idiot* with a roll of his eyes. "Not in the physical sense anyway. We'll simply have to maintain a certain proximity to each other."

"Proximity? Just how close are we talking here? Fifty feet? Ten? *Five?*"

"That will depend on us," says Tristan in a flat voice. "Unfortunately."

"Oh, yes," says Basil with a grin. "The better you get along, the farther apart you can be. Once you've come to some sort of peaceful arrangement, the spell will dissolve and you'll be free to go your separate ways."

The spell doesn't sound quite as awful as Tristan made it out to be, but by the look on his face, the whole binding thing is probably worse than it seems.

"What's the catch?" I ask. There's been a catch to just about everything in my life lately, so why would this be any different?

"The more we argue, the closer we'll have to be to each other to appease the spell," says Tristan. "I hope you'll enjoy sleeping on the floor in the boys' dorm."

Burke raises an eyebrow at Basil.

"Ah yes," says Basil. He pulls an old-fashioned pocket watch from his bag. "I'm going to adjust the spell enough that you can each sleep in your own rooms. It will only be active from 8:00 a.m. to 10:00 p.m."

"What about my classes?" asks Tristan. "We don't have the same schedule, and I can't afford to—"

"You do now," says Burke. "Your schedule has been adjusted to be identical to Selene's. Including tutoring with Basil."

"That's ridiculous!" yells Tristan. "I can't afford to miss out on my classes because I have to sit in beginner courses with *her*. It—"

"Is not going to interfere with any of your other classes. You will not be required to complete the coursework for the classes you attend with Selene, and your other teachers will provide you with your assignments and allow you ample time to complete them. Think of it as independent study if you'd like," says the director.

"My parents will hear of this."

Burke gives Tristan a wry smile. "You'd like them to find out about you getting into a physical altercation in the middle of class?"

Tristan's jaw tenses as he presses his lips together and casts his gaze on the floor. Apparently, Mommy and Daddy St. James wouldn't be happy to hear that. I suppose they have to draw the line somewhere. Blatant hatred of shifters? That's perfectly fine. But getting into a physical altercation? Total no-no.

Burke motions for Basil to continue, and the smaller man lights the candle before taking a piece of string and tying one end around my wrist and one end around Tristan's. Basil touches each of the objects on the desk in turn, mouthing words I can't hear, and then touches the string. A sudden pressure lands on my chest and squeezes before disappearing.

"It's done." Basil unties the string and then gathers all the spell components.

"Good luck." Burke rises to his feet. "I'm sure the two of you will learn to enjoy each other's company eventually." He speaks with a perfectly straight face, but I can almost hear laughter behind his words. "Now, why don't you two go eat some dinner and get to know each other?" He ushers us out of the office and into the hallway before closing the door behind us.

"And don't let the door hit you on the way out," I mutter under my breath in a bad imitation of Burke's accent.

"Funny," says Tristan in a voice that implies anything but. He strides off down the hallway, silently fuming. Once he goes past the third doorway, his steps slow. There's a tug at the center of my chest, gentle and testing. The feeling turns into a hard yank, and I stumble a few steps in Tristan's direction. The spell? He nods to himself, and there's another tug.

No. *He's* doing this. The spell might tie us together or whatever, but he's the one using it like a leash to pull me around.

Another hard yank.

"Stop that," I snap. "If you—"

"The dining hall closes in thirty minutes. Let's go." He doesn't even turn around.

The next time he yanks on the connection, he gets pulled backward a little. Probably from the spell tightening.

He tilts his head back and lets out a loud, exasperated breath. "If you'd like to be rid of this stupid spell, you need to cooperate with me."

"I think we actually need to cooperate with *each other*."

He turns to me, lips pursed. "Look, I can't afford to have you following me around for long. The quicker we get this over with, the quicker we both can go our own ways." He plasters on a smile complete with dimples. If his eyes weren't blank and bored, I might even call it a panty-dropping smile. "I'm so sorry we got off on the wrong foot. Do you think we could be friends?"

I gape at him. "Are you being serious right now?"

The smile on his faces grows strained. "Of course."

"I may be new to all this, but I'm pretty sure getting rid of this spell isn't as simple as that."

His face goes blank, and he shrugs. "It was worth a shot. Sometimes binding spells can be more literal."

"Had this problem often?" I snort. "I can't say I'm surprised."

He scowls and yanks on the spell again, pulling me closer.

"Can we stop at my room before dinner? I'd like to change."

"I'm sure you would." Those dark amber eyes move from my toes to my head. "But we don't have time." He starts walking but not before yanking on the spell again.

Asshole. I need to figure out how he's doing that. If he can use the spell to his advantage, I'm sure there's a way for me to use it to mine. Until then, I'll just let him take the lead. I smirk to myself. He seems to be more tolerable if he thinks he's in charge.

CHAPTER 9

I really thought Tristan was kidding about the whole 'we don't have time' thing.

He wasn't.

He drags me straight to the dining hall. No stops. No bathroom break so I can maybe salvage a semblance of normalcy by taming my hair and splashing some water on my face. Nope, it's directly to the dining hall, a large, semi-noisy room holding most of my classmates. There are various groups of students gathered around long tables, and it's generally what I'd expect to see at an OSA academy that's known for catering to the Coven Council and the old money families. The place still screams 'high school cafeteria' with a salad bar and plastic trays, but there's a sushi chef and a gourmet deli counter along with other made-to-order stations, and the dessert bar holds artisan pastries and handmade chocolates.

Tristan walks to the salad bar and loads up a plate without pausing or asking me what I want to eat. The dessert bar is calling to me with all its chocolaty goodness, but the spell won't let me go any farther than five feet or so from Tristan, and his path takes him nowhere near the sweets.

I have nothing against vegetables and load my plate up too, but after the day I've had, I think I deserve a little sugar. Not enough that I'm going to ask for permission like a child, though. Instead, I follow Tristan to one of the tables and sit down across from him without uttering any of my complaints. Hey, maybe I'll get bonus points from the spell for not complaining. That could happen, right?

The situation shifts from irritating to awkward rather quickly as the silence between us grows longer and longer. Am I supposed to make small talk or something? Will that help appease the spell? I can't imagine sitting here staring at my plate in silence will be helpful. I glance at Tristan. "So, do you—"

"Not in the mood," he says, not lifting his gaze from his plate.

Well, neither am I.

Okay then, back to silence. The awkwardness, that feeling of being surrounded by people but still alone and out of place, reminds me of being at the party while standing on the edges and having no one to talk to. It sucks. At least the party had music.

And Reid.

And people who didn't eye me with suspicion or outright disdain like the witches at the tables around us.

Not a single one of the three people who have actually been nice to me here are in sight, and that lost, lonely feeling with hints of homesickness hits a new high for the day. I don't know how long I can keep this up. I'm already failing at being a witch, and it's only my first day. My parents raised me to never give up, but I'm still so confused and I'm beginning to think this whole thing is hopeless.

And the fact that I'm magically bound to an arrogant asshat certainly doesn't do anything to boost my confidence. Sure, the guy's acted like a jerk from the second we met, but antagonizing him was not one of my best decisions, especially after everything Adrian and Devin told me. What's done is done though, and I need to find a way to make the best of this situation—or at least a way to endure it.

Sighing, I pick at the lettuce on my plate, more moving the leafy greens around than actually eating them. The longer Tristan and I argue, the longer we'll be stuck together, meaning my adjustment to life here at Ravencrest is only going to be harder and take longer if I can't make nice with the scowling boy across from me. I'm gathering the nerve to speak again when another boy drops into the chair beside Tristan.

This guy is one of the ones Tristan was with earlier: blond hair, blue eyes, and an attitude I'll call preppy with a side of money. "St. James, Gordon and I are headed off campus. You coming?"

"I can't," says Tristan, his expression blank and bored.

"Can't?" The guy looks at me and then back at Tristan. "You're ditching a chance to hook up with Tasha for the crazy shifter girl?"

Lovely. It didn't take long for that to become my new nickname.

"No." Tristan flicks his gaze toward the ceiling and releases a slow breath. "Desmond thought it best if she and I learned to get along."

And I don't have off-campus privileges yet.

A pause as the guy cocks his head to the side and furrows his brow. He takes in Tristan's bland expression, and I can practically see the guy replaying the words in his head before coming to a conclusion. "You're kidding me." He glances between us. "A binding spell? Can't you get rid of it? Flash those dimples of yours or something? That normally has the girls dying to 'get along' with you."

I fight the urge to roll my eyes. Does this guy think Tristan is some sort of lady killer? The new albatross around my neck is hot, but his personality definitely doesn't make up for it. I give the guy a tight smile. "Yeah, he tried that one. Didn't work."

"Maybe not yet, shifter girl." The guy snorts and turns back to Tristan. "Careful how close you get in your pursuit of getting along. You might get fleas."

Tristan closes his eyes and presses his lips together. He says absolutely nothing. I don't know why I'd expect him to defend me, but he could, at the very least, tell his friend to piss off or something.

The guy continues talking. "Wait a second. You're going to have to go to all her classes, aren't you?" He starts laughing, his face going red. "I bet she's in basics, isn't she? How are you going to keep your class rank without the advanced courses? Your parents are going to be *livid*."

Tristan's shoulders go tense, but his expression doesn't change. "I will deal with the spell and be back in my regular classes before the month is out. Until then, there's plenty of extra credit work I can do." His voice drops lower, and he gives his 'friend' a hard smile. "My parents never need to know about *this* just like yours don't need to know about last weekend. Right, Jason?"

Jason's expression mirrors Tristan's, like two predators facing off, both tense and waiting to pounce. They seem to come to some sort of silent agreement before Jason's attention moves to me. "Yeah, sure man. They won't find out from me." His gaze roams down to my chest. "Considering the circumstances, I suppose we can extend an invitation to your new buddy. You might need to give her a bath first though."

And that's it. I've had enough. "Look, douchebag, why don't you go back to your own table? I'm sure your little crew misses their leader or whatever, but clearly you aren't getting him back right now. And the more you piss me off, the less likely it is that you'll get him back anytime soon."

Weirdly enough, the idiot listens, but not without sending a malicious grin in Tristan's direction.

"Catch you later, St. James," Jason says as he walks away from the table, shooting a jaunty wave over his shoulder.

And Tristan? He visibly relaxes and goes back to his dinner. Like nothing happened. I study him as he eats, my own food forgotten. Most of their conversation had a veneer of civility, but I definitely caught the undercurrent of it. Verbal power plays like that are common among shifters, and I'm starting to wonder if witches aren't quite as different as they think.

"I take it that guy's not actually your friend?"

"Still not in the mood," he replies, but this time his words are a little softer around the edges.

It's almost like progress.

Or not.

Tristan insists on spending the rest of the evening studying in one of the common rooms in the boys' dorm and, as I have no books or notes or *anything* with me except the clothes on my back, I get to spend the time staring at the wall. Just like at dinner, the downtime isn't helpful. When I don't have the whirlwind of classes and information—and the occasional argument with Tristan—to occupy my brain, all my mind can do is dwell on how much I miss my family and how alone I feel here.

I hate this.

It's almost ten thirty before I make it back to my own dorm room, and the lack of sleep is catching up to me. Hard. All I want to do is crawl into bed and sleep for a week. But I still have homework, and I'm hoping Isobel might have some insight into this spell and how to get free of it. Tristan wants to be rid of me, but I want to be rid of him even more.

I reach out for the doorknob, but someone grabs my arm and yanks me down the hall. After spending all evening with the stupid binding spell, I'm kind of getting used to being pulled around against my will. But this is different. The person who has hold of my arm is a *shifter*, someone who belongs here even less than I do.

I glance back at my abductor. *Shifter girl from the party? What the hell?*

Shifter girl shoves me into a small, darkened room and shuts the door. There's the click of a lock before the light is turned on, and I'm left staring at a rack of cleaning supplies and an agitated shifter. I take an involuntary step away from her, and she growls with narrowed eyes.

I lift my chin, refusing to back down. She doesn't get to manhandle me and then growl at me like she's my alpha. "What the hell is this?" I snap out. "Are you following me or something? What the hell do you want from me?"

She paces a couple steps in one direction and then back, as if trying to decide what to tell me. She curls and uncurls her hands, and her nostrils flare with agitation. The longer she goes without speaking, the more questions form in my head. Who the hell is she? Why is she here? Did she have more to do with the binding on my powers being broken than I thought? She wasn't surprised, and she somehow seemed to know what was happening and what I should do...

She continues her silent pacing, and my anger flares.

"Look, if you're not going to say anything, I don't have time for this. I need to get some rest." I move to shove past her, but she stops me with a hand on my arm.

"I'm a student," she says.

A student? At the *witch* academy? Curiosity is enough to stop me. I pause, one hand resting on the doorknob.

"I'm Bitten," she continues. "Two months ago."

What? I drop my hand from the doorknob. Except for OSA sanctioned "punishments," it's illegal for a shifter to give the Bite to a witch, and even if it wasn't, what is she doing here now?

I turn to face her, crossing my arms over my chest. "How in the hell has no one figured this out yet? Can't they tell?"

She averts her eyes. "Short answer is no, they can't. Long answer is...I don't know why you *can*."

"So...what? Are you going to threaten me into silence? I'm pretty sure the next full moon will give away your secret without a word from me. Unlike Born wolves, you *have* to shift then, all Bitten do."

"I know that." Her gaze goes to the floor. "I wanted to be sure I didn't run into you randomly and you give me away somehow. I worked hard to get here. I'm not giving up my spot."

There's an edge to her words, one that makes them sound like a threat. I feel like I should be scared, but I've had just about enough of being threatened today.

I let out a harsh laugh. "Giving up your spot? And here I thought *I* was delusional about making it through this school year. How do you expect to complete your classes with no magic?"

"No magic?" She smirks. "Is that what they told you? The Bite takes away a witch's ability to use magic?"

I drop my arms to my sides. "Yes. Why?"

"It's not true. Not completely anyway. Sure, I won't be tossing energy balls or spells, but potions and wards I can handle."

My jaw drops. Can she possibly be telling the truth?

At my surprise, her face twists into an expression of disgust, and there's an unexpected bite to her words considering the circumstances. "The Coven Council would have everyone believe that shifters are the enemies of magic itself."

A Bitten witch who isn't anti-shifter? This girl is a mess of contradictions. "That's ..." The breath leaks from my lungs. "I don't know what to say." I drag a hand over my face. "Look, I'm spent. If this is the 'threaten Selene into silence' bit, can I just stop you now? Besides the fact that I have more than enough to worry about already, I don't care whether or not you're a shifter. Why should I? I *like* shifters. I have no idea how you're going to keep it hidden, but that's not my problem now, is it?"

"No, it's not." One side of her mouth curls into a wry smile. "But I'd appreciate it if you'd keep my secret. And maybe help out with my classes if I run into something I can't fake."

I pinch the bridge of my nose between my fingers. *If she runs into something she can't fake? Sounds like she definitely* will.

"Fine," I say, too tired to do much more than agree. "I don't know how much help I'll be. You know more about all this than I do, but...I'll do what I can."

"Thanks."

"I am curious, though. What the hell were you doing at that party and with Bridget of all people?" I pause as the picture becomes a little clearer. "She doesn't know either, does she? That whole thing where I thought she was picking on you for being a shifter...that was something else, wasn't it?"

"Yeah." She won't meet my eyes. "There was a time when you might have considered the two of us friends. I kind of ghosted her this summer, and she was pissed."

"Well, it appears you had bigger things going on," I say with a shrug.

"Much bigger." Her half smile turns into something closer to a real one. "I'm Penny."

"Selene."

She swallows. "I know." Her gaze moves away from me. "You're not what

I expected, not from what they told me."

"What *who* told you?"

She flinches. "Never mind. I've said too much. You better get back to your room."

She scurries away before I have time to ask anything else, leaving me with more questions than answers, but my head is way too foggy to bother trying to figure her out now. Maybe tomorrow I'll have the brain power to devote to finding some answers, but for now, I'm going to bed, homework be damned.

I find my way back to my room and successfully open the door. If nothing else, I've managed to master that little bit of magic.

Isobel glances up from the book she's reading at her desk as I enter the room. "I hear your day got even more interesting after I saw you last."

"I don't know if interesting is the word I'd use for it." I sigh and plop on my bed. "Maybe...stupidly awful or level-ten irritating."

She laughs. "It can't be all that bad tied to the hottest guy in school. I can think of at least three girls here who would pay for that privilege."

I shoot her a death glare. "Why don't you try it then? It's not nearly as fun as you seem to think it is. He barely speaks to me. I'm like some weird valet who has to follow him around but not actually do anything." I sigh. "And then there's the fact that he's a St. James and I'm, well, *not* a shifter, but they're who raised me, so the St. James family isn't exactly one I enjoy being associated with."

"What if I told you that you don't have to follow him around?" She flashes me a mischievous grin and lifts the book she's reading so I can see the title: *Advanced Usage and Implementation of Binding Spells.* "I plan to concentrate in Spells. I can probably make a tweak or two to make the spell work *for* you instead of against you. I can at least give you the upper hand on who's following who."

"So, I wouldn't have to get up early to make sure I'm dressed and ready before he summons me to his dorm?"

She nods.

"That is maybe the best news I've heard all day." I pause. "But why would you do that for me?"

"Us lowly peons need to stick together...and it's good practice." She smirks. "So you're okay with it?"

"*Definitely.*"

At her request, I give her a brief overview of what Basil did and answer some oddly specific questions about the color of the string and the candle before she nods to herself. She's bouncing with excitement as she tells me what she plans, something about symbolism or maybe syllables. Most of it goes completely over my head, but she's so enthusiastic about it I can't help but smile along.

"Basil is a master spellworker," she says. "The opportunity to work on one of his spells is...I can't even describe how cool this is."

And I probably wouldn't understand if she did since, well, my ignorance becomes more and more apparent as this day goes on. There's been something bugging me, and to save myself the embarrassment of asking in class, I might as well ask Isobel. "What exactly is the difference between a spell and, well, magic like what we were doing in PE and what happened to me last night?"

To give her credit, she doesn't laugh full out at the question. She bites at one fingernail and thinks for a moment. "I don't know if that's something I've ever had to explain." She pauses, and her brows pull together. "Think of it like this: magic is the energy, and a spell is how we manipulate it. Every witch has a...spark of something inside them that lets them access the magic in the world around them and kind of draw it into themselves. In PE, you were pulling magic and just throwing around the energy itself, something quick and easy. But a spell takes that energy and shapes it into something that performs a specific action. For example, if I wanted to create light, I'd need a spell, but only a simple one, a word or two depending on the desired effect. The more complicated the effect, the more complicated the spell, so for something like this, I need not just words but also other items to help me cast—like these candles and the watch you said Basil used to set the time constraints on the spell."

"Huh." That's about the most eloquent response I can offer. Her explanation isn't perfect, but I think I understand it. Emphasis on *think*.

Isobel puts the candles and other items she's gathered on her desk and starts doing whatever it is she said she was going to do. She lights the candles, moves things around, and mutters words under her breath. When she's done, I don't feel any different, but she looks ecstatic, so whatever she did must've been successful.

"You should be good to go in the morning," she says.

"Thank you so, so much." I bury my face in my pillow, once again neglecting to ask how everyone around here wakes up on time. I'll figure it out tomorrow.

She giggles, and I smile into my pillowcase. This place might not be so bad after all. Not everyone hates me, and I have at least one friend. Two, maybe three if I can count Adrian and Devin. I drift off to sleep with the sound of turning pages and a pencil scribbling across paper playing in my ears.

CHAPTER 10

A mild tugging sensation in my chest pulls me out of the most wonderful dream. I blink my eyes open and glance around the room in confusion. *What? Where?* My stomach sinks as the last day and a half comes back to me and I remember where I am and what that stupid sensation growing in insistence is: the damn binding spell. This must be some kind of precursor to when the thing fully kicks in at eight.

At least it will make for a handy alarm clock.

Still, I'm exhausted, and the last thing I want to do is get out of bed. No, the last thing I want to do is deal with Tristan and his whole 'do what I say' attitude. My chest grows tight as the spell pulls taut and the pounding in my head returns. I let my eyes slip closed with a sigh.

But...I don't have to get out of bed now, do I? I grin and replay Isobel's words from last night. If her tweak works, I can bring him to me. Once he's in range, the spell will back off and I'll be able to get a little more desperately needed sleep.

The spell yanks at my chest again, this time more like a summons from the king of bad attitudes. The spell is about to kick back in, and he's attempting to do what he did yesterday by dragging me to him.

Not gonna happen.

I close my eyes, concentrating on the connection, and try to remember Isobel's instructions. I pull at my magic, sending it to poke at the spell. Once I find a hold, I yank on the connection, hard enough that I feel Tristan stumble wherever he is and start involuntarily in my direction. He, of course, pulls back, but I'm not giving in this time. I'm not letting him dictate where I can go and when.

A couple minutes later, there's a knock at the door.

Damn, I should've thought about that. Now I actually *do* need to get out of bed. With a groan, I swing my legs over the side of the bed, stand up, then make my way to the door. I open it, give Tristan a vague wave, then crawl back into my bed and pull the covers over my head.

"Not a morning person, I take it?" The question has no bite to it, merely a polite observation—or as polite as Tristan can manage anyway.

Actually, I *am* a morning person, but in the past forty-eight hours or so I've barely gotten any sleep, and that's on top of all the other exhausting crap that's been going on. My head is spinning with all the questions I still have—about how I ended up with my parents, about my birth mother, about magic, about pretty much *everything*—but I don't have time to deal with any of that now.

I remove the covers from my head and glare at him. "Don't talk to me before coffee."

"That might be difficult unless you have a coffee maker somewhere in this closet of a room," he says. He ruffles his hair with one hand. His *damp and messy* hair that curls up slightly at the ends.

My gaze moves from the uncharacteristically untidy hair to his face, his cheeks slightly pink, and down to his clothes—a t-shirt and a pair of gray running shorts that show off his lean, muscular legs. He raises his eyebrows.

"Were you...running?" I ask in a voice that makes it sound like the activity is a foreign concept to me. It's not. But my tired brain has gotten stuck on this slightly rumpled version of the prissy perfect guy from yesterday and refuses to supply words that make sense.

"I do the three-mile trail around the lake every morning." Tristan lifts a water bottle to his mouth and takes a few gulps. The struggle to not watch his throat as he swallows is a losing one. My stupid brain is having trouble getting the message that the hot guy in front of me is not for us. "Now, as fun as this is, would you mind getting out of bed so I can shower, change, and prepare for the day?"

And just like that, my brain gets the message: *Pompous asshole.*

I huff out a laugh. "You're kidding me, right?" I, again, swing my legs out of bed and get up, this time to stand directly in front of Tristan, one finger pointing at his face. "You dragged me around all evening in my sweaty gym clothes. Why the hell shouldn't I return the favor?"

He rolls his eyes. "Look, I apologize if I upset you yesterday. It—"

"That is *not* an apology." I jam my finger into his surprisingly hard chest.

"Whatever. I need to change into my uniform. I'd *like* to shower as well. If we don't get going, we'll miss breakfast, and then where will you get your coffee?"

He has a point, but I'm not going to admit that. "Get out."

"What?" He seems legitimately baffled, his brows drawing together at the command.

"I said get out. I need to get dressed."

"Yes, you do." His gaze darts down to my bare legs. *Oh crap.* All I'm wearing is an over-sized t-shirt. There's a brief flicker of interest in his eyes before he shuts down all expression on his face. "I'll be outside." He turns and walks from the room, slamming the door behind him.

I take my time getting ready. I wash my face and then put on a few simple touches of makeup: a little mascara, eyeliner, and lip gloss. Next, I put my hair up in a ponytail and pull on one of the uniforms that were delivered yesterday. Mine aren't as tailored as everyone else's, but at least the new clothes fit and I won't stick out quite as much. I don't exactly have any proper shoes, so I pull my boots on. They make me look a little rocker chic, but they're certainly better than flip-flops.

At close to 8:30, I swing open the door and give Tristan a wide grin as he leans against the wall. "Sorry I took so long. I guess we don't have time to go back to your room or we'll miss breakfast."

He scowls at me, but the expression is quickly replaced with a placid smile. "I suppose I'll live."

Huh. I expected more of an argument. I eye him skeptically, but his face remains neutral, and he gestures for me to precede him down the hallway.

The walk to the dining hall is, like dinner last night, silent. After the initial irritation with me, he hasn't appeared so much as ruffled. Is this a kill them with kindness type thing, or is he actually trying to get along with me? Maybe he's just resigned himself to dealing with me.

Once at the dining hall, we both get our food—a stack of pancakes and some berries for me, fruit and yogurt for him—and take our trays to a table where, of course, we have to sit together. But then he gets up and offers to get coffee for me. It's odd, but being as I haven't caffeinated yet, I don't have to think much before agreeing.

I sniff at the cup suspiciously when it arrives, but the steamy warmth of it is too tempting to resist for long. I take a large sip, eying Tristan over the edge of the cup. His face has moved very little since the scowl.

"I didn't poison it if that's why you're giving me that look," he says in a bland voice, those honey-colored eyes darting up from his food to meet mine.

I take another sip and savor the yumminess. "Okay."

Silence falls between us. Tristan finishes the last of his food then sits in the chair, chin up, back straight, shoulders set as he waits for me to finish my coffee. I'm a little impressed with his commitment to the role of silent stick up his ass. He acts almost like a robot, as if he can't bear to show any weakness, not even emotion.

I tilt my head to the side and study him from the corner of my eye. If this is his normal behavior, then what the hell was yesterday? Was it just my presence that set him off so badly or the fact that he was hit by a girl or... what? I'm curious enough to ask, but I doubt he'd answer.

"I don't like this situation any more than you do, so if we want to go our separate ways, we need to try to appease the spell as much as possible." When I don't respond, he sighs and motions toward the coffee station, which is at least twenty feet away, something I hadn't noticed when he walked over there.

So *that's* why he offered, to suck up to the spell. "Does that mean you won't be forcing me to follow you around anymore?"

"As long as you're not honestly planning on insisting we don't have time for me to change before class."

"Well, I—"

"And good morning to you, my favorite witch," says Adrian as he slides into the chair beside me and puts an arm over my shoulder.

"Your favorite witch? You met me yesterday," I say in a dry voice. I pause a moment and then crack a smile. "I suppose I can count you among one of my favorites too."

Adrian grabs his chest and winces as if in pain. "One of? That's the best I get?"

"Yup. Isobel gets the top spot because she's my roomie and she brought me coffee yesterday. You still have a lot to prove before you get into the inner circle," I say with a chuckle. Adrian is, if nothing else, very entertaining.

His gaze moves to Tristan, and that mischievous glint returns. This is going to be interesting..."And what about St. James here? Is he one of your favorites?"

Tristan hasn't looked up, hasn't so much as acknowledged Adrian. Hell, the guy has barely acknowledged *me* for the past ten minutes.

"Unequivocally not," I say.

"Harsh," says Adrian. He kicks out under the table, and Tristan grunts. "How does that feel, St. James, having a girl blatantly *not* want you?"

"I'm sure you're familiar with the feeling," says Tristan. "How do *you* deal with it?"

Adrian laughs, full out, his head tilting backward and his mouth open. "I never realized you had a sense of humor."

Tristan rolls his eyes and goes back to ignoring us.

"So, what's your first class?" Adrian asks me.

"Tutoring with Basil."

Adrian chuckles. "That's sure to be interesting. Definitely better than sitting through Advanced Spellcasting with Mrs. Feng." His attention turns back to Tristan. "How are you going to keep up with your classes if you have to follow her around?"

"I'll manage," Tristan bites out.

"Really?" Adrian grabs a strawberry off my plate and sticks the fruit in his mouth. "It's going to be awfully hard to maintain your class rank without a full roster of advanced classes."

Tristan is silent, but his jaw tenses as if he's biting back words.

That's the second time someone mentioned class rank, and I still have no idea what they're going on about. I mean, I know what class rank is in theory. My high school had a ranking system too, but the one here sounds a lot more serious.

"What's so important about class rank?" I ask after a moment of debate.

"You sweet little newbie." Adrian pinches my cheek. "Your class rank here at Ravencrest determines so many things, like eligibility for the best job placements after graduation, and even more important, whether or not you're allowed off-campus privileges and other perks. St. James here is expected to be at the tippy top."

There's not a word from Tristan, but he grows even tenser, his fingers curling around the edge of the table.

"Of course, for the right amount of money, you can buy your way up." Adrian rubs at his chin for a second before breaking into a sardonic smile. "It will be interesting to see what your boy's rank might be without a schedule packed with advanced classes. If he manages to stay up there . . ."

"I will," snaps Tristan. "And my parents don't buy my achievements. Not like yours."

Adrian leans across the table until he's right in Tristan's face. "I can't wait to see you knocked down a peg or two this semester."

"Whatever," says Tristan. He turns hard eyes on me. "Can we go now?"

I hold up my half full coffee. "Soon. This is quite informative. And entertaining."

Tristan closes his eyes and visibly swallows. All expression leaves his face, and just like that, he's back to a blank-faced robot. The quick change would be impressive if it wasn't so...sad?

Adrian raises a hand, and Devin walks over to our table.

"You ready to head to class?" asks Devin.

"Unfortunately." Adrian hops to his feet. "I'll catch you later, Selene. Maybe I can show you that you're definitely *my* favorite witch." He winks and blows me a kiss.

Devin pulls on his arm. "Come on, lover boy, we're going to be late."

The two of them leave the dining hall, and I turn to Tristan.

"You know he's not serious, right?" asks Tristan in a bland voice. "Dumont flirts with everyone, so don't get your hopes up that you might marry your way into the Dumont family fortune."

I gape at him. "Did you just imply I'm a gold digger?"

He shrugs.

"First of all, I'm seventeen. I have no plans to get married anytime soon, and I could give a crap about the Dumont family fortune. Second of all, I can take care of myself, and even if I couldn't, the last person I'd ask for advice is you." I take a sip of coffee. "Despite what you may think of me, I'm not an idiot. Adrian's a friend. Unlike some people, he's actually been nice to me."

Tristan shrugs and stares at the table. "Whatever."

I drain the last of my coffee and stand up. "You ready?"

"Do I have a choice?" he asks with a forced smile.

"I suppose not." I shrug and pull my backpack over my shoulder.

He rises to his feet, brushing the front of his shorts like he's trying to make them look decent.

There is a tiny, *tiny* piece of me that feels a little bad for making him go to class in his running clothes and without a shower, but it's not like he didn't do worse to me yesterday. Plus, it's almost sickening how perfect he still looks. No one should be allowed to look this good after an early morning run. I smile to myself. Maybe I'll be nice enough to let him change at lunchtime.

CHAPTER 11

Tutoring with Basil is the class Tristan seems the most irritated about having to take and the class I'm hoping will give me the most insight into how the hell I'm going to make it at this school. Basil seems invested enough in my future, considering my birth mother chose him as her contingency plan, and he clearly knows his stuff if Isobel calls him a master spellcaster. If anyone can help me, he can. After yesterday...I have no idea if any of this will ever make sense. Magic is not as intuitive as everyone here makes it out to be, not for me anyway, and I have no clue why.

Basil also has answers about my birth mother. Answers I think I want, but I don't think I want them while Tristan is around. He's already an unwelcome intruder in my life and a constant witness to my screw ups. The idea of having such a deeply personal conversation with Basil in Tristan's presence feels...not right. It's something that will have to wait until after the spell is resolved.

Or until I decide Tristan is trustworthy, something that isn't very likely to happen.

My gaze strays to the boy beside me as I knock gently on Basil's office door. Tristan didn't say much on the walk up here, not even to complain that he didn't get to change. That carefully bland expression of his gives absolutely nothing away, but I know he must be more ruffled than he appears.

"Welcome, welcome, welcome," says Basil as the door swings open pulling my attention away from Tristan. "I'm so glad you two could make it."

As if we had a choice.

He gestures for us to enter and waves at the now empty couch in the back corner. "I cleared us some workspace."

The stacks of books on the floor are like a maze, except instead of hitting a dead end, one wrong step will get us buried in an avalanche of knowledge. I maneuver my way to the couch to take a seat. Tristan sits beside me, his thigh pressing against mine for a brief second before he scoots as close to his armrest—and as far away from me—as he can get.

Basil drags his desk chair over to the area in front of the couch. How he manages to maneuver through all the junk without knocking over so much as a single piece of paper is a mystery. He plops down and clasps his hands. "We're going to have so much fun!"

Fun? Okay then . . .

Tristan coughs into his hand and stares at the wall.

Basil jumps up and runs a finger down one of the stacks of books. "No," he mutters. "Not that one. Nor that one. Hmm . . ." He glances around the room. "Ah! Over there." He scurries to another stack to pull a book from near the bottom—once again miraculously not knocking anything over. How does he do that? He catches me watching and winks before returning to our 'classroom' area and handing me the book. *Origins: The History of the Fae.*

"Sounds...interesting?" I say. "Director Burke didn't mention anything about you tutoring me in history, just government and spells."

Tristan glances at the book, raises an eyebrow, and then goes back to staring at the wall. I guess he's not planning to participate.

"You wouldn't have gotten a full history of the supernatural in your human schools, and you should know some of the basics. For example, the basis of all magic is with the Fae, so I thought that a little bit of their history would be a great starting point," says Basil. "Most of our history courses don't bother with it, but I think it's important to learn as much as you can. You too, Tristan, so pay attention please."

"I've already taken all the required history courses. Fae history is not on the exam, and this is a non-credit course—at least for me. I'm only here because of this stupid spell." Tristan's voice is flat and dry, his face bored.

Basil shakes his head, his mouth downturned and his brow creased. "Ah, but what's on the exams isn't always the most important information."

Tristan scowls. "Basil—"

"Hush," says Basil in the harshest tone I've ever heard from him, which honestly isn't saying much.

Tristan sighs and rolls his eyes before leaning back on the couch and crossing his arms over his chest.

Basil turns to me. "Now, Selene, how much do you know about the origins of magic?"

"Not a whole lot. It has something to do with the Fae that came to our world thousands of years ago."

"Correct," says Basil. "The Fae arrived here some three thousand years ago, bringing their magic with them. All three supernatural races are their descendants, with each race getting a specific piece of Fae magic. Vampires get immortality. Shifters the ability to change forms. And witches the ability to connect with and manipulate magic itself."

"Witches are the most direct descendants," says Tristan. "That's why our connection to magic is the strongest."

"Not true," says Basil. "Although there are rumors of actual Fae blood being introduced into various witch family lines, those...influxes happened at least three centuries ago and have never been proven to be fact. Some witches have, however, used that type of misinformation in an attempt to place themselves above the other supernatural races. It's one of the reasons the highest positions in the Order are currently held only by witches and why the number of shifters joining the Order or even attending OSA academies grows smaller every year. A witch's connection to magic is no stronger than a shifter's or a vampire's. The other supernatural races simply have connections to different aspects of the Fae magic. The magic of the witches is merely the most *active* connection which is what allows us to pull magic from the world around us to fuel spells and such."

Tristan scoffs, clearly uninterested in Basil's explanation. Of course the jerk thinks witches are above everyone else. That kind of arrogance probably comes with being a St. James. "This is ancient history of a dead race. It doesn't matter to our current world, and I doubt this is what Desmond requested you tutor Selene in." He stands. "If I have to sit here—"

"*Sit down*, Tristan." Basil's voice has gone cold, and the smile drops off his face. "You have no idea what does and does not matter. History is important, and the history of our origins is even more so. I understand you have been taught differently, but you are ignorant of more than you think. These lessons are not just for Selene's benefit, but as the heir to the St. James family, they are for yours as well. If you are to follow in either of your parents' footsteps, it would behoove you to think beyond their narrow views."

Whoa. Go Basil!

"I don't have to listen to this." Tristan storms toward the door, but the spell tightens well before he reaches the exit and brings him backward, half-stumbling and falling onto the couch beside me. He shoots me a dirty look.

"Wasn't me," I say, fighting back a laugh and throwing my hands out to the sides. "*You* provoked the spell."

He releases a loud breath through his nose, and his jaw tenses before his face goes back to that placid, blank look he's so practiced at.

And class goes on. Basil rattles off a lot of names and dates that I probably won't remember while Tristan sits there not participating and barely listening. I hate to admit it, but a large part of me agrees with Tristan about the subject matter. History is not going to help me fit in or help me learn to use magic, and my hopes of learning all the secrets and becoming a super awesome witch under Basil's tutelage decrease every time he throws out another historical tidbit. Maybe the history portion of this class will be short and we'll move onto something more important tomorrow. Ninety minutes later, I'm more than glad to get out of here.

I'm hoping Wards class might go better today, but by the look on Ms. Anderson's face as I walk in the room, I'm pretty sure that's not going to happen. She clearly remembers me from yesterday—how could she not?—and even on time and not destroying the door ward, the look on her face makes it obvious she doesn't like me much. Tristan, however, she gives a warm, welcoming smile, one that he ignores as he strides toward the back of the room with me following along.

The rest of the class files in and finds their seats, and the teacher starts drawing diagrams on the whiteboard. She's going over last night's homework. The homework I didn't do. *Crap.*

My pen flies over my paper, copying the diagrams and trying to take down everything she's saying. A lot of the information goes right over my head, but some things makes sense, like when she explains pieces that have more to do with geometry than magic. The rest of the lesson might have made more sense if I'd had time to do the homework.

The teacher puts down her marker. "Last class, we talked about simple locking wards. Can anyone tell me what the next most commonly used type of ward is?" she asks as she paces from one side of the classroom to the other.

Every hand goes up. Except mine. And Tristan's. He's spent the class so far with his arms crossed over his chest as he stares at the wall.

"Protection," mutters Tristan.

He's probably right. No, it's almost a guarantee that he is, but I don't feel like making a fool of myself, so my hand stays down just in case.

"Rachel?"

"The second most common type of ward is a protection ward," says a girl in the front row.

"That's correct." Ms. Anderson moves back to the whiteboard and sketches out a triangle then draws a circle around it. "This form is the base for every protection ward. As you add to it, you create more or less protection or different kinds of protection. A protection ward can be combined with a protection spell, but only under certain circumstances. It's not something you'd want to try as beginners."

A quiet huff comes from Tristan.

"Now, I'd like you all to partner up like we did yesterday and go over some of the exercises in your books on page 103. Remember, for now I want you to concentrate on perfecting the *forms*. When we reach the point where you'll be infusing magic into the wards you draw, the forms need to be perfect." She walks back to the board and erases everything from earlier as the class, once again, bursts into motion and people pair up.

Do I *ask* Tristan, or do I just assume—

"Would you like to be my partner?" asks Bridget's sister whose name I still can't remember as she bats her eyelashes at Tristan. "I would love to have someone of your experience to help me."

"No," he says as he turns to me. "Do you have your textbook?"

The girl gapes at him, and her cheeks go pink. Her mouth closes then opens again as if she's about to say something, but nothing comes out. He actually shocked the words out of her. She stands there for another beat, still speechless, before walking off.

"Harsh," I say, fighting back a touch of amusement.

He gives me a patronizing smile. "I'm stuck with you, but I don't have to put up with other students below my caliber."

And there goes my admittedly petty amusement at the girl being turned down. Below his caliber, huh? I suppose it's the truth, but he doesn't have to be such an ass about it.

I return his smile with a sickly sweet one of my own. "I'm so happy you deign to grace me with your experience." I slam my textbook on the desk and flip to the required page. "Let's get started then."

He does nothing but watch me struggle over the problems. No input. No help. Nothing. Maybe I should have encouraged him to partner with Bridget's sister.

"You know this would go a lot quicker if—"

"I'm not here to do your work for you. If you're struggling with basic *theory*, you don't belong here anyway, Andras or not. Things will only get more difficult for you when the class moves into the practical aspect of wards. Why don't you just go back home to the shifters you love so much?"

My jaw drops, and I replay the conversation in Burke's office. *He wasn't there for that part. He doesn't know.* I let out a disbelieving laugh. "Believe me, there's nothing I'd love more than to go home, but that's not an option."

"Why not?" I'd think he cared if his tone wasn't so bland.

"Going home puts my parents at risk of getting in trouble with the Coven Council. You know, the thing your mom runs? And maybe OSA, too, if that new legislation your mom is pushing goes through." I grasp the sides of my seat to keep myself grounded. "So, if you really want me to go home, why don't you put in a good word for me with Mommy and Daddy?"

"This is not a situation I would bring to their attention," he replies.

I scoff. "Of course. You wouldn't want them to know how very far you've fallen getting stuck with me in beginner's classes. You can't possibly have them know you aren't absolutely perfect, right?"

His eyes narrow. "My parents don't think I'm perfect."

"Yeah. Right." I go back to my textbook and attempt to sketch out the next exercise.

But now he's irritated. "They *expect* perfection, but they have no illusions that I have achieved it." He studies his nails, lips pressed into a thin line. "And I was quite serious. This is not a situation that should be brought to their attention, so it's important this spell is gone by parents' weekend."

I shake my head and roll my eyes. There's no point in responding. We'd only end up in yet another argument. So, back to work I go, continuing to struggle through the exercise.

"You're doing it wrong," he says a moment later.

"Story of my life . . ." I shake my head again and then glance at him. "Make up your mind. Either you're going to help me or you're not, but you need to quit distracting me."

He studies me for a beat then shrugs and goes back to staring at the wall, ignoring me for the rest of class. I don't finish the assigned exercises, so they're another thing to be added to my plate this evening. Maybe Isobel will be around and willing to help. Clearly I won't be catching up to the rest of the class on my own.

Next up is a quick lunch in the dining hall followed by chemistry class, aka Potions. Turns out Tristan actually wasn't lying yesterday when he told me the location of the classroom. It's on the bottom floor near the back of the building. There are two-person tables in rows of four spread out across the room, with beakers and Bunsen burners and everything else expected in a chemistry lab. It all looks surprisingly normal and familiar.

Even better, Devin shoots me a friendly smile from one of the lab tables. He nudges Adrian beside him, and Adrian grins and doffs an imaginary hat. I head in their direction.

"Selene!" a girl calls out near the front of the classroom.

I turn to see Penny raising a hand from a chair next to the teacher's desk. *What is she doing here?* I reroute in her direction.

"Hey," I say tentatively as I approach. "Are you in this class?"

"Sort of. I'm Sergei—Dr. Nikiforov's TA for the semester." Her gaze darts to Tristan and back to me, and then she quirks an eyebrow in question.

I'm pretty sure the entire school knows about the binding spell by now, so what is she trying to ask? For me to get rid of him? For an introduction?

"Do you know Tristan?" I ask awkwardly, gesturing in his direction.

"Uh, yeah," she says. "By reputation only." Her smile falters, and her eyes narrow at the blond beside me.

"And this is Penny," I say to Tristan.

"Charmed," he says dryly.

Penny sends me another look I can't read, so I simply shrug and mouth 'sorry' at her. She nods and turns to greet the next group of students entering the room.

I make my way to the table next to Adrian and Devin to take a seat, Tristan beside me. He mutters something under his breath, probably about my seating choice, but tough luck for him. This is where we're sitting.

I lean over to speak to Adrian. "I thought you guys were in all the advanced classes."

"For the most part, but the advanced Potions teacher is a...definite *witch*. I opted for Nikiforov's class instead. He's a much better teacher, and he's everyone's favorite." He smirks.

I figure out the reason for his smirk when the teacher walks in a few seconds later. He's much younger than I expected, like in his late twenties. And quite good-looking. Silvery-blond hair tied back in a low ponytail, bright-green eyes, and dimples are totally not what I expected in a teacher at a stuffy old school like this.

"Hello, everyone. I hope you're ready to work today." His smile is warm as he claps his hands. He moves to the front of the room to sit on the large desk, his hands braced on either side of his legs. "To start off, I believe we have a new student." He winks at me.

A blush heats my cheeks to the point of inferno. Can't I just be done with all this dumb new student crap?

He leans his head back in a laugh, the sound like a brush of warmth across the room. "I'm not the guy who's going to ask you to come to the front of the room and introduce yourself or anything like that, but I would like you to tell me what you think you're going to learn in this class."

Huh? Isn't that obvious? "How to make potions?"

Tristan sighs.

The teacher hops to his feet. "Class? What do we learn here?"

Tristan mouths the words along with everyone else. "How magic and science come together."

Sounds like the same thing to me, but whatever.

Dr. Nikiforov ignores me for the rest of class, jumping right into the day's lesson. He moves more quickly than even the wards teacher, and by the end of the ninety minutes, I'm more confused than when I came in. Not good.

Penny catches up with me as I leave, and I must have a hell of a confused expression on my face because she says, "Don't worry about it. I can help you with this stuff. It's my concentration area, and I've already taken all the advanced courses available. That's why I'm a TA now."

"Concentration area?" Isobel mentioned something about concentrating in Spells last night, but she never explained it.

"Kind of like a major. You pick one area of magic to concentrate in, and that dictates what you take second year." Her gaze moves to Tristan. "Or you're a blatant overachiever and you concentrate in everything."

He raises his brows and shrugs. "There's no one subject that interests me more than another, and I'm expected to excel at them all."

"It's part of his perfect act. The illustrious St. James family expects nothing less," I say in an exaggerated voice.

Devin comes up behind Penny and waves. "You handling things okay so far, Selene?"

"Except for the addition of Mr. Personality over here, I'm doing okay I guess."

Adrian waggles his eyebrows and throws an arm around his roommate's shoulder. "You ready for some action?"

Devin rolls his eyes. "He means PE."

"Of course that's what I meant," says Adrian with a wink. His gaze darts between me and Tristan, and mischief dances in his eyes. "It's sure to be a *blast*."

CHAPTER 12

The next morning, Tristan shows up at my door at 7:59 already dressed and perfect. We barely talk beyond a perfunctory greeting, and classes go smoothly except for the fact I'm still way behind everyone else. And it seems I'm falling farther behind by the day. There are no arguments, no snide comments, no blatant animosity...but there is also no sign of the spell letting up.

Two days later on Friday, Tristan has a coffee in his hand that is unceremoniously shoved into mine when I open the door, and we go through another day of classes and putting up with each other with no change in the spell.

And then it's my first weekend at Ravencrest. I'm buried in work, still struggling to catch up to where I'm supposed to be, and the entire weekend is an endless stream of monotony and studying. I don't have off-campus privileges, so I'm left behind when Adrian and Devin head out. Isobel practically lives at the library, and the only time I see Penny is in Potions class or in quick glimpses when we briefly cross paths on campus. My only company is Tristan, and after those first couple days, nothing seems to ruffle his feathers. He's so boring I'm almost looking forward to my second week of classes.

Monday morning, Tristan has two coffees: one for me and one that he sips on as he leans on the wall outside my room while I get dressed. And another day passes with no progress on the spell. Things are weird, but we've come to some sort of silent arrangement. We don't talk to each other unless absolutely necessary, but we also don't argue. For the most part, we ignore each other, a difficult feat when we're within ten feet of each other for the majority of the day.

After dinner, we head back to my dorm room. Or, rather, I head to my room and he stands outside while he waits for 10:00 to roll around. An hour of Wards homework later, I sigh and slam my book shut. Potions is going okay, Basil's still working his way through a 'brief' history of the supernatural, and I've got the whole energy ball bit in PE down even if my aim is crap. But Wards...all this crap about lines and angles and degrees and how they all fit together just isn't getting through my thick skull. I'm hopeless.

"Trouble in paradise?" asks Isobel from her position at her own desk where she's working on her homework.

"Paradise? This place is Hell," I say as I walk over to my bed to plop down on it. "How do you manage to get everything done? How do you understand everything? How does *he* get everything done?"

"By 'he' I'm assuming you mean the tall blond nodding off outside our door?" Isobel looks at me over the top of her glasses, eyebrows raised.

"Nodding off?" I sit up. "What do you mean nodding off?"

"Exactly what I said. You've apparently run the poor boy ragged."

I give her an incredulous look. "Poor boy? Since when is he a 'poor boy'?"

"Since you drag him around with you everywhere," she said, closing her book. "I tweaked the spell to help you, not so you could torture him. I mean, you could at least invite him in so he doesn't have to sit on the floor every evening."

I glance around the room, the space feeling even smaller at her suggestion. I never even thought of that...

"Oh geez," she says. "You could go to the library or something." At my semi-skeptical look, she lets out a quiet laugh and shakes her head. "You guys will never get rid of the spell if you don't learn to work together. That's the whole point of it."

"I thought the point of it was for us to get along. We're doing that."

It's her turn for a skeptical look. "The two of you are just barely managing civil. I don't call that getting along. One of you is going to have to reach out. You're both stubborn, but he's had eighteen years of upbringing in the St. James household. He might not know how to let go of his pride enough to reach out."

"I guess this means it has to be me." I sigh then stand up and walk across the room. "If this backfires somehow, I'm going to blame you," I say right before I open the door.

She lets out a full-fledged laugh. "I wouldn't expect any different."

Tristan is sitting up against the wall, his uniform jacket bunched up on one side of his neck as a makeshift pillow. He isn't nodding off. He's fast asleep.

I allow myself a few seconds to study him, my eyes tracing over his features. There are dark circles under his eyes and stubble on his chin. Wrinkles crease his shirt and his pants. How did I miss all this?

Guilt floods into my stomach.

"Hey," I say, nudging him with my foot.

He springs awake with a jerk, his limbs flinging outward. He jumps to his feet, and his jacket falls to the floor. He flails his arms before crossing them over his chest and leaning against the wall as he gives me his best bored look. He doesn't pull 'cool and collected' off very well, not when I can see his quickened pulse pounding in his neck, and certainly not with the school crest marked in red on his cheek from lying on his jacket.

I laugh. "I guess my life is a little too boring for you."

He glares and doesn't respond. Typical Tristan.

"If you'd let me know you wanted to take a nap, you could've come inside or something."

His jaw tenses, and he releases a loud breath from his nose. "If you didn't insist on keeping me here, I wouldn't need a nap."

"Why are you so tired anyway?" I ask. "Is being perfect really that exhausting?"

"Why me . . ." He drags a hand over his face. "You've made it more than clear that for the purposes of this spell, you're stronger than I am, so you make me follow you around for fourteen hours a day. Have you ever seen me with an assignment or a textbook? When exactly do you think I do my homework and study?"

I open my mouth, stunned at the picture taking shape in my head.

He holds up a hand. "Six hours a night. That's what it takes for me to do the work necessary to keep up with the classes I'm currently not permitted to attend," he says. He straightens, his chest moving with quick, angry breaths. "I'm up till almost four every night, and then I have to be back here at eight. I don't need a bloody nap. I need a fucking good night's rest!"

It's the most emotion I've seen out of him since that first day.

"Why didn't you *say* something?" I ask, throwing up my hands.

"Say something?" He jerks backward and blinks. "Would you have *cared?*"

I grimace as the truth hits me. "No. Probably not."

"Of course not. You're too self-absorbed to—" The words choke off in his throat as the spell wraps tighter and pulls us closer together. "Perfect," he says between clenched teeth. "The one time I let my temper get the best of me, and the last week and a half becomes worthless."

I place a hand on his chest, and his gaze jerks to mine. "I'm sorry," I say, and the spell loosens again. "I got caught up in everything else going on, and I didn't stop to think that you might have stuff going on too."

He gapes at me as the spell loosens even more. Isobel was right. It had to be me.

Tristan sputters something that sounds like an apology.

"Would you like to come in and study or do your homework? I know our room's not that big, but you can use my desk. I'll sit on my bed."

"I...I don't have my books," he says, stunned.

"We could go get them," I offer. "I mean, there's only two more hours until the spell goes to sleep for the night, but that's two less hours you'd have to stay up, right?"

"Yes." A long pause, and then much softer, he adds, "Thank you."

My hand is still on his chest. *Ooops.* I take a step backward, heat filling my cheeks. "Okay then."

Tristan leads the way down the stairs and over to the boys' dorm, occasionally looking over his shoulder at me as if this is some big prank and I'm all of a sudden going to yank him back to my own dorm.

His room is on the top floor, and by the time we tromp up all those flights of stairs, my thighs are burning. Since that first day in PE, all we've done is run a couple laps and then shoot energy balls at targets or each other. I've gotten better at accessing magic and using it to make energy balls, but I haven't been getting nearly enough actual exercise, and it's showing. Tristan, however, acts like it's nothing. At my inquisitive look, he says, "I'm used to the stairs. Plus, I run every morning."

"Wait a second. Are you telling me you're studying for six hours a night and still getting up in time to run *and* take a shower *and* stop for coffee before coming to my dorm in the mornings?" I stop in my tracks, trying to calculate how much sleep the poor boy is getting. Oh God. *Poor boy.* Now Isobel has gotten me saying it. I feel even guiltier than I did earlier.

He shrugs. *Shrugs*, like it's no big deal. "It hasn't been ideal, but it isn't as if I've had a choice. I'm sure you've noticed that the past week I've been toting a cup of coffee for myself as well? It's not exactly something I'd drink unless I had to."

Not had a choice? Of course he had a choice. My brain stumbles over his words, trying to fully comprehend. "Why not just...not?"

"Not what?"

"Not run?" I bite at my lower lip. "Or not spend quite as much time studying. I've seen some of your grades. I'm sure your GPA could take a couple hits and—"

"That's not an option." The words are tight, guarded, and he immediately starts walking again without looking to see if I'm keeping up.

Okay then. Must be a touchy subject.

I jog to catch up—not that the spell would have let me stay very far behind—and don't ask any more questions. If he wants to tell me, he will. If not...it isn't my problem.

He stops at the last room on the left and uses the ward to open the door before he disappears inside. I hesitate. What am I supposed to do? I always made him wait outside. What if—

"You can come in," he says.

So I do. The room I walk into is on a completely different level—and at least two, maybe three, times bigger—than mine. For one, there's clearly only one resident here since there's one *queen-sized* bed. The space not taken up by the sleeping area holds a leather couch, a coffee table, an end table, and a sleek-looking entertainment center complete with a very large TV.

Tristan walks around a corner, and I follow to find a little office alcove with a desk and a bookshelf and another door I'm assuming leads to the bathroom. Judging by the rest of the room, he probably has fifteen shower heads and a whirlpool tub in there or something...

And I should not be thinking about him in the shower right now.

I let out a low whistle. "Is this the kind of room you get if you're family friends with the director? I might need to suck up a little more if so. I don't mind sharing a room, but I'd love to have something other than a twin bed."

"No, this is the kind of room you get when your parents are major donors to the school." His voice is flat, unemotional, but there's an undertone like he's almost ashamed or maybe embarrassed about it all.

Is that why he's so concerned about perfection? Because of his parents? Even though I suppose I'm kind of here on a scholarship, I know tuition isn't cheap. Paying the tuition is one thing, but giving the school enough money to land a room like this... That has high expectations written all over it.

He grabs a couple books off the shelf and shoves them in a bag. "Okay, I'm ready."

"Do you want to just study here?" I shuffle my feet, guilt flaring up again.

"But you didn't bring your books," he says. "And I only have one desk chair."

"Good point." I nod like he just said the smartest thing in the world. "We'll go back to my room then."

He gives me a strange look. "Why are you acting like that?"

"Like what?"

"Like you're uncomfortable with me."

"Huh?"

"You keep wiggling and glancing around. You won't even look at me."

"I feel bad, okay? I've been kind of a bitch to you, and although you may have deserved it the first day—or five—I shouldn't have kept pulling you around after me like a dog."

"Well, I haven't exactly been the picture of courtesy either."

"Sorry," we say, almost in tandem.

He cracks a smile, a *real* one, and I let out a small laugh. *Maybe he isn't quite so awful...*

The second the thought goes through my mind, the knot in my chest loosens considerably. *The spell.* It isn't gone yet, but I guess it's giving us a little more space. Another thing Isobel was right about: the spell isn't going to go away just because the two of us aren't arguing. We apparently need to have some self-reflection or something. I can do that. Maybe this spell can be gone by tomorrow.

"Let's go," he says. "I've seen your grades, and you definitely need some serious study time."

I press my lips together to hold back the words I want to fling at him. Maybe *not* by tomorrow then.

CHAPTER 13

Surprisingly, studying with Tristan is not so bad. Maybe it's only because he's the first person to explain some of the basic theory to me instead of automatically expecting me to know things like what a ward actually *is* (a kind of written 'container' for magic that holds it in place) or how potions work (standard chemical reactions combined with magic), but it seems like I've learned more from him in the two hours we spent studying—or rather, him helping me study—than I have in the past week and a half of classes. Or at least I understand more about what I'm doing wrong.

The next evening, after another grueling day of classes, we head to my room and hit the books right after dinner.

First up is Wards. Whether it's because Ms. Anderson hates me or because I simply don't get it, this subject is definitely kicking my ass. I did okay in regular geometry, but this one has magic on top of everything else, and in general, magic doesn't like to cooperate with me. Plus, the worst that can happen if you screw up in regular geometry is to get a question wrong, but if the angles or lines are wrong on a ward, it's...not good.

And we're about to move on from drawing and analyzing the forms to pulling magic and using it to infuse our wards, something I'm so not ready for.

Tristan sketches out a couple simple forms and explains them to me, how each line works, what the different angles and points of connection do. Clearly, super basic stuff that anyone who isn't a complete newbie to all this would already know, but the teacher never bothered to take the time to break it down like this. Tristan's way is immensely helpful.

I almost want to hug him. *Almost.* I stop myself just in time and settle for a warm smile sent his way.

The next day, Ms. Anderson gives a pop quiz. I don't get one hundred percent like Tristan, but I don't fail like I did all the others. I'm so ecstatic with my high C that I almost hug him again. It's a near thing.

He graces me with an actual non-condescending smile and congratulates me.

And the spell loosens even more. We can now be in different rooms in the same building as long as we're on the same floor. The situation still isn't ideal, but this is definitely an improvement.

He doesn't invite me to his room again, just brings his books with him every day so we can study. I have a sneaking suspicion he's still putting in another few hours after he gets back to his room. His grades are still perfect, and there's no way he could keep that up when he spends at least half our studying time working with me instead of doing his own work.

Two days later, Isobel walks into the room when Tristan is standing over me at my desk. His hand is on the back of my chair, his chest hovering near my shoulder, and he's explaining one of the homework problems in a low voice. The whole thing is way more innocent than my roommate's giggle makes it seem.

I shoot her a death glare and pull my attention back to what Tristan is saying.

"You see, if you draw the line at a forty-five degree angle, it won't leave that side of the ward open enough to draw the power it needs," he says, tracing one finger over the line I'd drawn.

I quickly erase the line and sketch out a new one, this time making the angle slightly wider.

"Perfect." He taps his finger on the paper. "That's the last one, right? I still have a couple things I need to review for chemistry."

"Yes. Thank God." I lay my forehead on the desk. "I'm never going to be good at this."

"You'll do fine once you get caught up with everyone else," says Isobel. She glances back and forth between Tristan and me, a mischievous glint in her eye. "So you two seem to be getting along well."

Tristan takes two quick steps backward, and his cheeks go slightly pink. Is he *blushing*?

"Well, we kind of have to, don't we?" I say, arching an eyebrow. "Isn't that the point of this dumb spell?"

Isobel laughs and sits on her bed before her attention moves to Tristan. "I must admit I didn't expect the mighty St. James to become such a fixture in our room when I tweaked that spell."

Everything but cold anger drops from Tristan's face, and his voice goes low, quiet. "What did you just say?"

"I . . ." Isobel stammers, her eyes wide. She leans away from the intensity of Tristan's glare.

"I asked her to tweak it so I'd have more control over it," I blurt out. It's not exactly the truth but close enough. But if I thought telling him I requested the tweak was going to redirect his ire away from Isobel, I'm clearly dead wrong as, if anything, his expression gets more and more pissed, all of it directed at my cowering roommate.

"What exactly did you do?" Another quiet question, but this time the words are more strained, as if he's barely keeping himself in control.

Isobel spouts out a long explanation about the tweak she made. She loses me after the first time she mentions the syllabic rhythm in comparison to the number of lines. The spell is clearly way beyond my basic understanding, but not beyond Tristan's. His eyes narrow to nothing more than slits.

"And how do you know altering the basic structure of the spell didn't make it worse? Didn't change the parameters?" He stalks forward, towering above her much smaller stature. "How do you know it didn't make me stuck with it even longer?" He's yelling by the end of the question, and Isobel cowers away from him.

"Hey!" I jump up, step in front of Isobel, and shove him away. "Don't you do your snarling asshole thing to her. If you want to blame someone, blame me."

"Oh I do," he says, his upper lip beginning that arrogant curl. "I thought this spell was taking much too long to resolve. It should have been as simple as me bringing you coffee and us having a couple civil chats, but now I find out you let your nobody friend alter it to your advantage. I don't think you even understand what kind of trouble this can cause. Do you know parents' weekend is only two weeks away? I can't be stuck with you when they're here. It's completely unacceptable!"

"Lower your goddamn voice!" I step forward, chin up, arms loose at my sides but ready to come up if necessary.

"Why should I?" he yells. "You have no idea what you've done. None." His fingers curl and uncurl, and he paces to the other side of the room and back again. He starts muttering under his breath, almost talking to himself.

"This was supposed to be done with by the time they showed up. They can't find out about this. They can't."

Tristan has stopped pacing, but his face is twisted into an expression I've never seen on him before. Is he *scared*?

I reach out and grab his arm. "Why—"

"We're not talking about this," says Tristan through clenched teeth.

"But—"

"I said drop it!" He jerks away from me, his entire body tense. He stands there for a second, doing nothing but breathing in slow, even breaths, as if he's trying to calm down. His lips thin, and he shakes his head. Then, without a word, he gathers up his books and papers before storming out of the room.

Of course, he can't go very far, but there's plenty of hallway well within the distance requirements of the spell.

Should I go after him? Probably not. I doubt whatever conversation might come of that would be in any way productive. And it might make things with the spell worse based on Tristan's attitude toward my not even half-asked questions.

So, I sit here and stare dumbly at the door for a couple minutes, waiting to see if he comes back. He doesn't. Not five minutes later. Not ten minutes later. Not ninety minutes later. He stays in the hallway for the remainder of the spell's daily time limit.

And I study. Well, kind of study, more like I stare at my book and pretend I understand any of it. It doesn't help.

By the next day, he goes back to being the taciturn robot that followed me around the first week. If it wasn't for the spell being so much looser, I'd think I'd imagined the past few days where he was almost...nice.

For a reason I don't really want to examine right now, it bothers me that he shut me out right when we were beginning to open up to each other. It doesn't seem to bother him at all, which only makes me irrationally pissed. Why do I care anyway? Did I think the two of us were going to form this undying friendship through the course of this binding spell?

I laugh to myself.

Ah, well, I guess it's back to the way it was before we started studying together, albeit with a bit less naked animosity. Probably only because Tristan knows if there *was* naked animosity, we'd never get rid of this stupid spell.

We spend our weekend studying in separate sections of the library. Well, I study anyway. I really have no idea what he does. Left to my own devices, I don't get nearly as much work done, but his prior help proves invaluable. I might not get all the questions right, but I understand why I get them wrong... about seventy-five percent of the time. Still, it's better than zero percent.

Sunday night finds the two of us back at the library after dinner, and my patience with Tristan growing thin.

The stupid potion formula in front of me simply isn't making any sense. I can't seem to get the equation to balance right, and I have no clue what I'm doing wrong. Once magic is tossed into the mix, chemistry isn't nearly as straightforward as it was in high school. If I could throw the book across the room without potentially damaging something, I would. Instead, I settle for slamming the book shut and stomping over to the table Tristan is sitting at with a different chemistry book open in front of him.

"Are you done pouting now?" I internally cringe. Not my best opening.

"Pouting?" he asks without looking up from his book. "Is that what you think I've been doing?"

"Yes."

"I've simply distanced myself from an uncomfortable situation. It might take longer to resolve the binding spell, but it will happen eventually. There's no need for us to . . ." His eyes dart toward me in a furtive glance.

"For us to *what?*" The temper that calmed a little at my idiotic opening ramps up again.

"To actually be friends," he says in a monotone voice.

I blink, too angry to form any words at all. So, he'd felt it too, that we were sort of friends?

He coughs nervously. "You are not as obnoxious as I first thought, and I don't think as poorly of you, but I don't think you and I are of the same... anything."

"That is the most ridiculous thing I've ever heard!" It really isn't, but my brain isn't functioning on all cylinders, so my reasoning is rather nonsensical.

"I don't want to argue with you." He sighs and drags a hand through his hair. "We'll never get rid of this spell if I do."

I have to admit, that hurts. He pretended to by my friend because of the spell and—

Wasn't that the purpose of the spell to begin with?

I'm so stupid. Here I am thinking we might be friends or at least casual acquaintances, but he's just trying to get rid of the spell. "I guess that's it then. We'll be stuck in this spell until hell freezes over."

"These things have time limits," says Tristan. "And I talked to Desmond. He promised me if the spell isn't resolved by parents' weekend, he'll take care of it."

Take care of it? If it's so easy, why doesn't Burke take care of it now? But I don't ask.

"Fine. Whatever." I cross my arms over my chest.

Tristan says nothing else, and after a few seconds, I return to my table and open my book.. At most I have another two weeks stuck in this spell. I can make do until then.

Right?

CHAPTER 14

For the next three days, Tristan barely says two words to me. If he thinks the silent treatment is going to solve the spell, he's totally wrong. Though the spell hasn't tightened, it also hasn't loosened, and I'm not sure what to do about it.

Isobel does her best to help me after she gets to our room at night, but she doesn't understand my difficulties, and her explanations aren't half as good as Tristan's, so I'm floundering in most of my classes.

Potions is currently my best academic subject, though that isn't saying a whole hell of a lot. I'm still struggling as the work gets more and more difficult, but my level of understanding doesn't increase. The science, I get. The magic? Not so much.

On Thursday, Dr. Nikiforov returns our recently graded tests to us at the end of class, leaving them face down on our lab tables. Tristan's sitting in the back of the room somewhere, so I don't see his grade or reaction. Adrian flips his over and shrugs, and Devin looks quite happy with his. Me? I leave it sit, the blank back of the test taunting me as I stare down at it.

My score could be okay, but it could also be awful. Do I really *want* to know? No. Not really. This unit test is a large part of my grade, and based on how very long it took me to complete and the fact that at least half of the questions didn't make any sense...I don't think I did very well.

Anxiety twists in my stomach, and I pick at one corner of the paper. I lift the edge and set it down again, trying to convince myself the longer I wait the better off I'll be. Not that that makes any sense.

Adrian and Devin shoot me sympathetic looks as they head out to their next class along with the rest of the students, but I stay at my lab table, warring with my internal desire to toss the damn paper in the trash and forget about it. What if—

Someone snatches the paper off my desk and waves it around.

"Oh look here," says one of Tristan's preppy frenemies. "A sixty-one percent."

Well, I passed. So there's that at least.

I slam my hands on my desk and jump to my feet. "Give it back."

"Why? You want your parents to hang it on their fridge or something? I bet it'll be the best grade any of those dumb—"

"Drew, give it back." Tristan is suddenly beside me, glowering at the guy.

What the hell? The ass has barely spoken to me in days, and now he's trying to be all knight in shining armor coming to my defense?

"Why should I, Tris?" Drew glances between the two of us. "You yourself said she was no better than dirt and didn't belong here. I think this test proves it. Not only can she not hack it at being a witch, she can't hack it passing any of her courses. Don't tell me you've gone soft on me."

Tristan said that? His gaze darts to me, and he gives a slight shake of his head. But not slight enough that Drew misses it.

"You have!" He laughs and crumples my test into a ball before tossing it across the room. The paper goes flying, hitting the rear wall and bouncing to the floor. "Find me when you've rethought your stance and want to come back to where you belong. Until then . . ." He leers at me. "I suppose you could find *some* way to enjoy yourself."

Is he suggesting what I think he is? Heat gathers in my chest, a ball of magic just itching to knock Drew to the other side of campus. My fingers curl around the edges of my desk as I fight to hold the magic back.

Calling up magic has never been a problem for me. The raging inferno of what Basil calls 'raw power' is always waiting in my chest. But *controlling* the magic is a different story, and I haven't felt this out of control since the night I manifested. I grit my teeth.

A few moments later, Tristan's hand lands on my arm. "He's gone."

"Yeah, I know," I bite out. "But my magic isn't, and it's pissed and looking for a target."

The room is empty; even the teacher is long gone. It's just the two of us, and the situation is quickly getting uncomfortable—for me at least. Keeping my magic from finding a new target in the boy leaning next to me is an effort.

And he's still staring at me.

He studies me and rubs at his chin. "The way you talk about magic...it's not like how other witches describe it. Maybe you've been going about this all wrong. I wonder . . ." He grabs the geometry textbook from my bag and opens to a random page, tapping his finger on one of the wards. "Pull a little bit of magic, and use it to look at the ward. Try to...let the magic guide you."

I want to roll my eyes. Like it's that easy? But I listen to him and stare down at the ward. The magic in my chest jitters, and I let a tiny strand out to trace each line and angle carefully, a new understanding of the purpose and the power of each position gradually seeping into me. Because my *magic* understands the ward, I do too.

My eyes go wide. I scan over the example on the next page and let my magic study that ward too. It's like all this time I've had the pieces but no way to put the puzzle together, and now, ever so slowly, I'm building the edges and filling it in until I can finally see the full picture.

I flip a couple pages back, to the most recent chapter we went over in class. The exercises that seemed completely unsolvable before now make a bit of sense. If only I had my last assignment with me to see if this new understanding worked on figuring out what I was doing wrong before.

"I understand it," I say. "I can't explain it, but I can see how it all kind of works together now."

Tristan smiles, a real, warm, open smile, the corners of his eyes crinkling and everything. It's like a physical hit to the chest. Sure, I've known him for a couple weeks now, but I never *really* looked at him. Or maybe he never looked at me like *that*?

"Everyone else has been raised with magic, known about it and been able to trust their instincts. But your instincts don't default to using magic. You haven't learned how to work *with* it. That's why you've been doing so poorly." He glances at the textbook. "Well, so poorly with wards anyway. It doesn't work the same way with potions or spell casting, but I think if you find a way to...connect with magic more, the others might start to come easier as well."

I rest my elbows on top of the textbook and lean my forehead on my palms. "But will it do any good at this point? I'm not so sure I'm going to be able to pass for the semester. I don't think I'm at the bottom of the ranks, but I'm definitely close."

"Nonsense," he says. "You still have midterms coming up as well as the whole second quarter. Granted, your grades might not be top of the Order material, but you'll be fine. Plus, there's still the tournament next quarter, which could definitely help with your class rank."

"Tournament?"

He cocks his head to the side. "Were you not aware of it? There's an obstacle course competition around the end of each semester. The participants get points for speed and skill and a good score can boost your class rank. It's optional for first year students, but it's certainly something you should look into. As long as you can gain a little bit of control, I think you could do very well in it."

As long as I can gain control...

"I can't fail at this," I say, my voice lower. "My parents are depending on me."

He averts his eyes. "I know."

My stomach rumbles, and I glance at the clock. A little after 4:00, almost two hours until the cafeteria opens for dinner. I don't know where the words come from—I blame it on my stomach—but my mouth blurts out, "What would you say about skipping PE and getting out of here for a bit?"

He blinks, and there's a long pause before he, very slowly and with a strange look on his face, says, "I'd say you're only inviting me because I have a car and you don't."

I shrug and focus on my desk as heat flares in my cheeks. "Well, that's not the only reason. I think I owe you for that little breakthrough. The town's not too far off, right? I think Isobel mentioned a pizza place."

"Okay," he says.

Even though I wanted him to agree and was hoping he would, the ease of convincing him is a bit of a shock. He doesn't even question the fact that I don't have off-campus privileges. I can't decide whether or not to ask if he's sure or just go with it.

"Grab your books," says Tristan. "We should still get some studying done."

"Yes, sir." I give him an exaggerated salute and shove my books into my backpack, a big grin on my face for the first time in days, one I'm not going to think too hard about the reason for.

Penny's standing outside the classroom as we exit, and I shoot her a wave. "Did I hear you say you two are going off campus?" she asks, her mild tone a contradiction to the strangely calculating gleam in her eyes.

"Yup," I say, and it dawns on me that what we're doing sounds an awful lot like a *date*, and I need to change that perception ASAP. Because no. "Do you want to come with us?"

Her face shifts from surprised to something that's almost derision before she plasters on a pleasant smile and slowly shakes her head. "I've got some homework to do," she says. "Maybe next time."

"Sure thing!" *What is wrong with me? Why am I being so awkward?*

By the way Penny widens her eyes, she must wonder the same thing, but she goes without comment and waves us off.

Tristan and I make our way to the garage for students just outside the back gate, someplace I've never actually been before, and he unlocks a dark-gray BMW with the click of a button. I toss my bag in the back and get into the leather passenger seat.

Like everything I've seen of Tristan's, his car is immaculate. There isn't a speck of dust on the dash and not a single piece of dirt on the floor mat.

After sliding into the driver's seat, he pulls out of the garage, headed on the road to town. The air between us is heavier now, making the twenty-minute drive seem much longer. This—skipping class and leaving campus—feels bigger than anything else we've done together. Have we officially crossed the line into an actual friendship?

Even on a Thursday and fairly early in the evening, the small downtown area is a little busy, and it takes a few minutes to find a parking space. Tristan smoothly parallel parks and then hops out. By the time I grab my backpack,

Tristan is opening my door.

My brows rise.

A blush tints his cheeks with pink. "Sorry. Habit."

Habit? That's certainly something to digest. Does he date often? Clearly he hasn't been lately, but—

Stop it, Selene.

I do not care about his dating life. Not one little bit.

I let him lead the way to the pizza place, a small space tucked into the lower floor of a larger building. The restaurant is packed, with nearly every table taken, even the outdoor ones. The second we enter, the most delicious scent assaults my nose, and my stomach lets out an even louder rumble than before.

Heat gathers in my cheeks, and I send a quick glance at Tristan to see if he noticed. He did. Of course. And is grinning like it's the funniest thing he's ever heard.

"Hungry?"

"Always," I say with an exaggerated sigh. "I swear my stomach is like a bottomless pit sometimes."

Tristan laughs and flashes two fingers at the hostess. She leads us to a small table in the front corner. Calling it a table is generous. It's more like one of those super tiny things at weddings people are meant to stand around and put drinks on, but shorter.

I pull my chair out before Tristan can do it for me and then sit with my back to the wall. He slides in across from me, our knees bumping underneath.

"Where are we going to put plates?" I ask, pretending to measure the tabletop with my hands. "I think we're going to have to eat directly from the pizza pan."

"I have no problem with that," he says with a shrug.

"Here's the true test, what toppings do you want on this pizza?" I ask.

We agree on the simplicity of pepperoni with extra cheese and sit back to wait for it to be delivered.

Our conversation peters out, and things grow awkward rather quickly. Tristan and I have been forced to spend quite a bit of time together, but it hasn't exactly been quality time, and I'm beginning to realize how very little I actually know about him.

I know his parents are assholes.

I know he's a stellar student.

I know he's rich.

But the stuff that really makes him tick? I have no clue.

This suddenly feels like a bad first date where we've run out of things to talk about.

The arrival of our pizza—a delicious-looking masterpiece—saves me from trying to make conversation, and I spend the next few minutes inhaling half the pizza and then eyeballing the last piece.

"Take it," says Tristan, nudging the plate in my direction.

"Are you sure?"

"Of course. I—"

Two hands land on Tristan's shoulders, and my eyes follow the hands up to their owner: a large, dark-haired man flanked by two others. All three of them are shifters.

"Didn't anybody warn you not to leave campus? Leaving the safety of those wards isn't healthy for a St. James," drawls the first man.

CHAPTER 15

The three shifters pay me no attention, the first man leaning down to speak directly into Tristan's ear. Whatever the man is saying is too low for me to make out, but given his opening line, I can't imagine he's saying anything good. The color drains from Tristan's face, and his whole body goes tense. Under the table, he grabs my knee and squeezes. Holding me in place? Asking for help?

The shifter's knuckles go white as he digs his fingers deeper into Tristan's shoulder. A low grunt makes its way past Tristan's lips but no words. I've been at the other end of shifter strength before, and that grip has to hurt like hell.

"Why don't you come outside so we can discuss your mommy's proposed legislation?" For the first time, the shifter's gaze roams over to me. "We wouldn't want to upset your pretty lady friend, yeah?"

Proposed legislation? This is about the new shifter laws they're trying to pass? How in the hell did they know to find Tristan here?

Tristan nods stiffly. He gives my knee another squeeze and rises to his feet.

The shifter leads him to the doorway, one hand still tightly gripping Tristan's shoulder, and the other two men follow behind.

For a second, I'm not quite sure what to do. Tristan likely doesn't want me to follow, but I'll be damned if I'm just going to sit here. There's a good chance those shifters could be part of the group rumored to be behind the recent attacks on witches. I can't let Tristan face them alone, not when this could be a genuine threat to his safety. We might not be friends exactly, but I don't hate the guy, and I don't want to see him hurt.

I fumble for my wallet, throw some money on the table (hopefully enough to cover the pizza), and then run out after them.

By the time I get outside, they've disappeared from sight. I glance up and down the sidewalk. Where to? Where would—

There. An alleyway off to the left.

I dash toward it, and as I turn the corner, there's the very definite sound of a punch being thrown.

"Hey!" I call out.

Tristan's back is against the brick, and he's half doubled over—probably because he's the one who was punched—and the three shifters are standing in front of him, blocking him in.

"I'll deal with this," says Tristan, slightly out of breath. "Just go back to the car. They won't kill me. It won't look good for their cause."

He's right. If these shifters are truly worried about the new legislation, they aren't planning anything permanent. But am I willing to bet his life on that?

One of the shifters flashes me a sharp-toothed grin. His eyes hold a feral glint I don't like. Sure, the renegade shifters haven't killed anyone so far, but who knows if these guys are part of that group? Even if they are, will they be able to pass up a shot at hitting the St. James family where it really hurts? Not to mention Tristan has a tendency to rub people the wrong way.

I wrack my brain, trying to come up with ideas. Shifters have so many traditions and rules. There has to be one I can use. Can I challenge one of them? No, that definitely wouldn't work out in my favor. So, what? Do I claim him or something? Can I do that?

He isn't pack. Technically, neither am I but...

"I name him a friend to the Donovan pack of the Blue Ridge region," I blurt out.

"What did you say, little girl?" asks the leader of the three shifters.

"I said I name him as—"

One of the others, a guy with stringy brown hair, grabs my neck, holding it tight enough to show force but not tight enough to cut off my air. He bares his teeth at me and snarls. I hold his gaze but tilt my neck to the side. I'm not trying to get into a dominance thing with him, but I'm not going to back down either. The leader makes a gesture with one hand, and his minion releases me.

I swallow, waiting.

The leader narrows his eyes and cocks his head to the side, not in submission, but in inquisitiveness. "Who are you to speak for the Donovan pack, witch?"

I pull my hair away from the right side of my head and tilt to show the small mark behind my ear. "I am kin to the alpha."

The minion moves closer to examine the mark, and inhales deeply. Scenting me.

"She's definitely a witch," he says. "She reeks of magic. *Strange* magic, but still witch. And that's a pack mark."

The leader rubs at his chin, eyes narrowed into slits. "I heard something

. . ." He advances toward me. "Donovan's on the outs with the witches, something about his sister kidnapping one, so he's holed up on his pack lands. He may claim you as *kin*, but even if the story's true, you don't have the authority to do what you're trying to do."

And now's when things get complicated. The guy's right. I have no standing to claim Tristan as a friend to the pack, but if I can pull this off...

I smile, willing my heartbeat to stay steady. No use tipping them off about how nervous I really am. My next words need to be solid, irrefutable. "As daughter to the pack beta, adopted or not, I definitely have the authority to name friends of the pack."

The leader eyes me, digesting my words silently.

"Who's to know if we take care of this problem anyway?" asks the second minion, speaking up for the first time. "Like you said, Donovan's practically in hiding, and there's no crime if there aren't any witnesses."

Shit. That is exactly the conclusion I hoped they wouldn't come to.

I can't call for first blood. There's been no definable insult to my pack, and something tells me these guys wouldn't honor it anyway. I'd lose a full-on challenge. Only one choice left then. I kick the guy in front of me in the groin, and he goes down with a yelp. Shifter or not, he's very much a guy, and Reid always says, "If in doubt, fight dirty."

The second minion snarls and jumps at me. He's fast, much faster than me, but I know how to use size to my advantage. I dodge and send an elbow at the side of his head, driving his forehead into the brick.

"Tristan, go!" I yell. I don't have time to see if he listens, because the second minion is turning, and the leader is starting toward me. Perfect. I fake a shot at the leader's face. He dodges easily and grabs the front of my shirt, slamming my back against the wall.

"Did you honestly think you could take on three shifters, girl? Your trainer was very good, that much is clear, but not good enough."

The other two are back on their feet, flanking their leader in much the same positions they had taken around Tristan. Just where I want them.

"You seem to have forgotten I've had more than one kind of trainer." I put my hands on his chest and push, magic ripping from my chest and going straight into his. He flies backward, his head cracking against the opposite wall. I shoot my hands out to the side, sending more energy at the other two. They both go down.

Now, *that* I can do. Sometimes having no finesse works in my favor.

"Wow," says Tristan from somewhere off to the side.

I glance at him, and he releases the magic he was weaving together with his hands.

"I've never heard of someone taking out three shifters like that. I didn't even see you pull any magic."

"Raw power has its perks," I say. "We need to get out of here before they wake up."

Tristan grabs my arm. "You didn't have to do that. There'll be... repercussions for you, won't there? With your pack or whatever."

"Did you think I was going to stand there and let you get hurt? That's really not my style." I tug my arm out of his hold.

"You didn't answer my question," he says in a harder voice.

I shrug. "If there are repercussions, I'll deal with them. They had no business accosting you like that. Connor will understand why I did what I did. He won't consider it a betrayal. What they're doing is illegal."

He lets out a dry chuckle. "And that fact has been so good at stopping them? How many witches have been attacked in the past few months? A dozen?"

Penny's face pops into my head. I never asked her about the circumstances of her Bite. Is it possible she was a victim of these attacks too? But then why doesn't she hate shifters?

"They're out of control," he says, his hands curling into fists. "I know you don't understand why my parents are doing what they're doing. I know you don't agree with it, but as it is right now, shifters have no consequences for their actions. If I'd ended up dead or Bitten tonight, those guys would have run to pack lands, hidden under the protection of an alpha, and gotten away with it."

"That's not true," I say as I follow him out of the alley. "No alpha would allow a major criminal to hide under those protections. It's against everything shifters believe in. They value family and loyalty and honor. They—"

"Tell that to my sister," he snaps. *His sister?* At my blank look, he continues. "The shifters that took Cecily didn't seem to hold those values. They grabbed her when she and I were having a picnic in the woods by our house and left six-year-old me wandering alone. There was no ransom demand; they simply sent back her fingers one by one. Since the culprits were within the boundaries of your precious pack lands and the region's alpha was not willing to let in any search parties, no one could do anything about it."

The words hit me like a punch to the stomach. I've never heard of Cecily St. James or about anything like what Tristan just described. The kidnapping, the brutality, none of it seems like something shifters would do...but how do I really know? Connor's the regional alpha, but besides a few exceptions he's mostly kept me away from the other shifters in the small local packs that live in his region, and I grew up sheltered from all the conflict with the witches since, at the time, no one knew what I am. What if I only saw the good parts of shifters?

And only saw the bad parts of witches?

Maybe life's not as black and white as I thought.

"That's why you hate shifters so much," I say softly. "Because of what happened to your sister."

His jaw sets into a firm line, and he looks at the ground. "Something like that."

"You know we—they aren't all bad, right?"

He lets out a loud breath. "I don't have the option of pausing to find out if the particular shifter I might be dealing with is a 'good guy' or a 'bad guy.' That's what drew my sister in. She thought he was a good guy. He wasn't."

"Is that why your mom is so adamant about the new legislation?"

"No." He shakes his head. "She just hates shifters. She always has." He sighs and drags a hand through his hair. "I know you and I will probably never see eye to eye on this issue, but please remember there are always two sides to the story, and growing up with shifters, you only ever heard one."

I have no response for that. Because he's absolutely right. My family—Mom, Dad, Connor, and Reid—they're honorable. They're good. They're loyal and honest and every other quality that makes them amazing people. But I can't say the same for *all* shifters, not after tonight.

And he can't say it for all witches either.

"You only heard one side too," I say softly.

His only response is a nod.

We arrive at his car a few minutes later. This time, he makes no attempt to open my door, and we sit in silence the entire way back to school. As he puts the car in park, he glances at the clock and lets out a sharp breath. It's only 6:30. We're stuck together another three and a half hours. He sighs, steps out of the car, and turns to lean against it with his back to me.

I climb out of the car and walk around to stop directly in front of him. "I'm sorry about what happened to your sister. I hope . . ." I let the words trail off because I have no idea what I hope for. That he sees shifters as a whole are not responsible for the actions of a few? That *I'm* not a bad person for defending shifters? That my family isn't filled with a bunch of blood-thirsty monsters?

"For what it's worth...I'm sorry too. This whole evening wasn't exactly what I had in mind." He smiles, strained but real. He moves as if to brush my cheek, but his hand lands on my shoulder instead. "I hope you won't hold all the drama against me. Maybe we can do it again sometime?"

Do it again sometime? Not so long ago, he declared that he and I will never get along and now...what? He wants to be my friend? But it's an olive branch all the same, the first one I recall him truly offering.

"That might be nice." I return his smile and release a slow breath. The spell pulls taut—*What the hell? We're getting along!*—then releases entirely. I rub at my chest, my mouth falling open, and notice Tristan doing the same. There's a strange emptiness in my chest, like there's a piece of me missing.

Tristan grins, obviously not feeling as weird as I am, full on dimples and everything and not at all strained. "It's gone. The spell's gone."

"I guess so." My voice is quiet, the jubilation that filled Tristan's words nowhere to be found in mine.

He tilts his head backward and mouths 'thank you' to the sky.

"So . . ." What's the protocol now? Do I invite him to study with me? Does he even want to? I have no idea what to do, so I settle on saying, "I'll see you around?"

"Of course." He nods absentmindedly, and I can see the wheels turning in his head already, probably creating a to-do list of some sort. He gives me one brief smile then a small wave with the hand by his waist. "I'm going to go study. In my own room for once."

And there's my answer. Now that he can, he wants to be as far from me as possible. Or something like that.

"Okay," I say awkwardly, when what I really want to say is 'stay.'

But he's gone before I can work up the nerve to speak, disappearing in the direction of the boys' dorm while I'm standing here trying to figure out what I'm feeling.

I walk to my room slowly, rubbing at my chest. I pull my books out and sit at my desk then move to my bed, but no matter what I do, I can't get comfortable. It's quiet. Too quiet.

Is this normal? Is it some sort of side effect like spell withdrawal or something? Because everything feels...off. *I* feel off. Maybe it's just me. Tristan didn't appear to be affected by the spell's absence at all. So, what the hell is wrong with me?

Tristan is irritating and arrogant and condescending.

But I kind of...miss him.

CHAPTER 16

The sound of a door slamming somewhere down the hall jerks me out of a dead sleep. Why is it so bright in here? Did I forget to turn the light off last night? I wasn't that out of it, was I?

I blink my eyes open. The brightness is daylight. It's at least mid-morning. What the hell? Where is—

The memory hits me. The spell is gone. Tristan is gone. My magical 'alarm clock' is gone.

And I'm really, really late.

There's no time for me to do anything but leap out of bed, grab a shirt, struggle into a skirt, and desperately search out a pair of shoes. My questing fingers find only the flip-flops I wore my first day of class. Hopefully that's not a sign as to how this day might go.

I sling my bag over my shoulder and yank open the door, pulling my hair back with my other hand, and run down the hallway, the sound of my flip-flops echoing in my ears. I scurry down the stairs and across the quad into the main building. Not until the door is closing behind me do I finally glance at an actual clock. Shit. I've missed breakfast and my tutoring with Basil as well, and Wards is almost half over. I push myself to go even faster, darting up the stairs two at a time.

The door is closed when I get to the classroom, but Ms. Anderson's voice drones on inside. I pause a moment to catch my breath and tuck my shirt in then try to open the door as quietly as possible. I don't succeed. The hinges let out a loud squeal, and every eye in the room turns to the doorway. It's like I'm cursed or something. In practically a shot by shot replay of my first time in this classroom, Ms. Anderson shoots a disdainful look in my direction, eyes narrowed, mouth twisted into a scowl. She makes a sharp gesture toward an empty desk in the front row and then turns back to the class.

I keep my gaze on the floor and make my way to the seat she motioned at, the accursed flip-flops making an awful racket the entire way. I glance up at my regular seat at the far end of the middle row. It's empty, as is the one next to it.

Didn't Tristan come to class?

The answer smacks me in the brain almost as soon as the thought crosses my mind. Of course he didn't come to *this* class. He's free to go back to his advanced classes now, no longer forced to follow me to the beginner ones. Meaning I'm entirely on my own in here. Again.

I plop my books down on the empty desk and slide into the seat. Rustling through my bag, I pull out a pen and a piece of paper then turn my attention to the whiteboard where Ms. Anderson is going over exercises from last night's homework.

The homework I didn't do. *Shit.*

This is simply not my morning. I rub my fingers over my forehead and then struggle to copy the diagrams already on the board while trying to pay attention to the explanations for the next ones. Splitting my focus does not work out well, and by the time Ms. Anderson passes out a pop quiz near the end of class, I find I might be more behind than ever, the rush of yesterday's breakthrough buried in the face of Ms. Anderson's brusque manner and my complete brain fart when I see the problems on the quiz.

I'd be surprised if I get any of the questions right, but my grade on this quiz is not something I have the energy to care about right now. My stomach is growling, and a headache is creeping up behind my eyes thanks to the fact that, along with missing breakfast, I didn't get my morning coffee.

I try the tracing it with magic trick Tristan went over with me yesterday. It helps, sure, but it does me no good when I get to the last problem on the quiz where I'm supposed to pick one of my drawn wards and actually use magic to infuse it. I imagine the infusion process is something Ms. Anderson went over in class before I got here, so I have no clue what to do. With the way my day is going so far, I might blow something up if I attempt to infuse one of the rather shaky looking wards I drew.

I'll just leave that last one alone then.

I drop my incomplete quiz on Ms. Anderson's desk and then rush out of the classroom before I have to face anyone.

Autopilot and my empty stomach take me straight to the dining hall. I'm a little early, so the lines aren't open yet, but I find a table anyway and sit down. I lay my head in my hands and curse myself for not remembering to set an alarm. I groan and shake my head.

How stupid is it that I preferred it when the binding spell was in place? At least then I was on time and Ms. Anderson's attitude toward me was always better when Tristan was around.

Twenty minutes or so into my pity party, a familiar voice hits my ears.

I glance up to find Tristan entering the dining hall, a wide—though clearly fake—smile on his face. He's surrounded by the gaggle of rich jerks he calls friends, and he doesn't so much as look in my direction. Nice to know *his* life's gone back to normal. I yank my gaze back to the table, but my eyes quickly find their way to Tristan again as the group passes by.

He's well-rested and perfectly put together. Obviously *he* didn't sleep in. Why didn't he—

"St. James, did you lose your puppy?" asks Jason with a grin in my direction as he catches me blatantly staring.

Tristan glances over, takes me in head to feet...and then turns back to his group without another word. As if I don't exist.

Jason smirks at me, an edge of malice to the expression. "I told you he was good. Took him longer than I thought it would to get rid of that binding, but I knew it would happen."

I'm stunned into a stupefied silence. Tristan was actually nice last night, and now he's back to acting like an ass? Just like that? Was anything he said last night even true? Or was it all an act to get rid of the spell? Could he have...*engineered* everything from the snatching of my paper to the shifter confrontation? My mouth opens, closes, then opens again, but no words come.

Was it all a joke to him? Tristan's words from the first day ring in my ears: *I'll be rid of the spell before the end of the month.*

Jason quirks an eyebrow. "You weren't part of the pool, right?"

The pool? I puzzle over his words for half a second before my brain makes sense of them.

The *betting* pool.

Tristan took *bets* on how long it would take him to get rid of the spell. No doubt yesterday was his bet, so he...I shake my head. I've dealt with assholes, but never one so backhanded as this. What was the point? Why would he...

My gaze darts to Tristan who's still standing there as if I don't exist. I could lose my temper. I could punch him in the face. But what would that get me?

Nothing except in trouble.

I rise to my feet and head to my room without a word, replaying every second of last night in my mind in an attempt to figure out exactly which ones were faked. And why.

His fear of those shifters wasn't fake, that's for sure, so that was probably real. But him coming to my defense when my paper was snatched? The, in retrospect, oh-so-convenient 'breakthrough' with my academic struggles? And later...the story about his sister? Was that real or some play for sympathy in an effort to manipulate the spell? Does it even work like that?

I want to punch him in his stupid smug face all over again. Why does this have me so angry? Is it because I kind of miss the asshole or because he fooled me?

It's definitely the latter.

Definitely.

How did he do it? He was so bad at it that first day. Did he bide his time getting to know me so he could figure out what might work on me? Or maybe it's like I thought earlier: he waited until whatever date he had in the betting pool to really put on the charm.

Back in my room, I slam the door behind me and sit on my bed, my hands clenched into fists in my lap. How was I so stupid to think any of that could be real? Me, friends with a St. James? I'm the biggest idiot on the planet. None of it was ever real.

My stomach growls. Oh crap. I didn't actually get to eat any food, and it's nearly 1:00 now. No lunch for me today. Another thing I plan to blame on Tristan.

I lie on the bed and stare at the ceiling as my thoughts race. My magic is also riled up, twisting in my chest like some wild animal anxious to get out. Too bad it wasn't so anxious about escaping when I actually needed it in class. Stupid magic.

Isobel comes rushing in a few minutes later. She pushes her glasses up on her nose. "Are you okay? Devin heard some of what happened in the dining hall, and he was worried."

"Sure. I'm fine. Why wouldn't I be? It's not like Tristan and I were actually friends or anything. It was just a stupid spell. It probably made me think we were friends, and now that it's gone, the feeling will fade."

"That's not how . . ." She trails off when I send a red-eyed glare her way. "Never mind."

She doesn't need to tell me. I might not understand exactly how spells work, but I know they definitely don't work like that, at least not that particular spell.

My roommate scores another point by not mentioning my red eyes or asking anything further about the boy who shall not be named. She seamlessly transitions to another subject. "I know you've mentioned you're worried about the finesse you'll need to control magic now that your classes are moving into more of the 'hands on' type stuff. I've been doing some research, and I'm wondering if having your powers bound for so long is what's causing your inability to pull and manipulate magic as easily as everyone else. How would you feel about me looking into it further? It might require some of your time too since I'll probably need to run a couple tests." The corners of her mouth twist upward. "It's win-win. I can use you as a subject of study, and you can use me to help you study your subjects."

I let out a reluctant laugh. Her joke wasn't that funny, but I'll give her credit for trying. "Sure. Where and what time?"

"How about—" My stomach lets out a loud rumble, and she reaches under her bed to pull out a bag of chips. She quirks an eyebrow in question. At my nod, she grins and tosses the chips in my direction. "How about I meet you at the dining hall for dinner and we can walk over to the library afterward?"

"Sounds good," I say through a mouthful of chips. "You're a lifesaver."

Isobel smiles and shakes her head before gathering up her books and heading to class.

I'm left in my room to kill another thirty minutes or so until Potions, and I spend every minute of that time thinking up all the things I *should've* said to Jason earlier. I hate when I can't think of any good comebacks until well after a conversation has ended.

I arrive at Dr. Nikiforov's classroom with only two minutes to spare. Penny waves at me as I enter. I return her greeting and make my way to where Adrian and Devin are sitting.

"How's it going?" asks Devin.

"Do you need help hiding the body?" Adrian adds.

"Fine," I say to Devin and then shoot Adrian a look. "I wish I could say I did, but no."

The two of them laugh as Devin snags his leg around my chair, dragging it over to their table. "You can partner up with us then. We're making a fertilizer potion today. It's supposed to allow a seed to sprout into a full-grown plant in only a couple minutes."

"Are you sure you want me and my abilities to have an effect on your grades?"

"I certainly have no problem working as a threesome," says Adrian, waggling his eyebrows.

I jam an elbow into his side. "Pervert."

He raises his hands and shrugs. "What? You're the one who read into that."

A laugh bursts past my lips, and I roll my eyes. "Hush. Class is about to start."

After a brief introduction to discuss the potion we're brewing today, Dr. Nikiforov hands out a list of ingredients and instructions to each group. Working with Adrian and Devin is different, mostly because the two of them keep up a constant stream of chatter and jokes, but we get everything mixed without any major events. Of course, that's the easy part. The potion will sit until our next class period when we'll add magic and test it out.

Hopefully I don't screw things up for everyone.

I drag my feet when class is over, not overly anxious to get to PE since it's the only class I still have with Tristan. He's been my partner for every class since the binding spell, and I've managed to become quite good at lobbing and dodging energy balls. It's one of the few things I can do well with any consistency, but I'm not so sure my temper isn't going to flare up and blast him across the field today.

I needn't have worried, though.

He's not in class and, according to Mr. Davis, Tristan's switched to another period and won't be back.

In less than twenty-four hours, he's gone from a constant presence in my life to a ghost.

I hate it.

CHAPTER 17

O n Saturday evening, my third weekend at Ravencrest and my
first without a grumpy blond shadowing my footsteps, I'm bored
out of my mind. All...three? four?...of the people I call friends
have off-campus privileges and are at some fall festival in town. After Burke
found out what happened last time I went off campus, I've been expressly
forbidden from going anywhere. Adrian offered to sneak me out in his trunk
or something if I wanted to go, but that didn't sound horribly appealing, and
I can't afford to be in any more trouble than I already am.

I think Tristan is under 'campus arrest' as well, but my plans do not
include hunting him down to see if he wants to hang out. He's the last person
I want to deal with right now.

After missing my tutoring session, Basil found me yesterday and shoved
a book in my hands with the instructions to practice the first two spells. I'm
not sure that anything I've learned up till now prepares me for spell casting,

but he didn't give me a chance to argue.

So, I'm sitting in my dorm room with the book open in front of me, giving the spell casting thing my best shot. I didn't have any problem pulling magic from the air around me like the instructions say to do, but shaping that magic into a spell is, apparently, not as intuitive as the book makes it sound, and I'm not anxious to torch my dorm room because I have no idea what I'm doing.

The unused magic for the spell tingles against my fingers, and the magic in my chest swirls, poking around and looking for an exit. The feeling is almost like one of those unsatisfying internet videos that leaves the watcher with the feeling of being almost there only to have everything jerked away before having the satisfaction of finishing.

That just sounds wrong.

A giggle escapes my mouth at my own comparison. Adrian must be rubbing off on me.

He'd probably love to.

I let out another involuntary laugh and then groan. What is wrong with me? Am I overloaded on magic or something? Is there such a thing as being magic drunk?

PE has always left me a little hyped up, and that's with me getting rid of the magic. I've been stewing in it for like fifteen minutes now, and there's only one way I know of to fix it.

Well, besides successfully casting a spell I suppose, which clearly isn't going to happen.

I tie my hair back, pull on a hoodie, and head outside to the quad. It's deserted. Perfect.

Using the magic I pulled for the spell, I start shaping an energy ball with my hands and then pause. I'm doing well in PE because it's always been about quantity of magic, not finesse. Could my problem with doing magic for my other classes be related to the fact that the only way I've ever successfully gotten rid of the stuff is by blasting something? What if I could...?

I release the half-formed energy ball, letting the magic dissipate into the air. Then, as discreetly as possible, I point my palm at the ground and will the magic inside my chest to dribble out and release the pressure there. Isobel grabs my arm just as the flow begins, which sends more of a blast then a gentle drip into the ground by my feet. Dirt flies up into my face, covering both me and Isobel in a shower of soil.

"Ooops," says Isobel. "I didn't realize you were...practicing?"

I shake my head. "Getting rid of the magic I pulled trying to do my spells homework, since I can't seem to actually cast a spell."

She eyes the gouge in the ground. "It looks like you're pulling way too much, but if you're having trouble casting spells, the problem should be that you're not pulling *enough*."

I shrug. "You and I both know there are all sorts of oddities with my powers. Speaking of that, did you find anything else out?"

"No," she says, shaking her head. "I think I've checked out every book in the library on binding spells by this point, and not a single one of them mentioned anything about a spell powerful enough to do what the one placed on you did. If Bridget hadn't blasted you when she did, your powers may never have awakened."

I stop in my tracks. "The spell was that strong? Who could have cast something like that?"

"Yes, and I have no idea."

"You have to have some idea. There can't be many witches powerful enough to cast a spell that strong."

"That's the thing. I don't know of *any*. Maybe as a group...but even then, that's *a lot* of magic."

"A group like a coven-sized group? Is this something the Coven Council could have done to me?"

"I'm not sure. I don't see the Coven Council hiding you away with shifters if that was the case." She pauses. "Unless they never wanted you—or your powers—found."

"But why?"

Another shrug. "I have no idea. That's why this is so frustrating. Nothing makes sense. I'll keep looking, but I don't know if I have enough access to find the information we need. Some of the more advanced books in the library are only available to second years."

"Second years?" She nods, and I smile to myself. For once, something is going right for me. "I know just the person to help us, the TA from my Potions class. I'll get in touch with her and set something up."

"Perfect," she says, smiling as she falls into step beside me.

"What are you doing back so early? I thought the festival didn't end until ten?'

She gives me a mischievous grin. "Oh, I forgot. I have a surprise for you."

"A surprise?"

"Yes! One I think you really need right now. Come on." She grabs my arm and hurries me along until we're back at our room and the door is shut behind us. Taking a pencil, she sketches a quick ward on the door.

For quiet? Maybe silence? I'm not entirely sure. The ward is not a type we've covered in class.

She pinches her fingers together and then rests them against the ward to charge it with magic. Then, she turns to me and grins as she pulls a black rectangle from the front pocket of her purse. A cell phone. "I picked it up in town. The school wards will fry it eventually, but it should last long enough for a call or two."

"You didn't . . ." My eyes burn, and I blink away tears. She has no idea how much this means. No. She does, and that's exactly why she broke the rules for me. I take the phone with shaking fingers, a lump stuck deep in my throat.

"I know how much you've been missing them. I saw the phone, and since it's parents' weekend next week and yours can't be here, I thought you might like to call them." She smiles again. "Although, I hope you have their number memorized."

I nod and press the button to turn the phone on. I might not know every number in my phone by heart, but I definitely know the important ones. The phone powers up with a familiar chime, and I carefully dial my house. The line rings once, and then I get the recording that tells me the number is no longer in service.

For a second, I feel like I might throw up. Where are they? What if something horrible happened to them? What—

They're in hiding.

Relief washes over me at the realization, and I know what number to call next: the Donovan house.

"Hello?" Connor's gruff voice is such a welcome sound that I can't even form words. "Who is this?"

"Connor," I choke out. "It's me."

"Selene?"

"Yes. I tried calling my house, but . . ."

"Your mom and dad aren't there, honey," he says softly. "And I can't tell you where they are for their own safety."

"I know," I say, the words sticking in my throat. "But it's nice to hear your voice too."

I can practically hear his grin. "You too, sweetheart. Is there any message you'd like me to pass along?"

"Can you tell them that I miss them and that I love them?" I pause, trying to find the right words. "And that no matter what happens here, they're still my parents."

"Of course," he says. "We miss you too." There's another voice in the background. "I do have someone else here who would like to talk to you."

There's the sound of the phone changing hands, and then a familiar voice comes on the line.

"Please tell me the rumors of you punching a St. James are true," says Reid with a chuckle.

I full out laugh, incredulous. "How in the world did you even hear about that? And aren't you supposed to be in New York?"

"Fall Break," he answers quickly. "And I have my sources," he adds in a sneaky voice. "So it *is* true then?"

"Yes. It's true. And I even kept my elbows down," I say with a smile.

"Hold on a sec." His voice drops lower, and it sounds like he's switching rooms. "You need to be extra careful over there. Some of those witches are... worse than I thought. Dad said there was an altercation between a couple witches and a group of shifters near Ravencrest a day or two ago. One of the shifters was hurt pretty badly. He's in a coma or something because of the force of the magic they used on him and—"

"They were going to *kill* us," I blurt out.

There's a long stretch of silence, and I picture Reid's face as he puts the puzzle pieces together.

"*You* were one of the witches?" he asks in a stunned voice.

"Yes. *They* came after *us*. Unprovoked. I had to defend myself."

Another stretch of silence.

"Reid? Are you still there?"

"Yeah," he says. "I need you to tell me exactly what happened so Dad can get on top of this."

I release a slow breath of relief. Connor will take care of this. He'll make sure everyone gets the story straight. "Tristan and I were having dinner when these three shifters came up behind him and grabbed him, saying something about his mother's legislation. They—"

"Wait a second. Tristan *who?*"

"St. James. But it's not what you think," I say quickly. "There was this binding spell because of the whole punching thing, and he'd been helping me study and sort of being nice so we went to dinner just to get off campus for a while." A pause. "Reid?" No response. I glance down at the cell phone. The screen is dark. The wards finally kicked in, and I have no idea how much of what I said Reid actually heard.

I feel sick.

On one hand, Tristan was absolutely right about how the shifters might spin the attack to get away with it, but on the other, Connor would have listened to me. He would have believed me. And I *know* he would have made things right. But what's going to happen now that Reid, and therefore Connor, has less than half the story and the part he does have involves a family with a reputation for being anti-shifter?

I replay the conversation in my head and feel even sicker. Depending on how much of my explanation Reid heard, he could very well think Tristan and I were out on a date. And that I sided with a St. James in an altercation that left a shifter seriously injured. I sit on my bed and rest my forehead in my hands.

"I can go back out and get another phone," says Isobel. "The stores don't close for another hour or so and—"

"No," I say. "I don't want you to risk getting in trouble and losing your scholarship. I can't ask you to do that for me."

"But—"

"No," I say more firmly. "Connor isn't stupid, and neither is Reid. Now they both know there's more going on than they're being told, and eventually I'll have a chance to fill them in. Our time is better spent trying to figure out what the hell is up with my powers so I don't fail all my classes and get kicked out. I won't make it past the first semester if I can't learn how to use magic and keep up with everyone else."

"You're right," she says. "Maybe we can go see if your TA friend is around? I think I have a lead on a book that might be helpful."

"Sounds good." But as soon as we step outside, I realize looking for Penny right now *isn't* a good idea. Tonight's the full moon, so she's off somewhere being furry, and I'm once again stuck with way more questions than answers.

Will Connor be able to set the record straight about the other night? Tristan mentioned repercussions for me, but will my actions actually end up having consequences for *Connor*? I'm technically still part of his pack, so another alpha could challenge him because he's protecting me, could use Connor's love for me as evidence of him being unfit to be regional alpha. That is, unless I go home, tell my side of the story, and own up to my part in everything.

But I can't. If I leave...that might make things worse for everyone.

And there's no way to know if the other shifters would even believe my side of things, not when the only other witness on my side is a St. James.

Isobel grips my arm. "Hey, you've gone a little pale. Are you okay?"

I cough. "Yeah. Fine. I don't think I'm up for any research tonight. Rain check?"

My roommate eyes me for a moment before nodding. "Sure."

We troop back into our dorm room, and then I bury my nose in my textbooks, willing the information to not only start making more sense but for it to take my mind off all my new worries.

CHAPTER 18

For the next week, I do little besides eat, sleep, study, and try to figure out what the heck is up with my magic.

And the first two only account for about five percent of the time.

My concerns about my parents and Reid and Connor, and the whole thing about those shifters, are still swimming around in my head, but all my worrying will be for nothing if I can't get a handle on my magic.

I don't understand it. I'm working my ass off. I'm not stupid. I have the power, but nothing comes to me like it does the others. I'm not failing my classes, but I'm not doing very well either. The academic portion of everything, like what the angles on each ward mean or why mixing two chemicals together creates the basis for a certain potion, I'm gradually beginning to grasp. But actually using magic to lock in a ward or finalize a potion? Not a clue. No matter how many explanations or demonstrations my teachers give, it feels like everyone else is on a completely different page in a completely different book, and I can't figure out why.

Neither can Isobel.

I'm beginning to think there's something very wrong with me, but I have no idea what it could be.

Basil glosses over the subject every time I ask if my problem has anything to do with the binding on my powers like Isobel theorized. He ignores my inquiries about whether or not my problem could have something to do with who my birth mother was and literally pretends he doesn't hear any of my questions about my birth father, who's a complete mystery. From anyone else, that would be telling, but from Basil? That's just how he is. He waves away half my questions and teaches me what he thinks I need to know. When I flat out ask why my magic doesn't seem to act like everyone else's, he fills my arms with a pile of books and sends me on my way.

Half the books are in languages I don't know, and the other half are so old they're practically falling apart. None of them appear to have any helpful information, but I haven't had time to spare them more than a basic perusal. There's simply too much other stuff I have to know *right now* to bother spending a bunch of time searching for an answer in those books, so they're sitting in a forlorn pile in the corner of my dorm room.

The one bright spot is that the potion I made with Adrian and Devin in class last week is, surprisingly, an amazing success. The three of us each had to infuse a vial full of our group's potion with our own magic, and I managed to not only get some magic into the thing without blowing anything up but to make it into one of the most effective potions in the entire class. The tiny seed practically exploded into a full-grown pumpkin within seconds of my pouring the potion over the dirt. If nothing else, I might have a future as a gardener.

Now...I just have to figure out what the hell I did differently for that potion and how to repeat it.

On Thursday evening I'm in the dining hall, chemistry book in front of me, trying to research just that when my ears pick up on a conversation at the table next to mine.

"... wearing to the banquet tomorrow?" asks a girl I don't know.

"I'm not sure. My father sent over a couple gowns, but they're from last year's line," replies a second girl.

The first girl wrinkles her nose as if that's the most despicable thing she's ever heard. "It's our first formal and—"

"*Formal?*" I wince at my very loud and half-involuntary interruption.

The second girl looks down her nose at me. "Of course. Both the Fall and Spring banquets are formal."

"And mandatory," says the first girl with a smirk.

I resist the urge to bang my head on the table. I know parents' weekend starts tomorrow, but someone couldn't have mentioned this stupid banquet before now?

The two girls return to their own conversation, a clear dismissal. Not that I mind, since I have nothing else to add and I'm too busy doing a frantic mental inventory of the clothes in my closet and drawers. There's nothing remotely formal. Not one single thing. What am I supposed to do? Wear my uniform?

I need to find Isobel. She's sure to have an idea. I jump up from my seat, toss my trash, and then jog outside.

It's dark and my brain is occupied figuring out whether my flip-flops or boots would be better to try to pass off as 'formal' as I round the corner of the dining hall, so it's no surprise that I slam directly into someone's chest. Tristan. *Of course.* That would be my luck. Who else would I run into like a clumsy idiot around here?

At least he's alone, so there's no witness to my humiliation. Or to the fact that I somewhat blatantly scan him over. The top two buttons of his shirt are undone, his tie crooked and loose around the collar. His dirty-blond hair is in disarray, as if he's been running his fingers through it, and his eyes are weary. The moonlight makes him paler than normal, and he looks exhausted, as if he's been working his ass off this week too. Who knows? He might have been.

He looks so tired and disheveled and simply not himself that I have a sudden urge to reach out and smooth his hair away from his face and fix his tie.

I resist.

"Hi," he says quietly. The corners of his mouth twitch like he wants to smile but isn't sure if he should.

I'm not prepared for the softness of his voice or his eyes. He's looking at me like we're friends, like he hasn't been ignoring and avoiding me for over a week. *Like he didn't manipulate me and place bets on how well he could do so.* I scowl and narrow my eyes.

"Selene, I—"

"No," I say, holding up a hand. "I don't want to hear it. I could have forgiven you for the manipulation, for the bet, for pretty much all of it, but for you to just stand there and let your friend talk to me, talk *about* me, like that after I stuck my neck out for you...No. Just no."

"You don't—"

"Understand?" I step forward, tilting my chin back slightly to glare directly into his eyes, hands on my hips. "I understand perfectly. You did what you had to do to get out of the spell, and you owed me nothing after that, not even basic human decency. That's fine." I let scorn and disdain take over my features, my upper lip curling. "You are a St. James after all. I don't know why I ever expected better. You're just as bad as everything I ever thought about your parents. Maybe worse. Perfect, pretty Tristan who always gets what he wants."

"I always get what I want?" he asks, the question carried on a huff of incredulity. "If only that were true . . ." Those honey-brown eyes close, and shame, pain, and anger play out across his features in quick succession. But when he opens his eyes again a second later, there's only pure determination and blazing heat.

I'm still puzzling over his words when, in one seamless movement, he slips a hand behind my neck, his fingers catching in my hair, and pulls me toward him, planting his lips on mine.

What. The. Hell.

Surprise locks me in place for two full seconds before it's replaced by a rush of yearning hunger. I lean into him, reaching up to wrap my arms around his neck. The anger hiding in his kiss shifts into something else, a push and pull between us that sparks with passion. His hands move down to curl around my waist, and he turns us until my back rests against the stone of the building without so much as pausing the delicious assault on my mouth.

He nips at my bottom lip, pulls back to look me in the eyes as if asking permission, and then presses his mouth back to mine at my nod. His tongue slips past my lips, and he makes an awed sort of noise as one of his hands moves up to cup my face. I match his intensity, tugging at his shirt and pulling him closer and closer until there's no space left between us. My entire world narrows down to nothing but the feel of his mouth on mine, his breath against my face, his fingers around my waist. And I am lost in it.

I've never been kissed like this before.

It's need.

It's want.

It's desire.

It's something close to desperation.

And it's Tristan St. James.

I can't do this.

The thought shoots across my mind and shatters the moment, sending my body into autopilot. My hands shove him away.

Tristan stumbles backward, his lips swollen and red, his eyes wide with surprise.

"I can't do this. Not with you." *Not with a St. James.*

His face breaks, his expression more open and honest and *lost* than I've ever seen from him. But just as quickly, the emotions are wiped away.

And me? I run to my dorm room like the coward I suddenly am, spending the entire time trying to forget the look on his face. First confusion, then desolation, then...nothing at all as his mask slipped back into place.

Lying back on my bed, I brush my fingers across my lips where the ghost of his kiss remains. I made the right decision. I know I did. But why do I feel so awful?

The door swings open and I jump to my feet, heart pounding in my chest. He wouldn't have...No. It's only Isobel.

My roommate takes a single look at me, and her brows go up. "What happened to you?"

"He kissed me," I say, fingers still resting absentmindedly on my lips.

"Who kissed you? Adrian? I saw him hitting on you at lunch. Do I need to, like, kick his ass or something? He—"

"No. Tristan."

"Tristan is going to kick his ass? How did . . ." Her voice trails off, and her eyes go wide. "You mean *Tristan* kissed you."

I nod, still too scatterbrained to do much else. She backs up and perches on the edge of her bed, and the two of us sit here saying nothing for a good five minutes.

Finally, Isobel clears her throat to break the silence. "So, what did *you* do?"

"Kissed him back and ran away."

"You . . ." Giggle. "You . . ." Another giggle. "You *ran away?*" She doubles over in laughter.

"Better than punching him," I mutter.

"I would say so," she chokes out, struggling to hold back another laugh.

The corners of my mouth twitch, and I let out a quiet chuckle that morphs into a loud snort and then into full-blown hysterics. Isobel manages to hold a straight face for all of a second before joining in, both of us rolling around our beds with tears leaking from our eyes. Five minutes pass before our mirth dies down. My stomach hurts from laughing so much, but it's a good kind of pain.

"He spent the last week and half ignoring me and letting his friends talk crap about me, and then he springs this kiss on me . . ." I lie on my back, staring up at the ceiling with my hands clasped together over my stomach. "I told him I couldn't do it. And I can't. Not with him. Not when things are so up in the air for me, for my parents, for shifters in general. It'd be like betraying my family or something."

"I'm not going to say that the situation isn't complicated, but I think you're overthinking it," she replies.

"Yeah, well, there are so many more important things for me to worry about right now. I don't have time for romantic drama too." I push up on my elbows. "Because you and I both know it would be drama city between Tristan and me."

Isobel presses her lips together and tips her head to the side in a half shrug. "You don't have to justify your choices. I'm not going to try to convince you to do anything you don't want to."

"Thanks," I say with a smile, a sense of relief washing over me. "You're the best roomie I could have possibly hoped for, and I don't know what I'd do without you." I glance at her from the corner of my eye. "Now, how is it that there's a *formal* banquet tomorrow and nobody's bothered to say anything about it until now?"

Her mouth forms an O. "I thought you already knew. It's a school tradition. The Fall banquet always happens during parents' weekend. I mean, all the info is in the admissions packet." I shoot her a look. "Which, of course, you never got."

"How in the hell am I supposed to find something to wear if I'm not allowed off campus?" I ask.

She laughs. "You know there's this thing called magic, right? And that you have some? Half the students here will just spell an outfit they already have into something for the banquet."

"We can do that?" I cry. "Why didn't you tell me this earlier? I could've magicked up some real shoes or something."

"First of all, there's a whole section in your spells textbook marked illusions, so it's not my fault you didn't know, and secondly, the spells aren't permanent and need to have some basis in reality. Like, you can turn a little black dress into a black gown, but you can't turn flip-flops into flats," she says. "Come on, I'll help you find something you can use." She smirks. "And, yes, I'll help you cast the spells tomorrow."

CHAPTER 19

lasses are canceled Friday since parents will be arriving throughout the day for the banquet this evening. I'm not looking forward to it today any more than I was yesterday, but I'm not going to complain about having a day off from class. I should spend the time studying, trying to catch up on homework, and maybe practicing manipulating magic, but I just can't bring myself to do it.

Instead, I'm going for a run. It's a gorgeous fall day, and I've spent most of the past week cooped up inside with my nose in a book. Way too much time has passed since I've been alone with only my breath and the pounding of my feet. Granted, we do some physical stuff in PE, but we've mostly concentrated on more magic-based things. I've been getting almost zero exercise, and I'm beginning to feel like a useless lump.

Thanks to Basil's whirlwind tour my first night here and Tristan's daily running habit, I know there's a trail around the lake behind the school and that it's about three miles long.

Three miles is, admittedly, longer than I should attempt after taking so much time off, and even after I set a slow pace, my legs and shins ache after the first mile or so. But my blood is pumping, the endorphins kicking in, so I push myself faster for the second mile. By the third, I'm alternating between a slow jog and a faster run before I walk the last half mile and then come to a stop at the end of the trail with my hands resting on my knees.

I'm hot, sweaty, and way more winded than I should be, and I might hate myself a little tomorrow, but right now I feel amazing. I might have to follow Tristan's example and try to fit in a morning run every day.

The thought of his name brings a different kind of heat to my cheeks as memories from last night replay in my head.

What the hell *was* that? It was so random and unlike him and...

I shake my head. Dwelling on this will kill my runner's high. I wasn't kidding when I told Isobel I don't have time for romantic drama. Not only that, but I barely *like* Tristan, much less feel anything stronger. Right?

My fingers brush against my lips. The kiss was nice, though.

Stop it, Selene.

I stretch out my legs and start the walk back to my dorm. It isn't until I reach the quad that I realize parents have already started arriving and the grounds are crawling with people, both parents and students, even though it's barely lunchtime.

One girl runs up to a tall man and hugs him tightly. A boy slings an arm over a middle-aged woman's shoulders, and the two of them laugh. So many smiles. So many laughs. So many families.

The elation from my run fades away and leaves me sticky, tired, and alone in a sea of people. Homesickness hits me like a punch to the stomach. Anger follows on its heels.

How is it fair that the people who've raised me and who love me can't show their faces for fear of being arrested? Yet, everyone else at this stupid school can—

I catch sight of Tristan walking across the quad, alone, his hands shoved in his pockets and his gaze focused only on the ground in front of him. He looks...lost. The memory of last night, of the conversation, of the kiss, replays in my head, and I internally flinch at what I said. He was vulnerable, *nice* even—not to mention the passion behind that kiss was scorching hot—and I kind of stomped all over him.

Maybe I should apologize? Or something? What could it hurt to talk to him? I ignore the voice in the back of my head telling me it could hurt quite a bit if he's back to his total asshole persona and rejects me. But maybe I sort of deserve it now?

I'm halfway across the quad, heading in his direction, before my mind fully forms the decision to do it. I give him a warm smile as I draw to a stop in front of him. "Hi."

He stops, his gaze darting up to meet mine, and a wan smile lifts his lips and vanishes again just as quickly. "Hey."

"I'm, uh, sorry about last night. I didn't mean—"

"Fine. Whatever," he says with quick, sharp words as a transformation takes over his face. His smile grows wide, and his shoulders straighten. "Mother, Father. Welcome. I'm so glad to see you," he says to a couple walking up from our right.

Crap. Meeting Tristan's parents was definitely *not* on my agenda today. I'm frozen in place for a moment before I force myself to turn and greet the enemies of shifters everywhere.

Allister and Bernadette St. James don't look much like what I've imagined. After all I've heard, I kind of expected horns or maybe tails, but they're simply an ordinary-looking middle-aged couple, albeit super polished and clearly rich. I want to hate them. In fact, I will myself to hate them, but they look so *normal*. Is it possible that all of the crap they've done has been in retaliation for what happened to Tristan's sister? Does it excuse them if it was?

"Hi, I'm Selene. I go to school here with your son," I say, unsure of what else to do. I stick my hand out and smile. The gesture is blatantly ignored.

After a beat, Tristan steps forward and places himself slightly in front of my body as if to hide me from them. "Perhaps you two would like to see the library first? Or maybe take a walk by the lake?"

But the attempted distraction, if that's what it was, is also ignored.

His father's eyes, twin in color to his son's, rake over me, so reminiscent of the day I met Tristan that it's almost like déjà vu. "Selene *who*?"

Tristan's nostrils flare. He's nervous. Or embarrassed.

"Selene Andras," I say, sticking out my hand. *Again.*

Allister visibly jolts but recovers his bland expression quickly. His wife? Not so much. Her eyes bore into me, and disgust ripples across her features. By their reactions, I'm assuming they might know who I am and how I grew up.

Bernadette, with obvious effort, softens her expression and offers up a tight smile. "Charmed," she says, a strong British accent lacing the word as she takes my hand and gives it a brief shake. *So she's who Tristan gets the accent from.* She not so subtly wipes her hand on her slacks when she's done. *And apparently some of his manners too.*

Tristan does nothing, says nothing, and the tension grows, as does the level of my awkwardness—and embarrassment. I'm completely out of my league right now. Shifters operate on a whole system of traditions and subtle power plays, ones that I learned to navigate early on, but this is entirely different, and I have no idea what to do. So, I stand here like an imbecile with a smile plastered on my face as the silence grows more and more strained.

"Selene, dear, I've been looking for you everywhere," says Adrian as he steps up beside me and rests one hand on my lower back. He presses his lips to my cheek and turns his attention to Tristan's parents. "Allister. Bernadette. Lovely to see you. I need to steal Selene away, but I'll speak with you at the banquet."

Adrian presses the tips of his fingers against my back and deftly maneuvers me away from the St. James family and toward the girls' dorm.

"Are you out of your mind?" he exclaims once we're inside. "Bernadette St. James eats shifter sympathizers for breakfast."

"I was just introducing myself. I thought—"

"Your optimism is so cute." He pats me on the head, and I scowl at him. "But, really, you should avoid them at all costs. I don't know how much their lovely son has told them about you, but, if they know who you are, they have the ability to make life here very unpleasant."

"What do you mean by that?"

"Well, on one hand you are, in their eyes, essentially a shifter, something they hate. On the other, you are part of the Andras line. I know Burke has been implying you're some sort of distant relation, but I'm pretty sure that's a cover story, right? That maybe you're something closer to a *direct* descendant of the main family line?"

I nod.

"Does *Tristan* know that?"

I think back over the past few weeks. Did I ever—*Yes*. The first day. I told Tristan who my birth mother was. I nod again.

Adrian shakes his head. "Then you can bet his parents do too. There's plenty of bad blood between the Andras and St. James families, particularly between the main branches of those family trees. There was a huge scandal involving his dad and Helen—" He catches the widening of my eyes. "Your birth mother?"

166

"Yeah," I say. My eyes go even bigger. If his dad and my birth mom...

"Not *that* kind of scandal," says Adrian. "You're definitely not related to the prissy jerk. Although, if others had gotten their way, you might have been. Helen and Allister were supposed to marry, but she ran off with another man well before that—*or anything else*—happened between her and Allister."

"So, I'm the daughter of the woman who jilted Allister St. James. Is that why Tristan was desperate to get rid of the binding spell before parents' weekend?"

He shrugs. "Maybe. Honestly, I don't know the guy all that well, but his parents run in the same circles as some of my family members, so I'm privy to a lot of the gossip."

"He was ashamed to be seen with me." I blink, shaking my head. "But then why did he—" I stop myself at the intrigued expression on Adrian's face.

"Why did he *what?*" He smirks.

"Nothing."

He opens his mouth.

"*Nothing,*" I repeat. Time for a subject change..."What about gossip about who she ran off with, who my birth father might be? Have you heard anything like that?"

"Nope. I don't think he was part of any of the major families, and therefore I doubt she introduced him around. For all anyone knows, yours was an immaculate conception." He chuckles and then leans backward to get a better look at something across the quad. His brows pull together and then rise. Amusement tugs at his lips, and there's a mischievous spark in his eyes. "It appears I was not the only one looking for you."

What is he...? I turn around just as there's a shout from somewhere across the quad. A familiar voice. "Selene! You better get your butt over here and greet me before I decide to go back home."

It can't be. I scan over the crowd until I find him standing at the edge of the quad.

Auburn hair, broad shoulders, a black hoodie. Reid's here!

My heart jumps in my chest, and my eyes are suddenly burning as I run full out across the quad, nearly crashing into at least five people. I blow past Tristan and his parents and leap into Reid's arms with a happy laugh. He catches me and twirls me around so quickly I feel dizzy.

"How? What?" I bury my face in his neck, breathing deeply the scent of pack, of family, of home.

"I wasn't going to let any uppity witches keep me from you." He hugs me tighter. "I know it's been tough. I'm so glad I could come."

"Me too." He sets me on my feet, and I lean back to stare up into his face. "But didn't your dad say you weren't allowed to visit me?"

Reid chuckles. "He said, and I quote 'I forbid you from visiting Selene when her parents can't.' I wasn't positive, but it's parents' weekend, so technically they *could* visit you. I decided to test it out to see if I had enough wiggle room in the command to come." He extends his arms out to the sides. "And here I am."

"You have no idea how happy I am to see you," I say. "It's been awful. This whole magic thing is way more difficult than I expected, plus mine doesn't seem to work right. I'm behind in most of my classes even though I study my ass off. There are like three or four people here I can stand, and everyone else is . . ." My gaze land on Tristan, and I go over the interaction with him and his parents again. *He's ashamed of me, embarrassed to be seen with me.* "Everyone else is a pompous ass."

"Well, have no fear, I am here." Reid winks and tucks me under his arm. "I heard a rumor there's a dining hall nearby. I could really go for some lunch right now."

I elbow him in the side. "When are you *not* hungry?"

"Never," he says in a serious voice. "I can always, always eat."

I lean my head back and laugh, my arm around his waist. "I missed you so, so much."

"I missed you too." He kisses the top of my head. In a lower voice with a hint of mirth, he adds, "We need to chat about this St. James thing, though. The phone cut out while you were talking, so please, *please* tell me you were not on a *date* with Tristan St. James."

CHAPTER 20

After lunch and an uncomfortable conversation about what I was doing with Tristan the night the shifters attacked us—during which I spent more than half the time trying not to think about the kiss and therefore blush—Isobel helps me spell some clothes for Reid and me to wear to the banquet. The result is...interesting.

I smooth my hands over the illusionary folds of my simple black gown. It's not perfect, but it's passable. I managed to take a knee-length black sheath dress I borrowed from another girl on our floor and turn it into a floor-length gown that shimmers in the light. The bottom is nearly sheer—illusion can only do so much—but it looks purposeful, as if the dress was meant to be see through to show off the tiny sparkles in the fabric.

My outfit is haute couture compared to my cousin's though.

Reid is beside me in a slightly too-small suit magicked within an inch of its life. Isobel borrowed it from a guy in one of her classes, the biggest one she could think of, but there's still a good three-inch gap between the arms of the jacket and Reid's wrists. And, like my dress, magic can only go so far, and it looks like Reid has some really wide sheer cuffs on both the jacket and the pants. He looks more than a little ridiculous, but he's taking it in stride, and in the sea of people around us, we don't stick out too badly.

For some reason I thought the banquet was going to be held in the dining hall, but instead, hundreds of people are lined up outside a large room on the second floor of the main building. The East Ballroom, according to the plaque outside the doorway. Does that mean there's a West Ballroom too? I don't understand why Ravencrest needs one ballroom, much less two.

The line inches forward and we're finally through the doors, finding ourselves at the top of a wide stairwell leading down into a large, well-lit room. It has polished floors and a soaring ceiling decorated with gilded molding. Round tables sit in rows along the floor, and there's a low stage and a podium in front of the floor-to-ceiling windows at the far end. This is everything I expected something called a ballroom to look like.

Reid makes a low whistling noise. "When they say formal, they mean formal." He glances down at the suit. "It would've been nice if the calendar on the website had been a little more specific."

"*That's* how you found out about this?" I ask. And then, "Ravencrest has a website?"

"Did you think I wasn't going to look into this place?" He grins. "They pretend to be like any super exclusive private boarding school and have event calendars up and everything. I'm sure humans would have a hard time finding the place, so they don't have to worry about anyone crashing their parties." He gestures at his chest. "Except maybe a very persistent shifter who misses his best friend."

"I missed you too, and at least we kind of match," I say as I gesture at the sheer bottom of my dress.

He snorts. "I suppose we do."

As we descend the stairs, I notice all the teachers lined up at the bottom, shaking hands with people as they work their way farther into the room.

"Is that an actual receiving line?" Reid snorts again.

There's a low laugh from somewhere behind us. "They do so love a little *extra* pomp and circumstance around here," says Adrian as he sidles up beside us. He's dressed in a slim-fitting black suit with thin pinstripes and a bright-purple shirt. His gaze roams over Reid with blatant interest. "I see your friend was able to find you."

Reid puffs his chest out and gives the shorter Adrian an assessing glare. Anywhere else and it'd be a challenge of a sort, but here it's merely Reid letting his alpha out to play. A test. "Reid Donovan."

Adrian's eyes light in recognition. "The cousin, yes?" He waggles his brows at me. "Are all shifters this"—his gaze roams over Reid's chest again—"powerful?"

I shove Adrian's arm. "Stop flirting with my cousin."

"Would you prefer I flirt with you instead?" He leans into me until his nose is inches from my face, a heated look in his eyes as he bats his eyelashes. I elbow him in the side. He laughs and pulls a small flask from inside his jacket. "Sorry"—he tilts the flask up to his lips—"I've had a bit to drink this evening."

I roll my eyes at the theatrics. "Reid, this is Adrian Dumont. When he's sober, I might call him a friend."

"You wound me," says Adrian with an exaggerated grab at his chest followed by a smirk.

We reach the bottom of the steps and the line of waiting teachers before Reid has a chance to respond. Most of them look bored, offering up forced smiles and bland greetings, but at the end waits Basil—in a powder-blue tuxedo.

Basil's eyes light up when he sees me, and he breaks away from his position in line to hurry over. He grabs my hand, shaking it vigorously. "I am so glad you could make it." His enthusiasm and his handshake switch to Reid. "And you! I've met your father, lovely man. I'm so glad you felt comfortable enough to come. I can't recall the last time we had a shifter at Ravencrest."

"This is Basil," I say, struggling for words. "He's my...tutor."

Reid nods. "It's a pleasure to meet you, sir."

"Wonderful, wonderful. Let me help you find your seats," says Basil as he links his arm with mine and leads us away from the receiving line.

Once we've made it to the row of tables near the back of the room, he pulls out a chair for me. And then one for Reid. My cousin raises his brows, and I shrug.

"I'm so sorry for the break in protocol," says Basil. "Many of us here are happy to welcome supernaturals of all races to Ravencrest, but there are some"—his gaze darts to another table where the St. James family is sitting—"who are not so welcoming, and I wanted to be sure to avoid a scene that might cause you embarrassment."

Reid says something in reply, but my eyes are locked on Tristan.

He's smiling, wide and happy, as he chats with the other people at his table, both adults and students. If I didn't know any better, I'd think I imagined the way he looked at me last night and the vulnerability on his face. Who is he really? Is he the blank façade he so often shows to the world or the lonely boy who kisses me like I'm the air he needs to breathe?

Bernadette turns, her eyes meeting mine and narrowing. I snap my gaze away and try to concentrate on what Reid is saying to Basil.

". . . do you think?"

Basil beams and nods rapidly. "Yes, I see how that could work." He reaches down and squeezes Reid's shoulder in a friendly manner. "Please let your father know I would love to discuss working with him on something like that."

"Nice guy," says Reid as Basil hurries back to the receiving line he deserted. "A little odd, but nice."

"Yeah," I say. "What do you think—"

A hand lands on my shoulder, and fingers press into my skin hard enough to hurt but not hard enough to leave a mark.

"Stay away from my son," says Bernadette St. James. She digs her nails deeper into my skin, and I hiss in a breath.

"I don't want your son," I snap, and in this moment, I really, really don't.

She gives me an appraising look with a cold smile to go along with it. "Your whore of a mother tried to weasel her way into the St. James family, did you know that? Threw herself at Allister and pouted when he didn't want her."

"That's not the story I heard," I say in a tight voice. "The way I heard it is she didn't want him at all."

Bernadette scoffs. "Helen was a disgrace to the Andras name." She leans closer. "And so are you."

Rage vibrates through me, but I refuse to lose my temper. She's not worth it. The sound of her heels clacking against the floor fades as she walks back to her table, and I let out a long, slow breath.

"What a raging bitch," says Adrian, plopping into the seat next to Reid.

"You can say that again," says Reid.

I rest my elbow on the table and lean my forehead on it. "You heard all that?"

The flask is out again, and Adrian glances at me over the top of it. He takes a swig and puts it away. "Darling, at least half the room heard all that. And the other half watched it."

Half the room? I glance around. Gazes pull away from me, people pretending they weren't staring. Students and parents alike whisper into ears, only some bothering to hide their smiles between their hands. Three tables over, my eyes stop on Tristan's profile.

His back is ramrod straight, and his face is blank. Bernadette walks up behind him and slides a hand over the back of his chair, leaning down to speak into his ear. He tilts his head, and smiles in response. I don't hear what he says, but his gaze darts to me for the briefest second before he returns his attention to his tablemates, unreadable once again.

Reid grabs a roll and butters it. "So I know what the website called it, but what exactly is this? Why all the fancy crap?"

"It's the *Fall banquet*," says Adrian in an exaggerated voice.

Reid gives him a wry look, and Adrian laughs.

"This is what Ravencrest has instead of a homecoming dance, you know, since we don't actually have a football team," Adrian continues. "It's important because this is when we get the first look at this year's official class rankings. In other words, tonight we get to see who's number one right now, and the parents get to see who the competition is. My bet's on that one to be top of the list." He nods toward Tristan and must notice my brow furrowing. "Oh, I don't mean he doesn't deserve it. He's not dumb, but I doubt Mommy and Daddy St. James will allow him to finish out the year at anything less than number one even if that means they need buy his way up there with a few well-placed 'donations' to OSA. This early in the year, it's more about seeing who doesn't belong up there than seeing who does."

"What do you mean by that?" I ask.

He waves at the crowd around us. "What do you notice?"

I study the room, the arrangement of tables, and take note of who's sitting where. "All the rich pricks are at those first few tables." A fake cough. "Except you, Adrian."

"Exactly." He takes another sip from his flask. "Up there, close to the podium, you have the major donors and the like, and the rest of the room is set up much like what they'd prefer the class rankings reflect. Call it a visual representation of how they think things should be."

"We're in the last row," says Reid.

Adrian taps his nose and points at Reid. "We're the riffraff."

"But you're . . ." I gesture at Adrian, his fancy watch, his perfect clothes.

"Yes, well, Ravencrest is the only school that would take me. They'd much prefer I wasn't here at all." He scowls and then shifts his face into a mischievous smile. "What is interesting, however, are the middle rows. Almost all of the scholarship students are there, much to the disdain of the people who provided those scholarships. Burke seats them up there to show where the real competition is. Tonight many of those students will top the list, maybe one of them will even knock Tristan out of the top spot, though I'd truly pity the person who got between a St. James and perfection." He leans over the table and gestures us closer. "The people in the front will use the information they gain from the ranking list this evening to see how big their 'donations' need to be. Or who they might need to...bring down a peg or two."

"Are you saying . . ."

"That those rich pricks will resort to almost anything to see their kids at the top? Why yes I am." Adrian leans back, his arms out over the back of his chair. "No one will get hurt. It's one of those unspoken rules. No permanent damage."

"There's a lot of wiggle room between 'getting hurt' and 'no permanent damage,'" says Reid. "Is my cousin in danger?"

Adrian shrugs, but he also chuckles. "I doubt it. The Andras name protects her to a point and"—his eyes go to me, and he smirks—"she hasn't exactly proven herself to be any sort of competition. She's not a threat to them, so they'll ignore her."

I blink. I guess there's one good thing about my grades being not so hot. I don't mind being part of the riffraff if it keeps everyone else off my back. But...I glance up at the tables in the middle again. Isobel is up there. What kind of horrible things do these people do that requires a 'no permanent damage' rule?

"But *why?*" I ask, flabbergasted by the whole thing.

"Because they already have everything money can buy, and they're all on some stupid quest to be the best of the best?" Adrian shrugs. "Sure, a higher class rank can lead to better job placement with OSA after graduation if that's the route you choose to take, but it's mostly about social politics and pedigrees. Academy class rank is pretty much the only trusted metric for how powerful a witch is, and the more powerful a witch is, the more desirable the alliance their parents might arrange."

"You're shitting me," says Reid.

"Nope."

"Witches still do the whole arranged marriage thing? What century are you guys living in?" Reid's gaze darts to me, and he does that bristly protective thing. "Selene is not on the market."

Adrian throws back his head and laughs. "I doubt any of these old money families want her type of trouble even if they knew how powerful she is."

"I'm not sure whether or not to be insulted by that," I say, eyeing Adrian as my lips twitch into a smile.

"Take it as a compliment," he says with another laugh.

We lapse into silence as servers bring around salads, dinner, and later dessert. I pick at all the food. Reid devours it. When he catches me glancing at him with raised brows, he shrugs and mouths 'it's really good.' At least he makes me laugh.

Adrian eats very little, sticking mostly to his flask, and his mood gets darker and darker throughout the meal. His speech is slurred, and he's swaying in his seat. How much has he had to drink? I scan the room for Devin. I might need his help to get Adrian out of here so he doesn't get in trouble.

But he's not here...

"Where's Devin?" I ask.

Adrian gives me a sardonic grin. "I was wondering when you'd notice." He takes another sip. How much can be left in that thing? "My family decided I was enjoying myself too much with my new friend. They had him transferred. I found out this afternoon."

Enjoying himself? "Were you and Devin...?"

"A couple?" He snorts. "Nothing that fun. Just friends, but I'm not supposed to have any of those, not until I 'see the error of my ways' and 'act like a true Dumont' or some crap like that. And there was also the fact that he wasn't of our same caliber according to my father."

"So, when you say they had him transferred . . ." Reid starts.

"They had him sent to another academy. With strict instructions that if he hoped to stay there or in any OSA academy, he would not contact me," says Adrian bitterly.

I place a hand on his arm. "I'm so sorry. I know you two were close."

He lets out a harsh laugh. "Yeah well, it seems anyone who gets too close to me is out on their ass." He glares at Tristan. "I'm sure it isn't much better for golden boy. He just hides it better." Another dry laugh. "Oh, and his parents actually approve of him."

If the Dumonts are worse than the St. James family, I hope I never have to meet them.

Adrian tips the last of whatever is in that flask into his mouth and then jumps to his feet. "I'm done with this." A salacious smile appears on his lips as his gaze goes to Reid. "Should you need any entertainment your cousin can't provide, please find me."

Reid coughs and gives him a mock salute. "I don't think that's going to happen since you witches seem to be quite an entertaining bunch, but I'll keep that in mind."

Adrian disappears through one of the side doors, and Reid looks at me with one brow quirked upward. "He's certainly a character."

"Yeah," I say, biting at my lower lip. "He's also the only person besides Isobel and Devin who goes out of his way to be nice to me. I don't like seeing him like that."

Sometime later, the last plates are whisked away and the volume of the music goes down. The lights dim, leaving a single bright spot over the center of the low stage. Director Burke steps up to the podium and smiles out at the crowd. He's never been exactly warm to me, but he's always been composed, and there's something in his stature that screams he's uncomfortable. It's unnerving. And unexpected. I wish Adrian was still here so I could ask if this is normal.

Burke's gaze roams over the crowd, stopping on Bernadette St. James. I can't see her face, but Burke's lips tighten and his jaw tenses, and it sends a cold feeling into my stomach. What has the St. James family used their money and influence to buy now?

CHAPTER 21

B urke clears his throat and smiles thinly at the gathered crowd. "Welcome, students and parents, to the Ravencrest Fall banquet. It's been my privilege to work with your children over the past few weeks, and I expect great things from them in the future. As you know, it is customary to release the current class rankings this evening, but we will also be announcing a new policy. First . . ." He gives the crowd another tight smile. "The lists."

A flat screen on the wall brightens, revealing two lists of names. It's odd seeing the tech since I've spent the last few weeks without even a cell phone, but I couldn't exactly expect them to handwrite the lists and still update them every day.

"The screen on the left is the first years' rankings, and the screen on the right is the second years'. Of course, these are not the final lists. Any one of you can rise or fall based on the merits of your academic grades and, for all second years and for those first years who choose to compete, your performance in the tournament. And this year that's a particularly good thing." He pauses, his lips pressing into a thin line. "Our admissions process allows for two hundred and fifty students to be admitted here each year. Beginning this school year, Ravencrest will be the pilot school for a new OSA policy which requires the bottom ten students in the first year class to be dismissed every quarter, except for the last quarter when the bottom twenty will be dismissed. Therefore, of the two hundred and fifty first year students here tonight, only two hundred will graduate."

Fifty students will be dismissed? Based on academic performance and that stupid tournament? I do some quick math in my head. That's *twenty percent* of the class.

I glance at the lists of names. The text is too small to read from here, but there's no way I'm not at the bottom somewhere, not with my grades, not with my continued inability to properly use magic. What am I going to do? It's been made clear that awful things will happen to my parents and to me if I'm not at this academy, if I don't become a happy, productive member of the Order.

Burke continues. "This comes as a surprise to many of you, those who thought they could coast through your courses here and still become members of the Order, but those of you with the drive and ambition to make it this far will have ample chance to prove yourselves good enough." His gaze darts out over the crowd, focusing on Bernadette again, and he gives a quick, sharp nod. "Please, enjoy the rest of your evening."

He steps down, and the voices in the room grow louder as the first few people stand and walk over to the list.

My throat has gone dry, and my fingers are twisted in the tablecloth like it's some weird sort of lifeline.

"What's wrong?" asks Reid. "You've gone pale."

"Mom and Dad…If I'm dismissed, there will be consequences."

"Okay, but you're not in any danger of that, right? I know you said you were behind, but you're not *that* far behind, right? You've always been good at school."

I laugh, a sound more pained than amused. "Regular school, sure, but I'm new to all this nonsense about wards and potions and magic. I've barely gotten a handle on my powers, and I'm only now starting to understand the *basics*. Not to mention, there's an entire area of history I missed out on learning because I went to human schools."

"But you're supposed to be one of the most powerful witches of this generation or something, aren't you?"

"What? Where did you hear that?"

"That Basil guy mentioned something about it earlier."

"Powerful, maybe, but I have no finesse, and doing anything with magic other than blasting things with energy has been near impossible." I meet his eyes. "I'm barely passing my classes." My gaze strays to Tristan. "I had help… kind of, but that's gone now."

Reid curls his hand over mine. "You've got this," he says. "And if you don't, you have time to fix it. You're smart and capable, and I know you could be the most badass witch here if you put your mind to it."

Though I appreciate the sentiment, the words don't make me feel better. At all. He has no idea what it's been like for me here, so his faith seems misplaced.

"Might as well go see how bad it is," I say as I stand.

Making my way across the room feels like walking to my execution. When I reach the first year student list, I start at the middle and run my eyes down and down and down…all the way to the impressing number two hundred and twenty-two. Well, I'm not the last in the class, so that's a plus,

---

but if I don't bring up my grades, I'll be cut before the end of the year—something I absolutely cannot afford to happen.

I move my gaze to the top, just to see the competition...at least that's what I tell myself. Adrian is at number eighty-four, Devin at fifty-three even though he's no longer here, and Isobel? My breath stalls. Isobel is at number one, *above* Tristan who's at number four with a couple names I don't recognize in between them. What does that mean for her? Would they really...No. Adrian was drunk. He had to have been exaggerating. His words replay in my head: *I'd truly pity the person who got between a St. James and perfection...*

A familiar cologne tickles at my nose as Tristan steps up beside me to read the list for himself. Only a second passes before his whole body goes rigid. He inhales sharply and swallows before spinning around and returning to his parents, jaw tensed and gaze fixed firmly on the floor.

His mom grabs his arm, giving it a shake. And not an encouraging one. Or even a friendly one. Her knuckles are white, and her fingers dig into the fabric of Tristan's suit jacket.

I can't see his face, but he hangs his head low like a chastised dog. His whole form screams of discomfort and unease, and his mother's mouth is twisted with anger as she hisses something into his ear.

Isobel steps up beside me and follows my line of sight. "Why don't you just go talk to him?"

"I think he's a little busy right now." I watch as Bernadette and Allister herd him toward a door in the back corner.

"He's been watching you all evening," she says. "Except for when *you've* been casting not so subtle glances at *him*."

I hold up a hand. "Nope. Not happening. We're not having this conversation." I tilt my head toward the lists. "Congratulations, by the way."

Isobel flushes. "Thanks. It's just the preliminary ranks, and there's no way

I'll still be there by the end of the year, but as long as I'm in the top twenty or so, I'm guaranteed good job placement with OSA."

She follows me to my table and gives Reid a wave as she seats herself in the chair Adrian vacated.

"So . . ." says Reid.

"Two hundred twenty-two."

He lets out a whistle, and Isobel flinches. I guess she hadn't looked at my ranking—or hadn't gotten down that far.

"So, we'll work out a more rigid studying schedule for you, and I can—"

"You can't spend all your time tutoring me," I say with a pointed look. "You already do enough. I'm not in danger of being cut this quarter, and all that research you've been doing will eventually pay off. We're bound to find something out about my magic and why it's not working correctly. Once that problem gets solved, it'll probably come easy to me considering Basil is constantly mentioning how powerful I am."

I lapse into silence, my head running through what I need to do to make it through this quarter, as Reid and Isobel converse around me. My eyes stray to the door Tristan went through with his parents. At least ten minutes have passed, and they haven't come out yet. What could they possibly be doing in there?

"Selene," says Reid in an amused tone that tells me this isn't the first time he's tried to get my attention. He pointedly looks from my face to the door I've been staring at. "I've never seen you moon after someone like—"

"I'm not mooning," I snap. "I'm...worried."

He holds up a hand. "Whatever it is. Your eyes follow him, and you constantly search him out in the room. St. James or not, there's clearly something going on there. And if he didn't have an awareness of you just as intense as yours of him, I'd be trying to talk some sense into you. Hell, I might try anyway. I mean, hello, he's a *St. James* . . ." He smirks. "Still, I have a feeling you're not going to hear another word I say until you go over there and figure out what's going on, so go."

I open my mouth.

"Go," says Isobel. "You know you want to."

She's right. They both are. So, I go.

The door leads to some back hallway, maybe a maintenance passage. There are various fixtures that look like they have to do with the operation of a building. One might be a boiler, and there are pipes overhead and things that look like fuse boxes on the wall. The St. James family is around the corner somewhere, out of sight but not out of my hearing.

". . . embarrass us like that? That little nobody has no business being better than you in any way," hisses out Bernadette, the words sounding somehow colder in her crisp accent. "How could you let this happen?"

"I don't know," Tristan replies in a strained voice, his own accent more prominent now.

"You don't know? How can you not know? Haven't you been attending your classes? Doing your work?" Bernadette's heels clack against the floor as if she's pacing, and in my head, I imagine she's flailing her arms about.

I know why his grades might have slipped: the binding spell. Odds are this is when he blames it all on me or on Isobel since his mother's ire seems to already be falling her way. But he doesn't.

"I've done everything you've asked of me. My grades are nearly perfect," he says.

"Nearly perfect? That's not good enough. You can't let that little wench beat you."

"I'm sure you can buy my way to the top like everyone else's parents if that truly worries you," says Tristan with an edge of sarcasm.

But Bernadette isn't hearing it. "We've already wasted enough money on you. Too much if you ask me."

"I'm sorry. I'm trying my best. I—"

The sound of a smack echoes through the narrow space as Tristan's words cut off.

Did she just . . . ?

"Don't you talk back to me. Your sister never would have let this happen." The words are hissed and edged with ice.

Allister finally speaks up. "There's no need to bring her into this, dear."

Dear? He calls that horrible woman dear?

"I'll bring my grades up. This is only the first—"

"You *will* be the top of the class, Tristan, or there will be consequences. I have put too much work into negotiating an arrangement with the Daoming family. You will *not* mess this up."

Arrangement? She can't mean...marriage?

"Yes, Mother." His voice is quiet and strained. The edge of anger has worn off, and he's back to that robot tone.

Bernadette's voice drops low, harsh. "As to the next matter, what, pray tell, have you done to have that Andras bitch sniffing after you so fervently?"

"I don't know, Mother," he snaps. There's an edge of annoyance in his tone now. "I did what you wanted me to and tried to find out about the shifters and where they might hide, but she doesn't know either."

What the hell? He was spying on me and reporting back to his mom?

Tristan continues, "Do you want me to keep encouraging her? Seduce her maybe? Would that make you—"

Another smack.

"Don't you dare speak to me like that." I can almost feel the chill in her voice. "You are to have no further contact with her, and if you expect me to continue paying your way, you will be at the top of your class. Is that clear?"

"Yes, Mother," says Tristan in a low, sad voice.

"Come, Allister. I need another drink."

"I'll be out in a minute, dear," responds Allister. "I'd like to speak with Tristan for a moment."

The clack of heels comes in my direction, and I duck behind the might-be-a-boiler thing before Bernadette rounds the corner. She straightens her dress and smooths a wayward hair behind her ear. Spots of red rest high on her cheeks, but her face is carefully blank in an expression I recognize well. It's the one her son so often wears. As she exits the hallway and returns to the ballroom, I turn my attention back to Tristan and his dad.

"I don't understand what more she wants from me," says Tristan, an edge of pleading in his tone. "I'm doing the best I can."

"I know you're trying. Your mother loves you," replies Allister. "She only wants what is best for you."

"But not if what's best for me isn't best for *her*." Tristan's voice breaks a little on the last word, and he sniffles softly.

"You know that's not true," says Allister, his tone chastising. "Now, pull yourself together and meet us outside. There are still a few people I'd like you to speak with."

"Yes, Father," says Tristan.

I duck behind the machinery as Allister rounds the corner and makes his exit. As far as I can tell, Tristan hasn't moved. There's not so much as the sound of shuffling feet. Should I leave like nothing happened? How can I be sure Allister and Bernadette are away from the door? They might be waiting for Tristan.

Indecision leaves me trapped as Tristan finally comes into sight. His shoulders are tight and his hands are curled into fists, but his face is a mask of nothing. He strides past me, his cheeks red. Did she smack both cheeks in some horrible attempt to make the marks even? Did she think they would be less noticeable that way?

Some sound of sympathy escapes my throat, and he spins around. His eyes widen when he catches sight of me, but his face quickly goes cold again. He grabs me by the shoulders and pushes me against the wall, his face inches away from mine.

"How much did you hear?" he rasps out.

"Nothing," I stutter, too shocked by his sudden nearness to think of anything else.

His eyes narrow, and he studies me. There's rage on his face, but his eyes...they're empty. There's nothing. "No one hears of this," he says under his breath. "No one."

"Of course. I . . ." My hand comes up to rest on his reddened cheek, and for a moment, just the barest hint of a second, he leans into my touch, his expression softening as he closes his eyes, but then he yanks his face out of my reach and releases my shoulders.

His face twists into a sneer. "I can't do this. Not with *you*."

My own words spit back at me, dripping with rage and disgust, are gut wrenching, but not half as bad as the look on his face. Because the rage and disgust aren't directed at me; they're directed at himself. He storms back to the ballroom without another word, and I'm left staring after him, my mind a swirl of confusion.

I knew the St. James family was bad. I'd heard enough things about his parents even before coming here, and even though his father doesn't seem quite as bad as his mother...they're utterly vile people. The only question is whether they've already turned their son into something just as vile, or is there time enough to save him?

And why do I want to?

CHAPTER 22

Any illusions I have about the kiss or about the moment I thought we had are dispelled the next morning in the dining hall. Tristan blatantly ignores my wave, my greeting, and me in general. It's as if I no longer exist. He hardly even looks at me, and when he does, it's as if he's looking through me.

He's taken his mother's decree to heart then.

It hurts and I hate that, but I have enough problems of my own without trying to take his on too.

After an uncomfortable night on my dorm room floor, Reid is more than a little grumpy. He follows my gaze to Tristan and stares after him. "He's not worth it, Selene. I didn't say anything last night because you weren't going to listen to me then. I'm hoping you will now."

"Tristan is—"

"Look, I'm not saying he's necessarily a bad guy, but he's not worth that look on your face." I fiddle with my fingers on the table, and Reid places his hands over mine, waiting for me to look at him before continuing. "He's not worth the *risk*. Things at home are...tense. Any desire the local packs had to work with the witches to come to a compromise was destroyed when you put that shifter in the hospital. Now, I *know* what the real story is, but the only thing anyone can focus on is the fact that a St. James was there. I don't know what's going to happen, but there's a lot of grumbling, even from the local packs under Dad. And that makes Tristan a target. Being around him, getting any deeper into whatever it is between you two, puts *you* at risk. I need you to be smart and stay safe, at least until some of this blows over. After that, feel free to go for it." He sighs and squeezes my hands. "I can't see him ending up as anything but exactly like his parents, but if you see something there . . ."

"I'm not sure what I see." I glance up and meet Reid's eyes. "But I'm not an idiot. I've got enough going on with my classes, and I certainly don't need to add in any other stressors. If you think it's dangerous, I'll keep my distance."

He grins and goes back to his food.

I sit and ponder the lie I just told. I really don't know what I see in Tristan. He's moody and arrogant and at least half the time he acts like an ass, but there was something in his eyes the night he kissed me. Like, for once, I really saw *him* underneath all his layers of armor. And if he chooses to open up to me again in spite of my idiotic comment when I pushed him away and his parents high-handed decree forbidding him to associate with me, I'm not going to turn him away. If nothing else, the poor boy needs a friend, a *real* one, otherwise Reid may be right and Tristan may turn out exactly like his parents.

My cousin has to leave after breakfast, and it's all I can do not to latch myself onto his legs and beg him to stay. I didn't truly realize how much I missed him until he was here, and it's a hard goodbye. I'll see him again—I *know* this—but I have no idea when. Once Connor gets wind of this visit, I'm sure he'll make his 'no visiting Selene' command a little more specific.

Reid wraps his big arms around me and hugs me tightly to his chest, planting a kiss on top of my head. He promises to find a way to get in touch and that he'll come to visit again, but they feel more like empty reassurances. And then he's gone, headed to the home I no longer have and the family I desperately miss.

My eyes burn, and it's only Isobel's solid presence at my side that keeps the tears at bay. She grabs my hand and gives it a squeeze, knowing without words how much I need her support. I'm not completely alone. I can do this. And I have three long weeks ahead of me to study my ass off and get my grades up so my parents' sacrifice isn't all for nothing. I will do this even if it kills me.

By the end of the first week, my eyes are in a perpetual state of grittiness and lined with dark circles. It's pathetic really. I've caught up with most of my classmates as far as the basics go, but even with Isobel's help—and thank goodness she has the time to help—I'm barely pulling a C in most of my classes.

And I'm not the only one feeling the pressure. Only ten students are getting cut at the end of this quarter, but by the way everyone's acting, it feels more like half the class is getting cut.

The first student dropped out the day after the announcement, simply packed his bags and left. He was some guy I've never met who wasn't even that far down on the list. The rumor is he cracked under the added pressure. Two more students drop out in the following week, also because of all the pressure. I can definitely understand that. The pressure isn't doing me any favors either.

But I *have* to stay. I *have* to pass. My parents' future depends on me. So, I go through the motions in my classes. I go to my room and study, study,

study. I do very little else. Occasionally, I remember to grab a meal.

By the end of the second week, I'm about to start pulling all my hair out. My grades have improved as far as things having to do with magical theory. I can draw wards. I can create the necessary chemical solutions to use as potion bases. But infusing anything with magic—the practical side of it—is still a struggle. My success with the fertilizer potion must've been some sort of fluke. I haven't blown anything up, thank goodness, but half the time my wards and potions don't turn out right, and I still can't figure out what I'm doing wrong.

And, unfortunately, a large portion of my midterm grades are made up of practical applications. Like activating a protection ward and making a mild healing potion.

On Friday evening the weekend before midterms, three weeks after the banquet, three weeks after that disastrous confrontation with Tristan and his parents, and three weeks of classes and studying and homework, I'm making the slog back to my room for yet more studying, when Penny finds me and drags me between the buildings.

I haven't talked to her much since the full moon, and she looks harried. Her eyes, lined with circles, are darting all over the place. Suspicious. Anxious. Worried.

"I need your help," she says, shoving a small bottle into my hands. "I need you to activate this potion."

"What? Why?"

Penny's brows pull together, and she bites at her bottom lip. "It's not working. I don't know what's wrong."

"What's not working? I don't understand."

"The magic...it's gone. I wasn't doing anything too strenuous before, just some simple wards and potions for my classes, but now I can't do even that."

I glance down at the bottle in my hands. "I thought you said—"

"I know what I said, but it's not working right. They told me—" She pauses and gives me a tight smile. "I mean, I've been doing fine up until now. I don't understand . . ."

"I wish I could help but—"

"You can help!" She curls my hand around the bottle. "It's no more complicated than that fertilizer potion you did in class."

"Penny . . ."

"*Please*," she says. "If I don't turn in this potion, I'm going to fail."

I eye the bottle. The liquid inside is an unfamiliar deep-purple-black with swirls of silver. It's rather pretty in a way. "What kind of potion is it?"

"A sleeping potion," she says quickly. "It's my midterm project, my own creation. It's supposed to work without some of the side effects of the more common sleeping potions."

Penny's trustworthy, I guess, but can I trust her about this? *Should* I? Something doesn't feel entirely right, but she seems desperate, and I don't want her to fail. I wouldn't exactly call her a friend, but I'm not comfortable standing by and doing nothing if there's something I can do to help.

I eyeball the viscous fluid again. "I'm willing to try. I can't guarantee it's going to work, though."

"Thank you. Thank you. Thank you." She grabs my hand and jumps up and down. "I can guide you through it. It shouldn't be too difficult. I know you can handle it."

I'm still not entirely convinced this is a good idea, but if she wants to risk her grade on me doing this, I guess that's on her. "Do I use a standard activation like we're learning about in class, or do I need to do something special?"

"It's not quite standard but close. In class, you're pulling magic from around you; for this you need to use your internal magic."

"Internal magic?" *No one's mentioned anything like that before. Could it be similar to the spark Isobel talked about that lets a witch connect with the magic around them?*

"Yeah. Instead of drawing magic from outside yourself, you need to pull it from within."

My brows draw together. "That explanation doesn't really clear things up."

She huffs. "I'm not sure how to explain it then . . ." She flaps a hand in my direction. "The night of the party, where did you feel the magic coming from after Bridget zapped you?"

I rub my knuckles on my sternum. "Right here. In the center of my chest. It felt like it was cracking open."

"Take the magic from there. Use that magic to activate the potion."

"Okay . . ." I say hesitantly. This probably won't work, but I suppose it's worth a shot. I concentrate on the feeling of magic in my chest. This magic is wilder than the stuff I draw from outside myself, but it's also more familiar somehow. Drawing on it and sending it out to my fingertips and into the potion is almost effortless. *Nothing* I've ever done with magic has felt this easy. The liquid flashes black for a second before settling into a navy-blue color that looks much more like I expect for a sleeping potion. I hand it to Penny. "Is this right?"

Penny takes the bottle, holding it up to the light and turning it from one side to the other. Her face breaks into a wide grin. "It's perfect," she says. "Thank you so much. You have no idea how much this means."

"You're welcome then. I'm glad I could help." I pause. "That activation technique...is that something I can use in class? For some reason, it seemed so much easier than what Dr. Nikiforov has been teaching us."

"Yeah. Sure," she says, still staring up at the potion. As if catching what she just said, she focuses in on me and adds in a forceful tone, "But don't tell anyone else about it. You might get in trouble for using the more advanced technique when you haven't been properly prepared for it."

The idea that I could be penalized for using a technique that works for me whether or not it's one I've been taught is strange, but I'm not going to take that risk. "I'll keep it quiet," I say with a small smile. "As much as I've struggled, that method was *simple* for me, and I need all the help I can get."

Penny tilts her head in my direction. "Good luck on your midterms next week."

"You too." I shoot her another smile and a wave then head toward the girls' dorm.

My mind races with all the possible applications of this new method, and for once, I'm anxious to crack open my textbooks and do some work. If I can get my Potions grade up, I might not have to worry so much about my Wards grade. I enter the dorm and jog up the stairs, excitement zinging through my veins. My room is mere steps away when my arm is grabbed again. This time by Isobel.

"Dinner," she says in a stern voice. "You haven't been to the dining hall for days."

"That's because I need to study, and it's too noisy there. I snagged a few snacks, and those have been holding me over just fine. There's another bag of chips under my bed somewhere," I argue, even though I'm not looking forward to yet another meal of the stale, over-processed slices of potato.

But she's not listening and, now that I think about it, subsisting on a bunch of prepackaged junk has been kind of nauseating. I allow her to drag me to the dining hall, but the second I walk in the door, I regret it. The tables are full of various groups, but it's the group in the corner that draws my eyes. The popular rich kids.

And reason number two why I've been avoiding the dining hall...

Tristan is one of those popular rich kids laughing and joking around an open box of donuts. We haven't spoken since the banquet and, for the most part, have managed to completely avoid each other, but he showed up at the dining hall for the first time in ages at the beginning of this week and has been here every meal since. His uniform is flawless, his eyes bright, and he has a ready smile for just about everyone. The cracks in his façade so evident a few weeks ago are sealed, and he's wrapped in a new veneer of perfection.

It kind of makes me want to punch him.

Not because I want to hurt him, but because I want to knock some sense into him.

Jason catches sight of Isobel and me and he smiles. "If it isn't the mutt and the nobody," he drawls. "Shouldn't you two be studying or something? I hear the mutt isn't doing so well."

My face goes hot, and my magic churns into a frenzy. I spin toward him, my mouth opening to rip him a new one.

"Leave it, Jason," says Tristan in a sharp voice.

In the back of my head, I know he's kind of defending me, but it was a half-assed defense—if that's even what it was—and it's not enough to stop my ire transferring to Tristan.

"I can take care of myself," I snap. "Go back to your ridiculous friends. I'm sure you're enjoying all this time slacking off since you're guaranteed top spot anyway, right? Mommy and Daddy are going to pay for it." I scan the rest of them. "Along with all the rest of you."

Tristan's brows go up. "Nobody has to buy my way on to the list," he says. "I'll earn the top spot purely on my own merits."

I take a step backward, the absurdity of that statement nearly bowling me over. "Really now? I wouldn't be so sure of that." My eyes narrow. "I mean, you've practically sold your soul to get up there, so . . ."

"Sold my soul?" His voice has gone flat, and that bored, stoic facial expression locks in place.

Jason stands and holds his hands up. "Hey now, let's not argue. I apologize." He grabs the box in the middle of the table. "Donut?"

There's got to be a catch here, so what is it? I eye the donuts. They look normal enough, and there's a few missing, so *somebody's* eaten them. I glance at Tristan. He averts his eyes.

Isobel shrugs and reaches for a donut, but Adrian grabs her wrists as he steps up beside her.

"You don't want to do that," he says. "They're spelled."

"Spelled?" Isobel asks.

"Yeah," he replies. "Probably a sleep spell or maybe a confusion one. If you eat one of those donuts, your midterms might not go so well."

"Then why . . ." My gaze darts around the table. No one has a donut on their plate or anywhere else near their own food. "You're giving them out to other students. To throw them off." A growl enters my voice as my anger rises again.

"Don't take food or anything else someone offers you this close to midterms," says Adrian. "I thought you'd already been warned and that's why you hadn't been here."

In the scheme of things, spelled donuts is probably the tamest way I've heard to game the ranks. It's little more than a juvenile prank, but still...

I focus on Tristan. He just finished saying he'll get to the top spot on his own merits, but he wasn't going to stop Isobel. He was going to let her take one of the donuts so that she'd be off her game during midterms. *He's just as bad as the rest of them.*

How did I not see it sooner? Was I so blinded by an attractive face, sugared words, and one single kiss?

All my attention narrows in on him as if there's no one else in the room.

He finally looks up to meet my eyes, and whatever he sees there creates a flicker of emotion on his otherwise blank face, not quite fear, but something close to it, and then a flash of resignation.

"I was so damn *stupid*," I say. "I thought you were different. I thought you were better, but you're nothing but a pretty wrapping for an empty soul. Maybe nobody *has* to buy your way on to anything, but certainly nobody *wants* to. Isn't that what your harpy of a mother said, that she'd wasted enough money on you? That's what you are to her—*a waste*." My voice goes low, and cold rage laces every word. "A waste of time, a waste of money, and a waste of space. I was a fool to ever think you were any more than that."

I don't stay to see what effect, if any, my words have on him, simply grabbing Isobel's arm and pulling her out of the dining hall and back to our dorm room with Adrian not far behind.

As of this moment, Tristan St. James no longer exists to me.

CHAPTER 23

M idterms week is hell, full of back to back days of exams and skill evaluations and, by the end of it, I've barely seen my bed, barely seen my roommate, barely seen *anything* but my textbooks, teachers, and tests.

But...I think I do okay. Using the new method Penny taught me, I'm able to fly through my Potions exam and successfully infuse the required potions during the skill section. Wards doesn't go quite as well, but my lines and angles for the drawing portion are pretty good. I ace the PE exam—if target practice can be called an exam—and I just finished Basil's exam. Now, all I want to do is crash.

Too bad I find a note summoning me to Burke's office as soon as I get back to my dorm. Getting called to see the director right after finishing the last midterm? Not the most confidence-inspiring thing. Have grades already been tallied? Not everyone has finished taking their midterms. The advanced classes still have a couple tomorrow. But maybe...I have no freaking clue what this could be about. And I'm too tired to debate with myself about the possibilities. No matter what, this meeting probably doesn't mean anything good.

I sigh and make my way to Burke's office.

Seth is on the phone, but he hangs up when he sees me and gives me a weak smile. "He'll call you in soon."

Great. I'd prefer Burke not call me in at all, but I'm not going to tell Seth that. All I do is smile back. Well, I try anyway.

Another ten minutes pass before Burke's voice comes echoing out of the intercom on Seth's desk. "Send her in."

Deep breath. I can do this. The distance to Burke's door suddenly feels much too short, and all I want to do is turn around and run out of here. Another deep breath. I open the door and walk inside.

Burke's at his desk, elbows resting on the wood and fingers steepled under his chin. He doesn't smile.

My stomach drops. This is looking worse and worse.

I slide into the chair in front of the desk and twist my fingers together in my lap. "You asked to see me?"

"I'm going to get straight to the point, Selene. Your grades, though improved, are not up to par, and at this point, I'm worried under the new policy I'll be forced to dismiss you from the school at the end of the semester."

"But...I've been trying. I don't know what else I can do. I don't understand why it's all so difficult for me." Exhaustion and disappointment add a pleading note to my voice.

His face softens, and he leans back in his chair with his intertwined fingers resting on his chest. "There's an option we haven't explored yet, but the situation is delicate, and based on my previous observations, I wasn't sure if it'd be something you were open to."

I huff out a laugh. "I'm open to pretty much anything at this point. This isn't my favorite place in the world, but I'd like to stay to protect my parents if nothing else."

Burke nods. "I'm sure you're aware of the rumors that a few well-placed... donations can improve your standing in the ranks, correct?"

"You mean the bribes paid to OSA? Yeah, I'm aware."

He grimaces. "I suppose that would be the more accurate term, yes." A pause. "But it is what it is at this point."

"My parents can't afford to bribe my way up the list, and neither can the pack, so what exactly are you suggesting?"

He sighs. "There's something I've been keeping from you, and I apologize for not informing you of this earlier, but I didn't want to make things even more difficult." His gaze goes to the top of his desk, and he leans forward to slide a file folder across to me.

"What's this?" I pick it up and shoot him a questioning look.

He merely tilts his head at the folder.

Okay...I open it and skim the single sheet of paper inside. It's contact information and some general background on Nikolas and Thea Andras. Who are apparently my biological grandparents.

Burke waits until I glance up at him to speak again. "As I told you when you first arrived, the Andras family is old and powerful. Nikolas has the financial means to make the expected donations in order for you to maintain your place here." He pauses. "Nikolas is aware there is a student here using the Andras name, but he, like everyone here besides Basil and myself, is under the impression you are something like a third cousin who is using the name with my approval. I have not disclosed your true relationship to him, nor will I if you request me not to, but if you decide to accept his help, you will need to reveal your true identity. He and Thea might expect a relationship with you. Helen was their only child, which, technically, makes you their only heir."

"I . . ."

"You don't have to decide right now. If nothing else, I believe you are safe this quarter, but it is a near thing. You certainly wish to consider entering the tournament next quarter to help boost your rank." He clears his throat and stands. "Now, I need to check on a few things down the hall." He makes a pointed glance at the phone on his desk. "I'll be back in about ten minutes."

I'm still trying to put everything together when he walks out of his office and shuts the door behind him, leaving me to watch after him completely confused. Did he want me to call them *now*? That can't be right. He said I didn't have to make this decision yet.

I'm safe this quarter, so maybe I should leave my...grandparents out of it unless I absolutely have to contact them.

I place the folder back on the desk and twist my fingers together again. The room is too quiet for my racing thoughts. Maybe there's something else he wanted me to see? I pull the folder toward me, but something catches my eye before I can open it. There's a sticky note by the phone's handset that says A & G M with a phone number I don't recognize.

Is that . . .? Did he . . .? It couldn't possibly be...I pick up the phone with shaking fingers, press the button for an outside line, and dial the number on the sticky note.

The call is answered almost immediately. "Selene?"

"Mom?" Her name is barely choked out past the lump in my throat.

"It's so good to hear your voice, baby girl." Hearing hers is even better.

"Is Dad with you? Where are you? Are you safe?"

She pauses. "He is, but it's better that you don't know where we are for now. We are safe though."

I want to argue that what would really be better would be me with them instead of here, but I don't. Because as long as they're safe, they're where they belong. And maybe I am too? "When can I see you?"

She sniffles, and her voice goes thick with heartache. "I don't know."

"I miss you," I whisper.

"We miss you too. I'm so sorry this—"

"You have nothing to apologize for. You're my parents, my family; you did what you thought was in my best interests. I can't blame you for that."

She's crying now, and I hear Dad's voice in the background as he takes the phone from her.

"Hey there, sweetheart," says Dad. "How are you holding up?"

I let out a sad laugh. "Not so well, but I'll live. Director Burke...how?"

"Desmond has been passing us information since you arrived, but he wanted to give you a chance to adjust before letting you know he could contact us."

"But I haven't done very well at adjusting, right? That's why I'm getting your phone number now."

Dad laughs. "We always knew you were different. Helen told us as much, but no one understood what she meant. We still don't. I know everything there is not what you'd like it to be, but you can trust Desmond. He's on your side."

"But he's a witch, and he's good friends with the St. James family."

"I know, but he's not a bad person. Let him guide you. He knows what he's doing."

I'm not going to be buddy-buddy with the guy, but if Dad says Burke is okay, then I guess I'll go along with it. "He'll be back soon, so my time's about up—or does it matter? Since he already knows and all that."

"If he were to be questioned, he has to have plausible deniability. Lying isn't an option in the face of a truth potion. So, yes, it matters. And you can't discuss this conversation with him or specifically tell him you've spoken with us at this point."

Footsteps approach the office door, and Burke loudly says something to Seth from right outside.

"I've gotta go," I say. "I love you both."

"We love you too. Take care of yourself."

I'm hanging up the receiver just as Burke walks through the door. I swipe at the tears on my cheeks, and Burke gives me a knowing look. Clearing my throat, I snatch the folder off the desk and jump to my feet. "Thank you...for the information." I wave the folder around. "And I'll think about what you said."

"Good," he says. His lips curl into a warm smile. "I want you to succeed here. There is a lot of good you could do for the Order. OSA needs open-minded people like you."

"I'll, uh, be going back to my room to think about things now," I say awkwardly. "Have a nice evening."

He dips his chin in acknowledgment as I rush out the door.

The trip from the main building to the dorm is a blur, and it isn't until I finally lie face down on my bed that I allow myself to really consider the effects of tonight's events. I'm so, so grateful I got the chance to talk to Mom and Dad, but I have no idea what to do with this other information on my grandparents. I wish I'd had time to ask my parents what they thought about it. All of a sudden it's like, 'yeah sure, Selene, buy your way to the top with the grandparents who know nothing about you.' How selfish is that? Am I willing to essentially sell my integrity, sell my soul even—the same thing I accused Tristan of doing—in order to make it to the top of the class, or even just to make the cut?

I might end up not having any other choice. If I don't get my grades up on my own, I'm going to have to call these unknown people and throw myself on their mercy. Their *financial* mercy, which is even worse.

But I want to talk to Isobel about all of this first. She hasn't steered me wrong yet. I haven't seen her since breakfast, but she should be wrapping up the last of her midterms soon.

I sit up and drag a hand over my face. My stomach rumbles. Too bad dinner is almost over and I'm not in the mood to make a mad dash to the dining hall. Chips for dinner it is. I walk over to my desk to grab my last bag, and a sheet of paper with Isobel's handwriting on it catches my eye.

Meet me at the library tonight at 7:45. I found something—something that could change everything. And good luck on your midterms!
—Isobel

I glance at the clock. There's almost an hour until I'm supposed to meet her so I lie down on my bed with one of the books Basil gave me, intending to finally try to decipher it...and jolt awake what feels like seconds or possibly centuries later.

My mouth is dry, my eyes gritty, and my head foggy. I have enough brain power to look at the clock and process the fact that I'm almost thirty minutes late to meet Isobel.

Crap.

I grab a hoodie and dash out the door and down the stairs. The quad is empty, and in the dark night air it's almost eerie. I run across to the main building, unlock the ward, and let myself in. The path I take to the library is also deserted as is the library when I reach it, a sign on the door proclaiming the library is closing early today. As in it closed thirty minutes ago.

So where the hell could Isobel be? I glance up and down the hallway. Empty. I slowly make my way down the stairs while my mind churns with questions. The no cell phone policy has never sucked more than right now. If this place didn't have to be warded all to hell, then I could just text her, but no, it has to be all difficult.

Where the hell is she? She said she found something big...What if something happened to her? What if she found something that put her in danger?

No use getting worked up until I'm sure. I run back to our dorm room, my heart pounding in my chest. She's not here. Nor is she in any of the common rooms downstairs.

Where else would she go? The boys' dorm? Not likely. The practice field maybe? The physical stuff has never been her forte, so she might want to get in some extra practice or something since she hasn't taken her PE exam yet.

The field is as deserted as everywhere else, and I'm turning around to leave when a flash of movement catches my eye. On the far side of the field, there's someone—no, *multiple* someones—running through the woods. A place they definitely don't belong.

Moving closer, I squint, trying to make out who it is. There are three of them, one supported between the other two. I don't recognize the others, but there's only one person I know of small enough stature to be the person in the middle: Isobel.

"Hey!" I yell. "What the hell do you think you're doing?"

Yelling is a dumb thing to do. I would have been better off following them to see where they were going, but I can't take it back now. I run full out toward the figures in the woods. They break into a run too, practically dragging Isobel along between them.

They're fast, but I'm faster, and I quickly gain on them. They must notice because one of them pauses long enough to rip some magic from the air and toss a blast at me. I dodge to the side and throw myself to the ground, but it's a close miss, and the smell of singed hair tickles my nose. That was definitely an energy ball, but way more powerful than any I've been dealing with in class. Who are these people?

I shove to my feet and continue chasing them. I can't let them get away with Isobel.

It's witch number two's turn to toss something my way, another energy ball, large enough that it hits my side even as I dodge. But that's not the worst of it. The worst is the second bit of magic thrown by witch number one that I *dodge* directly into. The force of it spins me around and sends me to my ass. Not a shot to kill—thank God—but definitely a shot to stun.

And stunned I am. That second burst of magic has all my nerves jolting with energy, but in a completely useless way. Like I've been hit by a freaking taser or something. I manage to get my hands under me and try to stand, but my legs give out, and a hot wave of pain crashes against my spine. What the actual hell? That wasn't just an energy ball. It was a *spell*. I didn't even hear the witch say anything. How powerful does someone have to be to cast without words while running? I'm clearly way out of my league, but I can't let them take Isobel.

Another attempt to stand brings yet more pain.

They're getting away.

I raise my hand and send a burst of wild magic in their direction, but my aim is off. Way off. And the spell is messing with my muscles. They're slowly freezing up, starting in the area where the spell hit and spreading outward, and every movement brings a jolt of pain.

Another wild burst of energy flies from my hand, but the action does little more than rustle the leaves in the vague direction of where the two forms run off with Isobel. Then, the muscles in my arm freeze and I fall face down on the ground, dirt pressing against my lips. I can't even see the witches anymore, but I know they're gone.

And they've got Isobel.

CHAPTER 24

I'm not sure how long it takes all my muscles to freeze. I don't have a watch, and most of my attention is on trying to make sure some of the more important muscles are working correctly. Like my heart. And my diaphragm.

Is my pulse slowing? I swallow, and my throat feels thick. Oh shit, that's a muscle too. Saliva pools in my mouth and drips from the corner of my lips into the dirt. My breathing feels too fast, but I can't tell if that's a physical symptom or my slowly growing panic.

Throwing a spell that could *kill* me wouldn't have been so easy...right?

Black spots linger at the corner of my vision, and the best I manage are shallow pants. The weight on my chest, imagined or factual, gets heavier and heavier by the moment. If I could just...I try to buck my body so I'll roll over, but the action doesn't work how I meant it to. Instead of being on my back, now I'm on my side.

Still, breathing seems a little easier.

Who knows how long passes before my chest expands in one full, real breath and then another and another. I'm so grateful for the air I barely notice the dirt in my mouth.

Another unknown length of time passes before my fingers twitch, followed quickly by muscle spasms that aren't pleasant but are strangely welcome all the same. Eventually, I shove up onto my hands and knees and then onto shaky legs.

Night has fallen, and I can barely see anything around me in the woods. The air is quiet, only the sound of bugs and an owl or two breaking the silence.

I scrub at my eyes with the back of one hand. What do I do? How in the hell am I going to figure out where they took Isobel and get her back?

Why did they take her? Could it have been because of me? It certainly wouldn't have happened if I was there, so it's at least partially my fault.

Stray tears track down my cheeks as I shuffle toward the dorms, my thoughts scattered and half nonsensical. There has to be someone who knows what to do. Shouldn't there be? Basil or Desmond or...someone.

Over an hour after I ran into the woods, I finally make it back to the quad. My legs are still stiff and not working right, though the paralyzed feeling is fading away. Where to first? What do I do? I pause to rest, one hand gripping the back of a bench.

There's tightness in my chest that won't go away, and my stomach really wants to give up its contents all of a sudden. What kind of spell did they hit me with? I shake my head to clear the lingering fogginess, but it's not going away. *Shit.*

I sit on the bench and put my head between my knees. I thought this was over. Why is it coming back? My chest tightens again, this time painfully, and heat races down my limbs.

Someone jogs up beside me. "Hey, are you okay?" It's Penny. *What's she doing out here?* She rubs a hand over my back. "You're burning up."

"They took Isobel. Something's wrong. They hit me with a spell, and I don't know . . ." I raise my head to look at her. "I don't feel right."

Her eyes widen. "Your eyes . . ." She leans away from me, a hint of fear on her face. "They're different."

"What do you mean?" The question is more of a cough as my throat grows tight.

She studies my face. "For a second there they flashed gold, but it looks like they're fading now."

What the hell?

Along with whatever weird eye thing, my unease is fading too. Then, as my body begins to feel like my own again, the effects of the spell disappear completely. That was all kinds of weird.

"I need to find Burke. Someone took Isobel. I think something bad is going to happen to her."

"Okay...and how would Burke help with that?"

"I don't know! He's an adult. They're supposed to do adulty things and know how to solve problems." The emotional reaction held back by the spell comes in full force, and hysteria rises in my chest. None of this makes any sense. None of it.

"Let's go then. I think I saw a light still on in his office."

His office? At the back of the building? What the hell was she doing there?

But I don't have time to allot those questions more than the tiniest of brain spaces, so I brush them away. *Later. I can ask her about it later.*

The two of us make our way into the main building. The lights inside are off, but the lock opens for us, and we go inside and head toward the stairs.

Two thin strips of lights line either side of the stairwell, enough to see by but also making the stairwell that much creepier. Four flights up, that hallway is deserted too. Why is Burke in his office this late? Is he always in his office this late?

We reach room 419, and Penny was right. There's a hint of light at the bottom of the door, a clear sign that Burke is in his office...or someone is anyway. I knock gently, but there's no response. I try again, louder this time. A voice calls out for us to come in. I push the door open and enter the office, shocked to find Burke and Tristan sitting across from each other at the small table in front of Burke's bookshelves with a chessboard between them.

Tristan is the first on his feet. He rushes toward me and grabs my arms. "What's wrong? Are you okay?"

Words won't come. I've been nothing to him for weeks, and this sudden concern, the worry creasing his brow...it does not compute. My brain can't even handle figuring out what the hell he's doing here.

I take a step backward—I can't deal with him right now—and my gaze goes to Burke. "Someone took Isobel."

Burke springs to his feet. "Took her? From campus?"

I nod, and the motion sends a small wave of dizziness over me. Whatever the hell this is, I don't have time for it. "I was supposed to meet her at the library but after"— my eyes go to Burke—"the wonderful news earlier, I went back to my room and accidentally fell asleep. I was only a little bit late, but they already had her. I chased them, but they threw something at me that I've never even heard of much less experienced."

"What do you mean?" asks Burke, stepping forward and taking my arm.

"The first witch threw a simple energy ball, and I dodged it. Then, the second witch threw one, and I dodged that one too, but I ended up directly in the path of some spell from the first one. I didn't even hear them say anything. Can you cast spells without words? Is that even possible?"

"It's possible," he says as he leads me to a chair. "But rare. There are only a few witches I know with that kind of power. What did the spell do?"

"It paralyzed me starting at where it hit me and then traveling through the rest of my body. I'm not sure how long it took to wear off, but…Why are you looking at me like that?"

Tristan's face has gone almost green, and he takes a step back, his eyes firmly fixed on the ground.

"Tell me more about the spell. What did it affect? Your whole body or just one component, like your muscles?" prompts Burke in a soothing voice.

I think about it for a moment. "My muscles maybe? During the worst of it I had trouble breathing, and my heart felt like it was only pumping once a minute. Why?"

His gaze darts to Tristan. "Because I know of the spell and who designed it."

"Who?"

"My mother," whispers Tristan. He clears his throat and speaks again, this time louder. "That spell was her second year project." He lets out a huff of disbelief. "She's also one of the few who could cast it without words."

"Are you saying . . .?"

"That my parents are likely the ones who took Isobel? Yes. I am."

Tristan's parents? They're the ones who kidnapped Isobel? But *why*?

Everyone in the room stares at me. I'm sure they're waiting for whatever they've already figured out to hit me. And it does.

"Are you kidding me?" I yell, jumping to my feet and advancing on Tristan. "Your batshit crazy mother *kidnapped* my roommate so you could be number one?" My rage turns to Burke. "I know the competition is fierce and people do dumb things like spell donuts to make people miss tests, but *kidnapping*? What the hell kind of school do you run?"

Burke gives me a tight smile. "I don't control the parents."

"But you control the goddamn wards, you control access, you control

..." I throw my hands up in frustration. I don't know what to do with this anymore. I turn back on Tristan. "Are your parents completely whacked? They're so worried about their precious boy not being the best that they resort to kidnapping? What kind of sense does that even make?"

"Why are you yelling at me? Do you think I *asked* them to do this?" He drags his hand through his hair, leaving it to stick up in unruly tufts.

"I wouldn't put it past you," I say with a bit of a snarl. "After all, you—"

"You know what she's like," he hisses in a pained voice, and then, quieter, "You know what she thinks of me."

What she...? A waste. That's what she thinks of him.

"She wouldn't do it for me," he continues. "I don't know what her motives are, but it's just as likely she hoped to throw *you* off. She'd do almost anything to be rid of you. Or maybe it's some twisted warning to me because she knows—"

"Are you saying this is *my* fault?" I clench my teeth to hold back the other words anger is begging me to spit at him.

"No!" He drags a hand through his hair again. "None of this is coming out right." His eyes find me and hold my gaze. "I'm sorry. For everything. I just...I'm fucking sorry."

I'm not sure what exactly he's apologizing *for* at this point, but there's true sincerity in his voice and his eyes, and this isn't the time to hash out all our issues. So, I'm just going to go with it.

"Will you help me then?" I ask.

"Help you do what?" Tristan raises his brows.

"Your parents took my friend, and I'm *not* letting them get away with it. I'm getting her back. I'm sure it'd be easier with your help, but I'll do it alone if I have to."

"Not alone," says Penny from beside me. "I'll go with you." I send her a questioning look, and she shrugs. "I owe you one—at *least*—and I've been to the St. James estate before, so I know how to get there."

"Wait a second," starts Burke. "This is a horrible idea. I'm sorry, but I cannot condone this sort of vigilantism. In the morning, I can go through the proper channels and—"

"The spell the harpy hit me with...If I wasn't who I am, if I didn't have this weird raw power thing going on, what might have happened to me? Could it have killed me?" I have a good idea what the answer to my question is, but I need Burke to confirm.

"Yes," says Burke hoarsely. "Bernadette designed it to take down rogue vampires. It was meant to physically incapacitate them so they could be killed, but on a witch, the spell alone would . . ."

"It's settled then. She's completely lost it." *Not to mention I've had it with this idiocy over rankings and kidnapping is like fifty steps too far. It's time someone put a stop to it, and it's a bonus that I get to take down Bernadette in the process.*

"I cannot—"

"Sorry about this," I say as I send a blast of energy at Burke, knocking him over and sending him sliding a few inches across the floor. I cringe. I didn't mean to hit him quite *that* hard. He doesn't get up, but his chest rises and falls normally, so he should be fine.

"Let's go," I say to Penny. "I'm not leaving my friend with that crazy witch any longer than necessary."

We make it all the way down to the quad before someone grabs my arm.

"Are you planning on helping me or trying to stop me?" I ask without turning around. "Because I can tell you the latter would not go so well for you."

"I'm going with you," says Tristan quietly. "I...I don't want to see you hurt, and my mother is less likely to react poorly if I'm there." A note of teasing smugness enters his voice. "Plus, I believe I'm the only one of the three of us who has a car, and there's also the matter of the St. James family wards."

CHAPTER 25

Forty minutes later, Tristan's car, headlights dark and engine off, coasts to a stop at the bottom of a meandering driveway in front of a large residence on the Western edge of Albemarle County. The house—if something named Oakwood Manor can be called a "house"— is a monstrosity of beautiful architecture. Every eave, every window, every whatever those things lining the roof are called is put together in a picture of perfect symmetry. It's as if one of those fancy regency-era manors fell out of the sky and landed in the middle of Virginia, and the *Downton Abbey* theme song plays in the back of my head as I stare in awe.

Tristan's staring up at the house too, an unreadable look on his face as his white-knuckled hands grip the steering wheel like some sort of lifeline. And maybe for him it is. If he doesn't get out of the car, he doesn't have to face his parents and what they've done by taking things a step—or fifty—too far. He can continue on in his perfect life with his perfect—

No. That's not right. Nothing has ever been perfect for him. He's just pretended it has been.

But for all his faults, for all his arrogance, he's here now, and he's going against his parents. As horrible as they are, that's still gotta be hard. And confusing. I rest a hand over one of his and wait for him to look at me. When he does, I squeeze his hand and give him a smile. The smile he gives me in return is strained.

"Let's go get Isobel," says Penny as she hops out of the back seat in a strangely upbeat action.

That's right. We have a job to do. I slip my hand away from Tristan's and exit from my own door.

Tristan walks up beside me a couple seconds later, his eyes still glued to the house with a contemplative look on his face. "They'll probably be keeping her in the basement," he says. "It's warded, but I should be able to get past them."

I glance up at the huge house, trying to picture what this basement might look like and where it might be. "What about servants or whatever? Do we need to worry about being seen?"

"No. They sleep at the opposite end of the manor from where we're going in."

My question was meant as a joke...kind of. I don't know why I thought they wouldn't have actual servants in a place this big. I can't picture Bernadette doing any cleaning, especially not scrubbing the miles and miles of baseboards that must be in this place and, based on my observations of Tristan, I'm sure everything in there is squeaky clean.

Tristan leads us around to the back and points to a low balcony about eight feet above the ground with a sliding door leading into the house. "My room is the best place to enter. My parents sleep in a completely different wing, and I set the wards on that door myself so they aren't tied to any of the others."

"Sounds reasonable to me," I say. "What do you think, Penny?"

She nods. "Shouldn't be too hard to get up there." She runs and jumps, grabbing the bottom lip of the balcony and hoisting herself over the edge. It's the type of skill she shouldn't be showing off if she doesn't want people to know her secret. She turns back to us and leans over the edge. "You next, Selene. I can grab your arms and help pull you up."

Tristan bends down to make a step with his hands, but I'm already running at the balcony or, rather, the side of the house right next to it. I jump, leading with my left leg and pushing into the wall and then away as I shove off and use the momentum to propel myself upward. My right leg lands in another step further up the wall, and I shift to the side to grab the edge of the balcony and pull myself over.

Penny and Tristan both stare at me as if I have two heads. I give them a little smile and shrug. "Reid's into parkour. He taught me a few things." In a lower voice only Penny can hear, I add, "And I needed to downplay your little feat of athleticism."

She gives me a tight nod. "Understood."

Tristan is...not as graceful as the two of us. He has the upper body strength to pull himself up, but it takes him a couple tries to get enough height on his jump to get a good hold. He makes it up eventually, though, and then we're in.

In the darkness, I can make out very little, only enough to know his room is sterile, no pictures, no decorations, no personality. It's kind of sad. He rushes us through without comment and leads us out of the room.

The hall is quiet and dark, the only light the slant of moonlight through the windows lining the wall. The light is just enough to see by, and I can't help but gawk at the money practically dripping from the walls. Every corner is clean, every tiny side table or whatever they're called is polished to a perfect shine and clearly antique or at the very least super pricey.

I feel out of place just walking down the hall, but Tristan...he looks like he belongs here. His shoulders are back, his chin tilted high, as if he owns the place. Which I guess he kind of does, or at least his parents do. I don't think I could ever fit in at a place like this.

He leads us farther down and takes a left into a slightly narrower hallway, once again lined with perfect molding and tiny, fancy tables interspersed between every third doorway. A gilded frame catches my eye, and I stop. It's a portrait—a painted one of course—of the St. James family. Bernadette, Allister, a young Tristan, and a teenage girl. I lean closer.

Tristan can't be more than six in the picture, and his smile is wide, dimples on display, not a care in the world. The contrast between the boy he was then and the one he is now is almost unsettling. What happened to turn him into someone who's alone in a crowd and rarely breaks into a real smile? And the girl...she looks somewhat familiar, but I can't place why. Maybe it's because she resembles Tristan so much, but something in the back of my mind tells me that's not the case.

She must be Tristan's sister, Cecily, the one taken by shifters and, if I had to guess by Tristan's age, this portrait wasn't painted that long before she disappeared. She looks sad and empty, much like the older Tristan does now. It could just be because it's a painting and doesn't quite catch the emotion of the picture, but it's a very good painting. Bernadette has a flare of ambition in her eyes and Allister's have that same blandness his son's so often do, so I have to believe the emotion, or lack thereof, on her face is deliberate. But why?

"My mother hates that portrait," says Tristan from beside me, the words brushing against my ear. I jolt in surprise, and he places a hand on my lower back. He uses the other hand to point at the painted version of himself. "She said it was 'uncouth' that my teeth are showing."

"That's your sister, isn't it?"

"Yes, that's Cecily," he says softly.

Penny moves up on my other side, also studying the portrait. "She looks familiar. Where is she now?"

"Dead," says Tristan. "Not long after that was painted."

Penny's brows pull together, and she tilts her head to the side. "I could've sworn . . ." She lets the words trail off and shakes her head. "I must be thinking of someone else."

The three of us continue to a door at the end of the hallway. The hinges creak as the door opens, revealing the top of a stairwell going down into complete darkness. I'm coming to hate stairwells. What happened to nice one-story ranches? I search for a light switch, but there isn't one.

"How are we—"

I feel Tristan pull at the magic in the air and glance over to find him forming it into a ball in the palm of his hand. As he concentrates, he whispers a couple words, and a gentle glow emits from the ball. A light spell.

He leads us down the curling staircase, me behind him with Penny bringing up the rear. About halfway down, my foot slips on the edge of a step, and I stumble forward. Tristan spins to grab my elbow and prevent me from plummeting headfirst down the stairs. Instead, I end up chest to chest with him, our faces close. A blush fills his cheeks. The light goes out.

"Thanks," I say, a bit breathless, more from adrenaline than him. At least that's what I'm going to tell myself. I almost fell down a flight of stairs for goodness sake. I have every reason in the world to be worked up.

"No problem," he says. I can't see his face in the darkness, so I imagine a smile to go with it. He guides my arm back to the railing and then calls up the light again. If he's curious why Penny isn't doing it, he doesn't ask. Eventually her secret will come out, and I'm not looking forward to Tristan's reaction to that information. I suppose it's good that Penny is here with us. Tristan finding out about her might go over smoother if I can use her helping us now as an example of "good" shifter behavior.

At the bottom of the stairs, Tristan hits a switch and releases the light spell. Wall sconces lining a hallway with three doors on either side flicker on. The place is so dungeon-like that it's almost cliché. But, like, a classy dungeon if that's a thing. There's no damp, moldy stones, and besides the air being slightly musty, it feels much like the rest of the house. Except underground. With no windows. Who the hell designs a place like this in a fancy manor house?

I go to step around Tristan, but he puts up an arm to hold me back.

"The wards," he says. "I need to unlock them before you go any farther."

Heat gathers in my cheeks. Of course there are wards. How stupid can I be? Did I think we were just going to stroll in, take Isobel back, and leave?

Well, kind of.

He waves a hand through the air and mutters an incantation under his breath. Something about revealing the truth of it, and the wards around the doorway shimmer into view. Holy crap. They're the most complicated wards I've ever seen, nothing at all like the piddly little things I've been working on in class. His parents must be really powerful.

I look from the wards to Tristan. "Can you get past them?"

He gives me a 'what do you think' look and starts concentrating on the first one. It takes him only thirty seconds to unlock, but the next one looks much trickier. Way more advanced than anything I've worked on before, and we've never even learned to *take down* wards in class. I look at Tristan with new eyes. He's that much farther ahead of me? That much better?

The second ward falls.

Even Penny looks at him with something like respect in her eyes, and she knows a hell of a lot more about all this than I do.

"Is this the kind of stuff covered in second year?" I ask, a little worried I'm going to be expected to pull off things like this in less than a year.

Penny shakes her head. "This is master class material, but he shouldn't have enough time with his powers fully active to be at this level."

"Then how . . ."

She winces. "There is a sigil and even a few spells that can wake powers early, but no matter the method, the experience isn't pleasant. For him to be at this level of skill, they had to have done it when he was like seven or eight." She casts her eyes to the ground. "My parents had me awakened at sixteen, and even at that age it was like fire ripping through my veins."

Seven or eight? It must have happened not long after his sister disappeared. How disturbingly awful. The kid loses his sister, and then his parents put him through something like that. They really are monsters.

The third ward falls, and Tristan pauses for a second before taking a small step backward. "The next one's a blood ward. I can't tell if it's keyed to only my parents or to any St. James."

"What happens if you try to take it down and it's keyed to only your parents?" I ask as I squint at the ward, trying to see what he's seeing in the shimmery red lines.

He huffs. "I don't know. Could mean pain. Could mean death."

"Your parents would put up a ward that would kill you?"

He gives me a droll look. "My *mother* could give a crap about me, especially right now. If the choice was between me dying and me figuring out their plan and showing up to rescue Isobel...she'd have no qualms about at least severely maiming me."

The words are so matter of fact that they somehow emphasize the horribleness of it all rather than lessen it. This is the kind of family he was raised in? A shudder travels down my spine. I'm suddenly grateful for my birth mother leaving me, for the binding spell, for getting to grow up loved and cherished. I wouldn't want to have been raised in the witch world if this is the way they treat their children.

Even Penny's story about having her powers awakened is a cautionary tale of how not to raise a kid.

"So, what do we do?" asks Penny as she leans against one wall. "We've come kind of far to give up now."

"We can't go back without Isobel," I say, even more sure about that than before. If the St. James are so awful to their own children, I can only imagine how they must be treating Isobel. My mind conjures a picture of her chained up and hanging from a ceiling somewhere. Granted, in a very nicely furnished and spotless room, but still chained up like some sick centerpiece.

"I'm not planning to," says Tristan, his voice determined. He pulls a small knife from his pocket and places the blade against his palm.

"Wait," I say, stepping forward and grabbing the handle of the knife. "If you're going to do this, you should at least be smart about it. The palm has got to be the worst place to cut. It doesn't heal well, and the constant movement will keep you in pain. I don't know why it's so popular in movies. It's dumb." I pause. "Unless you specifically need palm blood...Is that a thing?"

Tristan shakes his head, amusement hovering on the corners of his mouth.

"Good." I grab the knife from him and prick the tip of one of his fingers, then squeeze gently to bring up some blood. "Is that enough then?"

"Yes," he says. His attention turns back to the ward, and his face moves from amused to strained as he places his bloody fingertip at the top of the triangle and starts re-drawing the edges of the ward with his own blood. The task is almost complete when the lights in the hallway go out, plunging us into total darkness.

Tristan shoves me behind him and quickly calls up one of those magic light balls. The light illuminates our newly arrived company: Bernadette St. James.

"Hello, Mother," says Tristan in a clipped tone. Not the greeting I would have gone with, but who am I to complain?

She has eyes only for her son, dismissing Penny and me without a second glance. "I'm very disappointed to see you here, Tristan. When I felt the wards go down, I hoped I was wrong, that you wouldn't lower yourself to continue consorting with the Andras girl." She sighs. "But here we are."

CHAPTER 26

Bernadette's words are calm with nothing more than the tone of a disappointed parent, but Tristan goes rigid, his entire body vibrating with tension. He takes a sharp breath in through his nose, and the muscles in his jaw tense. He's angled in front of me, one hand holding the light spell that casts his scowl in shadows.

"I believe I was quite clear on this matter, was I not?" scolds Bernadette. "You were to have no further contact with the Andras girl."

"And I abided by your rules until you went too far," says Tristan.

Bernadette *tsks*. "I cannot let you shame the St. James name by—"

"You *kidnapped* someone!" I exclaim as I step out from behind Tristan, unable to stay quiet. "Isn't that something that shames the St. James name, or is that just normalcy for you all? You're delusional, lady."

She glances at me, looks me up and down, and then waves away my comments with a flick of her hand. "I forbid you from taking down that ward," she says to Tristan, and only Tristan, in a tone like she's speaking to a young child. "I was planning on having her returned tomorrow anyway. Why don't you run along back to school?"

"I'm not leaving her with you," I say, an angry growl entering my tone.

"And we're not letting you get away with this," says Penny with an entirely different kind of growl in her voice. "We're not letting you get away with *any* of it."

What is Penny doing? She's about to blow her own cover. I grab her arm, digging my fingers in. "Get a hold of yourself."

She shakes out of my hold. "Why?" she asks. "This is the whole reason I'm here."

I'm still trying to interpret her words when she shifts.

Except for the whole ripping out of her clothes thing, Penny's shift is seamless and near silent, a surprising feat for someone newly Bitten, and the beautiful silver-gray wolf left in her place takes up over half the width of the narrow hallway. She angles herself in front of me and Tristan, a growl rumbling in her throat as she takes a step toward Bernadette.

I expect at least a little fear, so I'm shocked to see nothing but derision on Bernadette's face.

"You brought one of those abominations with you? How dare you bring that creature into my house," she hisses, her nostrils flaring as her composure cracks.

Behind me, Tristan takes a step backward, the space left between us cold and empty. "I didn't know," he whispers, half in fear and half in awe. "She's a second year student. She's a witch. She can't be—"

"The thing is a Bitten wolf, you fool. Even worse than one of the natural-born ones. And you had the audacity to bring it here?" She steps forward and Penny matches her, still growling but making no other effort to advance. Bernadette sneers again. "Oh, please, you think your pathetic little noises are going to scare me. You're Bitten, and it must have been recently for you to have made it to your second year at Ravencrest. Your strength is no match for my power."

Bernadette makes a sweeping circle with one hand and *yanks* magic out of the air before shoving her open palm forward and sending the magic in a single concentrated bolt right at Penny.

Penny doesn't have time to dodge. She takes the hit directly in her chest and goes flying backward, knocking both Tristan and me to the ground. Bernadette hits Penny again, and the wolf slides across the floor and crashes into the wards. The smell of burned hair hits my nose, and Penny makes a noise I don't ever want to hear again. A cry of such deep agony that it sounds like she might be dying.

"Stop it!" I yell as I rise to my feet. "You're going to kill her!"

Those cold blue eyes turn to me, a new spark in them, one of pleasure from dealing Penny pain. "Like I should have done to you?"

"Mother! Stop this!" Tristan yells, shoving up to his feet. "*Please . . .*"

But Tristan's words have even less effect than mine. Her attention is firmly fixed on me, and she's gathering magic again, though not as quickly and violently as before. Which means she's probably cooking up something worse than what she did to Penny and plans to use it on me.

Tristan pushes me out of the way and stands in front of me, arms out and blocking my body. "Stop this!"

She doesn't listen, and the spell meant for me slams into his chest with a burst of light. He falls to the ground, his mouth gaping open, unable to draw breath. He claws at his chest and throat, making a horrible choking noise. She barely spares him a glance. Her own son lies gasping on the ground, his lips turning blue, and she barely even looks at him.

And there's no time to do anything for him because Bernadette is amping up again.

"You mongrel! Look what you made me do!" Bernadette screams, flames behind her eyes. She's completely lost it. She pulls more magic and tosses it toward Penny who's managed to drag herself far enough away from the ward that she's no longer screeching in pain.

There's a part of me that's resistant to spells or something; the fact that I fought off the paralyzing spell earlier proved that. At least I hope it did. *So maybe I can...*Instinct alone has me drawing on the magic in my chest and hastily constructing what I hope is a shield of some sort as I step in front of the blast. *This might hurt.* It does, but the shield also works. The blast of magic ricochets off and careens into the wall, creating a large divot with cracks spidering out of it. That was a shot to kill.

But the deflection has thrown Bernadette off her game. "How did you do that?" she yells, frustration evident in her tone. "You shouldn't be able to do that. That's too advanced for someone like you."

There's no point in conversation, no point in answering her questions, no point in holding off. Copying her earlier motion, I yank some magic from the air and throw it at her. She dodges out of the way, but it's a near miss, and she's up and throwing another blast my way before I have a chance to adjust for her new position.

Sure, I'm powerful, but she's much more experienced. The best I can do is keep her occupied with blasts of energy. If I let her get her bearings, she can toss a whole lot worse at me, so I send a constant stream of energy blasts her way. It's working. She's too busy dodging and deflecting to have enough time to pull together a stronger spell, but I'm tiring fast, and Tristan's gasps have faded into a quiet wheeze. He needs help, and if he doesn't get it soon, I'm not sure what might happen.

Would she let her own son die? *Maybe. But I* won't.

Which means we're pretty much at a stalemate and—

Penny leaps over my head with a snarl, flying over Bernadette and landing on Allister who must've come running at some point when he heard the commotion. Allister goes down, the weight of the wolf on top of him pushing him into the floor. Penny snarls again, her saliva dripping onto his face. Then, she glances at Bernadette, her threat clear. *Stop, or I'll rip his throat out.*

And at that, Bernadette pauses. She drops her hands to her sides and smooths her hair away from her face. "Please. Don't."

Sure, for her husband she'll stop. But not her son.

I drop to my knees beside Tristan, frantically trying to feel out the spell that's wrapped itself around him. Basil gave me only a single lesson on breaking spells. To do it, I have to find a loose thread, a seam, *something* to grab hold of to unravel. I can't find anything.

But I'm going to try anyway.

I grab at the magic making up the border of the spell itself and *pull*, draining away the magic and drawing it into myself. A wave of dizziness washes over me, and my breath comes in short pants, my heart racing. What the hell was that? How did I do that?

Tristan must be thinking the same thing because he's giving me an odd look. But at least he's breathing and the color is coming back into his cheeks.

"Get the wards down," I cough out. "Find Isobel. I need to do something about Penny."

He grabs my arm. "My father. Please don't let her . . ."

I don't know what to say, so I nod. Jumping to my feet, I turn to face Bernadette. She's muttering something under her breath as one hand moves behind her back, her attention focused on Penny.

I step in front of Tristan's mother, blocking her view of Penny whose teeth are still hovering over Allister's throat. "We're taking Isobel. Nothing you do now can change that. But this doesn't need to get any worse. Stop with the spells. Stop with the fighting. Just stop."

"Tell it to release my husband," says Bernadette with a curl of her lip. Her attention moves to Tristan, who's still working at the last ward. "If you stop now, I won't make you regret this. You can come home and still be our son. If you continue on the path you're on, we'll have no choice but to cut you off. No money. No car. No fancy school."

"Then do it," says Tristan in a hard voice. He makes one final swipe with his hand, and the last ward falls.

"If you—"

Allister screams.

And so do I. "Penny!"

Behind me, Tristan lets out a choked noise and whispers, "No."

The wolf has her jaw wrapped around Allister's arm, teeth in his flesh, blood trickling against his skin. She bit him. Penny *bit* him. She snarls again and lets go, taking slow steps backward until she reaches the wall, then sits down on her haunches, her canine lips quirked in a satisfied smile.

Bernadette's face twists with rage, and my hands come up preparing for more fighting, but her expression shifts to *anguish*. She falls to her knees at her husband's side. "What have you done? What have you done?"

I slowly lower my hands to my sides, and Tristan walks up beside me. In the corner of my eye, his face is ashen, shed of all color. We all know what this means. Allister is Bitten now. He'll be turning furry. I glance at Penny, but it's not the end of the world, right?

"There are still things he can do," I tell him. "Wards...potions . . ."

Tristan scoffs, a new coldness taking over his demeanor. "Is that the kind of nonsense your 'pack' is spreading?"

"It's true. Penny said—"

"She lied," he says in a flat voice. His gaze finds mine, his eyes hard and unforgiving. "And so did you. You knew about her, didn't you? Knew about her and didn't tell me. Knew about her and let her come here and . . ." His gaze strays to his father, still lying on the ground.

Tristan takes a hesitant step forward, but Bernadette holds up a hand and twists toward him, nothing but scorn on her face. "This is all your fault. Take your imbecilic little friend, and get out of here."

"But . . ." He takes another step forward.

"Leave!" she yells as she cradles Allister's head in her lap. "All of you." She turns rage-filled eyes on Tristan and makes complicated motions with her hands. Her son's eyes go wide and he moves back, bumping into me in his haste. Her lips are moving with words I can't hear, but I can feel the magic gathering in her hands, the way she's wrapping it all together into something truly awful. She pulls back a hand as if lining up a pitch. And throws.

Tristan covers his face with his arms and flinches away. I grab his shirt, pulling both of us down to the floor as Bernadette's spell flies over our heads and slams into the ceiling.

Someone yells a long string of strange words and magic freezes me in place, freezes *everyone* in place. A parade of black boots stomp down the stairs, and an entire unit of OSA officers fan out into the hallway around us.

CHAPTER 27

Outside, the previously quiet lawn is in chaos with patrol cars parked haphazardly in the grass and numerous OSA officers swarming around. A pair of them have Penny, now human again, in silver handcuffs, and they're loading her into the back of one of the cars. I want to argue, to speak up for her, to do something, but...she knew the consequences and did it anyway. Her actions were deliberate, purposeful, and *malicious*.

"I want that animal put down!" hisses Bernadette as she points in Penny's direction.

Through the back window, Penny gives her a grin, all teeth, all mocking. There's a hardness to her I don't recognize, a level of rancor I'd never noticed before, and it's filling in pieces of a picture I'm not so sure I want to see. She's been friendly enough, but she's never been particularly helpful before, and she barely knows Isobel.

Why did Penny come here? Was it solely to take a shot at the St. James family? And why would she lie about the Bite and what happens to a witch's magic? What purpose would that serve? To stay at Ravencrest? To earn my trust? What the hell is going on?

There are too many questions, too many possibilities, and nothing makes sense. A thought niggles at the back of my mind. I'm missing something, and my thoughts are too all over the place to figure out what that is right now.

Bernadette follows along as another officer leads Allister to an ambulance and helps him sit on the back while a medic looks at his arm. The medic shakes his head, and Bernadette covers her mouth with her hand and squeezes her eyes shut. Allister merely looks pale and drawn, resigned.

My gaze moves to Tristan, standing off to the side, looking lost and so very alone. His mother won't look at him, won't speak to him, and everything around him is moving at double speed while he just stands there. He's deflated, like everything that kept him upright has been stolen from him. And maybe it has. The steel in his spine, the hardness in his eyes, where did that all come from if not his horrible, awful mother who now looks through him as if he doesn't exist?

"You should talk to him," says Isobel's soft voice from beside me. She's sitting with her back against the side of the house and her knees drawn up into her chest. The medics looked her over and, besides being a little dehydrated and generally weak, said she's fine. I'm not so sure. Her eyes are slightly unfocused, and there's something...off.

"He doesn't want to talk to me," I say. "The whole thing with Penny. It's not what he thinks, but he's not going to listen to me." *He doesn't look like he wants to listen to anyone.* "Besides, I want to talk to you. What do you remember? Were you in the library when they took you?"

She tilts her head to the side, and her lips part. "I'm not...I'm not sure."

"Well, try to think about it. The officers will want to take a statement or something so charges can be pressed." I smooth a hand over the top of her head. "I'm glad you're safe."

She bites at her bottom lip, worry pulling her brows together, as she nods absentmindedly.

Thirty minutes pass and the officers haven't spared me or Isobel a glance. Two of them spent a while talking to Bernadette and another one talked to Allister, but so far no more handcuffs have been pulled out. It's as if...they don't plan to arrest them at all.

"Wait here," I say to Isobel. "I'm going to see what's going on."

Another absentminded nod.

I flag down the closest officer. "Are you guys going to take statements from us or whatever? I don't mind waiting, but Isobel's been through kind of a lot this evening."

"Statements? For what?" The woman gives me a blank look.

My gaze darts to Bernadette. "So you can press charges...for kidnapping. Or, like, attempted murder? I don't know. Isn't that what you're supposed to do?"

"You've been watching too many human cop shows, kid. We're not the same thing as the police. We're only here to investigate and take custody of the rogue shifter."

"But they...she . . ." I gesture toward Bernadette. "She kidnapped my roommate and tried to kill me."

The officer shrugs. "Not our department." She leans closer and says in a soft voice, "And even if it was, they'd never give the order to arrest Bernadette St. James. Not on the word of a couple teenagers. Sorry, hon."

I gape after her as she walks away. Bernadette is going to *get away with this*? How is that possible? How is that *justice*?

"I know what you're thinking, and it's not worth arguing with them," says Tristan as he places a hand on my lower back and guides me toward Isobel. "I've spoken with Desmond. We should return to campus." His voice isn't hard, it isn't angry...it's empty.

He takes advantage of my stunned state and leads me and Isobel to his car, opening the door for my roommate and helping her get settled before walking around to get behind the steering wheel. I slide into the passenger seat and watch as the officers speaking with Bernadette and Allister shake their hands and give orders for everyone else to disperse. Tristan pulls away as his mother helps his father into the house, and Isobel is asleep in the back before we reach the end of the driveway.

This situation is just as bad as what the St. James family thinks shifters do to avoid the laws. The witches are no better. What a bunch of hypocrites.

For the first half of the drive, I stare out the window, stewing in my anger and resentment. I want to yell and scream, but not at either of the people in this car, and I'm not even sure who. How is this system so messed up? How did this start? And how do I find a way to *fix* it? I sigh and shake myself out of the endless circle of questions in my head, asking instead one that I might get an answer for. "What's going to happen to your father?"

Tristan's hands tighten on the steering wheel, and his knuckles go white. "I don't want to talk about it."

"But what—"

"Let me rephrase, I don't want to talk to *you*," he bites out. "Your rescue mission was a success, and I doubt my mother will bother with you from here on out. We aren't friends. That hasn't changed. So, let's just leave it at that."

"I'm—"

"Yes, yes, you're sorry. I get it. I don't forgive you." His voice cracks. "Just stay away from me once we get to campus. Okay?"

I bite back my excuses and explanations, ignore the stab of hurt his word cause, and nod. "Fine."

The rest of the ride is silent. Once he parks, Tristan turns the car off, gets out, and walks away without another word, leaving me to turn around in my seat and gently nudge Isobel awake.

"Hey, we're back. Do you think you can make it to our room, or should I get someone to help us?" I ask.

"Back?" Her brow creases. "Back from where?"

That's...weird. I get out, open her door, and kneel on the ground by the side of the car so I can get a closer look at her. "The St. James house. They kidnapped you? Remember?"

She shakes her head slowly. "No...I . . ."

"What *is* the last thing you remember? The library?"

"The library?" Her eyes are unfocused.

"You left me a note? To meet you at the library because you'd figured out something important?"

There's no spark of recognition, only confusion. "What are you talking about? What note?"

"The note you left in our room tonight."

"Tonight?" Her face is blank. "What day is it?"

I run a hand over her head, no bumps, no bruises. There's not a mark on her, but this confusion isn't normal. "It's Thursday. The end of midterm week?"

She presses her forehead into her palm. "I don't know. Why can't I remember?"

I gently squeeze her shoulder. "You might have gotten hit in the head. It'll be okay. Why don't I take you to Director Burke, and he can take a look?"

Her frightened eyes meet mine, and she nods. I help her to her feet and link arms with her. Since Tristan spoke with Burke, I can only assume he's still in his office, so that's where I take her.

Burke raises a brow when I enter and sends me a wry look. "Had you listened to me earlier, this situation may have turned out better."

I scoff. "Are you telling me if we'd waited and gone through the proper channels or whatever, they'd have arrested Bernadette tonight?"

He averts his eyes. "No. I can't say that."

"Then I did the right thing."

He coughs.

"Sorry about the whole blasting you with magic part of it, though." I usher Isobel forward and into one of the chairs. "There's something wrong. I think she hit her head or they did something to her...She doesn't remember anything."

"Doesn't remember?" He jumps to his feet and comes over to lean down in front of Isobel. He studies her face, looking closely at her eyes, and then glances up at me. "Use the phone on my desk. Dial extension 921. That's Basil's quarters. Tell him I need him down here."

This is sounding worse and worse.

I follow Burke's instructions, and ten minutes later, Basil comes rushing in dressed in flannel pajamas covered in dancing cows. Like Burke, Basil carefully studies Isobel's face, paying particular attention to her eyes. He whispers a few words under his breath, and a ball of light appears in his hand. He stretches the light into a rod shape and uses it like a flashlight, shining it in Isobel's eyes and moving it from side to side.

"I don't see evidence of any spellwork, so it must be a memory potion," he says. "I don't know which one for sure."

"Memory potion? You mean they wiped her memory? Exactly how much of it?"

Basil shakes his head. "I have no idea. I haven't seen one in some time.

They're quite difficult to make and highly illegal." He shares a look with Burke. "Do you want me to try to trace it?"

Burke gives him a stiff nod. "Of course. If you can."

"What do you mean by trace it?" I ask.

"Basil can use a spell to find the origin of the potion, trace it back to the witch whose magic activated it. It is not a well-known spell, and there are only a few witches who can perform it," explains Burke. "It's also not an exact science, and it only works a quarter of the time, but it's worth a shot."

Basil makes the necessary preparations to perform the spell and gets to work. He places a small black stone in a circle of candles and begins lighting them one by one.

Bernadette would know about tracing. She's not stupid enough to use an illegal potion that might be traced back to her. So where did the potion come from?

A chill travels down my spine. Penny. A second-year student who specializes in potions.

Basil waves his hand with a flourish, letting out a stream of foreign words. Greek I think. The black stone brightens, glowing with harsh silver light. It pulses once, twice, three times, and then goes dark. Basil shakes his head.

"No luck," he says.

But I'm pretty sure I don't need the tracing spell to tell me who activated the potion: *Me.*

Penny would also know about the possibility of tracing and would take precautions. *Like having a witch ignorant about almost everything activate the potion for her.*

I study my roommate. Is it possible she figured out Penny's secret and that's why Penny dosed her? But I've known Penny's secret for a while, so why would Isobel figuring it out trigger such a drastic action? Or was it something else? There were more than a few times Penny started to say things and stopped herself. She alluded to things 'they' told her on more than one occasion. What could that have been about? Assuming I'm right and this memory potion is Penny's doing, what secret could Isobel have possibly uncovered that would make Penny resort to something like this?

And how will I get to Penny to ask?

"I'll have Selene take you to the infirmary for now," says Burke as he crouches down to Isobel's eye level. "The confusion is a common side effect of memory potions and should clear in the next day or so, and then we can figure out when you were given the potion and how much of your memory is missing. I expect the gap in your memory will be anywhere from three days to two weeks depending on the strength of the potion." He pauses and squeezes Isobel's hand. "You may or may not ever be able to regain the lost time. It's why the potions are illegal."

Isobel nods, her eyes going glassy. "What about my midterms? The ranks? It's almost the end of the quarter, isn't it?"

Burke straightens and goes to his desk, a strained look on his face. "I have the final rankings here ready to post in the morning." He pulls out a tablet and sighs, his hand over the screen. "I haven't looked at them yet."

He walks over to hand the tablet to me. I start scrolling.

1- Jason Barrington

2- Tristan St. James

3- Sasha Kensington

More scrolling...

81- Adrian Dumont

More...

201- Selene Andras

More...

232- Isobel Cardosa* (Incomplete Midterms)

Isobel loses even more color from her face. "Incomplete? But . . ."

Burke shakes his head. "You had three midterms today. You only showed up for one."

"But she was *kidnapped*," I argue. "Can't she take a make-up test or something?"

"The two midterms she missed were this afternoon, hours before the kidnapping," says Burke.

Hours before the kidnapping? That means Isobel *skipped* two midterms.

"But where...Why? . . ." There's a whimper in her voice, her expression lost and scared.

"We're okay," I say to Isobel, grabbing her hand. "And I promise you we'll get you back up to the top where you belong. I'm not going to let the St. James family keep us down. Even if it means I have to use every tool at my disposal to do so."

Tomorrow, I'm calling my grandparents. I wouldn't do it for myself, but I'll be damned if I let Isobel lose her place at Ravencrest. If anyone deserves a place at the top of that list, it's her.

Selene's story continues in...

SPELL LINKED

For updates and other fun, join TK's Reader Café on Facebook:

www.theresakay.com/booklink/743601

A NOTE ABOUT REVIEWS

If you enjoyed this book, please consider leaving a review.
Every single one helps, even if it's only a sentence or two. Thank you!

Amazon: www.theresakay.com/booklink/943192

Goodreads: www.theresakay.com/booklink/943203

Bookbub: www.theresakay.com/booklink/943206

ACKNOWLEDGEMENTS

Before this book, I hadn't finished a book in *two years*. That's not to say I hadn't written anything. I'd written a lot actually. More than 40k words in fact. And pretty much every single one of those words made up one of fifteen different beginnings for a completely different story.

This book started as a tiny voice in the back of my head, one I kept pushing away because I was going to write my ancient Rome fantasy dammit despite the fact that I still hadn't managed to find the perfect beginning, but then I decided to just do it. I needed something fun and tropey to play with and I simply adored these characters. Selene is very different from Jax and it's been interesting getting to know her.

I'm a pantser, but I knew if I wanted to release this series in one year instead of the three and a half it took me to get the Broken Skies series done, I needed a map to keep me from getting lost following all the little tangents my brain cooks up. So, thank you to Frankie Blooding for taking my concept for this series and my mish-mash of "well maybe" and "what if" and drawing that map for me.

Even with a map, I still had plot bunnies to chase down and that's where Regan came in. Our story chats, pep talks and in group progress posts were what got me to "The End" for the first time in two years.

Another big thank you to Kelly P. who read my disjointed and sometimes confusing draft chapters as I wrote them. I couldn't leave it in the story, but I'll put it here just for you. <more kissy stuff>

As always, many thanks go out to the other Rebel Writers: Stormy, Caylie, Kat, Alex, and Leigh. It's been five years now and even though so much has changed, the positivity and support never has. I never could've done any of this without every single one of you.

Some newcomers to my acknowledgement section, the Cville Spec Fic Writer's Group (or whatever we're calling ourselves these days): Stephanie, Bruce (who also beta read this book), Rae, Jo, Leeyanne, Megan, and Emily. Even when we're just geeking out about books or games, you guys are always tons of fun to hang out with.

I had a great group of beta readers who made this story so much better with their feedback: Lenore, Jen, Carla, Lillian, and Kirsten.

Special thanks to some of my other writer and blogger friends who've always been willing to lend a hand or answers my sometimes random questions: Rysa Walker, Meg Watt, Robin Mahle, Elle Madison, and Kelly St. Clare.

Thanks to Christian Bentulan for another set of gorgeous covers. You're always a joy to work with.

Thanks to Nadége Richards for making the insides so pretty.

Thanks to Krystal Dehaba for helping make this story better with your top-notch editing. You didn't edit these acknowledgements, so there are probably typos in here somewhere . . .

I'm sure there are people I'm forgetting and for that I'm sorry. Just know that I appreciate each and every person who has helped me either with this book specifically or through the years as I've navigated the waters of the indie world.

Last, but definitely not least, thanks to my readers who've stuck with me and are joining me for this journey into something new.

ABOUT THE AUTHOR

Theresa Kay writes stories that feature flawed young adult and new adult characters in science fiction, urban fantasy, or paranormal worlds, all with a touch of romance thrown in for good measure. She's constantly lost in one fictional universe or another and is a self-proclaimed "fangirl" who loves being sucked into new books, movies, or TV shows. Living in the mountains of central Virginia with her husband and two kids, she works as a paralegal by day and spends her free time reading tons of books, binging Avengers movies, anime, and Doctor Who, or playing Tomb Raider and Assassin's Creed.

WWW.THERESAKAY.COM

Keep track of my newest releases:
Newsletter: www.theresakay.com/booklink/327701
Amazon: www.theresakay.com/booklink/327718
Bookbub: www.theresakay.com/booklink/329342

Made in the USA
Las Vegas, NV
21 September 2022